# Praise for *The Blue Moon*

"Lorena McCourtney has crafted an entertaining…mystery with endearing characters and a setting so charming that if Sparrow Island actually existed, I'd be on the next ferry!"

—*Kathy Herman, author of the Baxter, Seaport, and Phantom Hollow Series*

"*The Blue Moon* casts its mysterious glow over Sparrow Island. Lorena McCourtney once again pens a cozy mystery that charms as it intrigues. A great rainy day read."

—*Lyn Cote, author of the Women of Ivy Manor series*

# About the
## Mysteries of Sparrow Island Series

*The Blue Moon*
by Lorena McCourtney

*Whispers through the Trees*
by Susan Plunkett & Krysteen Seelen

*Flight of the Raven*
by Ellen Harris

Meet Abigail Stanton, an ornithologist, bird watcher and keen observer who brings a sharp eye to bear on the secrets that lie hidden on Sparrow Island, a place of extraordinary natural beauty in the San Juan Islands. Fate has brought Abby back to the island—and the life she thought she had said farewell to forever. But Abby, inspired by hope and faith, soon discovers that life on Sparrow Island is full of intrigue and excitement when she opens her eyes to the mysterious ways God works in our lives.

# The Blue Moon

LORENA McCOURTNEY

GuidepostsBooks®

New York, New York

*The Blue Moon*

ISBN-13: 978-0-8249-4725-5

Published by GuidepostsBooks
16 East 34th Street
New York, New York 10016
www.guidepostsbooks.com

Distributed by Ideals Publications, a Guideposts company
535 Metroplex Drive, Suite 250
Nashville, Tennessee 37211

### Acknowledgments

Every attempt has been made to credit the sources of copyrighted material used in this book. If any such acknowledgment has been inadvertently omitted or miscredited, receipt of such information would be appreciated.

All Scripture quotations are taken from *The Holy Bible, New International Version.* Copyright © 1973, 1978, 1984 International Bible Society. Used by permission of Zondervan Bible Publishers.

Library of Congress Cataloging-in-Publication Data

McCourtney, Lorena.
  The Blue Moon / Lorena McCourtney.
    p. cm. — (Mysteries of Sparrow Island)
  ISBN 978-0-8249-4725-5
  1. San Juan Islands (Wash.)—Fiction. 2. Ornithologists—Fiction. 3. Diamonds—Fiction. 4. Jewelry—Fiction. 5. Superstition—Fiction. I. Title.
  PS3563.C3449B58 2007
  813'.54—dc22

                                        2007006066

Cover art by Tom Newsom
Design by Marisa Jackson

Printed and bound in the United States of America

10 9 8 7 6 5 4 3 2 1

*SPARROW ISLAND IS FICTITIOUS

# Chapter One

AFTER TEN MINUTES OF searching, Abby Stanton found a coupon for a free latte from the Springhouse Café, a photograph she needed for the new exhibit and enough stray paper clips to make a daisy chain around the island. Oh, and there was that earring she'd been missing for weeks! She pounced on it gratefully.

What she had *not* found, however, was the scrap of paper on which she'd scribbled the name of the reference book she needed.

Hands on hips, she stared at her desk in frustration. A handsome desk of solid walnut with decorative walnut burl inserts and a lovely patina of age, it had numerous pigeonholes, drawers and trays for keeping everything tidy and organized.

So how, she wondered in exasperation, had everything become so disorganized and untidy? Mail, notes and reminders overflowed the pigeonholes. Magazine clippings, computer printouts and letters to be answered or filed filled the trays. A leaning stack of manila folders threatened to fall to the floor.

*But I'm not really an untidy or disorganized person*, she protested as she studied the clutter. She kept her bills paid, the oil in her car changed and her teeth flossed. The dust bunnies under her bed never got large enough to attack.

But once she took a moment to reflect, she knew why things had gotten a bit out of hand here. She'd been out of the office a lot recently, nursing both an injured owl and a gull at the conservatory, and making numerous treks into the woods because of reports of an injured eagle. The number of guests here at The Nature Museum was light on these occasionally stormy days of fall, but she'd also spent more time than usual on the floor working with those few visitors because Wilma, the woman who usually staffed the reception desk, had cut back her hours to help with her daughter's new baby.

Abby also had to admit she preferred these outside activities to office work.

But the owl and gull had now been released into the wild, and Ida Tolliver had come to help out part-time in the museum. So the time had come, Abby decided with a sigh. Time to dig into this mess and—

"Hey, how about a cup of coffee and a roll? I brought some of those yummy cinnamon rolls from the café."

Abby turned as Ida stuck her head in the office door. Tempting, so very tempting. But she shook her head resolutely. "Thanks, but I've decided it's time to clean up in here. I've misplaced an important piece of paper."

Ida glanced around without comment, although Abby suspected she was thinking that an interisland ferry could be misplaced in this mess.

"Hugo might like one though," Abby added, referring to the man who was both curator of the museum and her boss.

"I asked him, but he said no." Ida's expressive, violet eyes looked troubled. "I wonder if something's wrong or if he isn't feeling well. He seemed kind of . . . preoccupied. He just waved me off."

"Oh?" That didn't sound like the usually cheerful, always thoughtful Hugo. Although Abby also knew that Hugo Baron wouldn't be apt to tell Ida, or anyone else, if he wasn't feeling well. "Perhaps he's working on the government report that's due in a couple weeks. They can be complicated."

"Could be. Oh, I didn't tell you! Yesterday Eclipse actually let me pet him for a minute."

"That's great. He'll be eating out of your hand in no time."

Eclipse was the name Ida had given to the black cat that had been hanging around the museum for the past couple of weeks—nervous and skittish as a wild animal but also hungry—and Ida had been setting food out for him with the intention of taking him home if she could catch him.

Suddenly Abby spotted a ragged corner of colored paper sticking out of a manila folder on the desk. It didn't look as if it belonged there. She snatched it. "Here it is! This is what I've been looking for." She waved the scrap happily. "It's the name of an out-of-print book I need on ornithopters."

"Ornithopters?" Ida repeated doubtfully. "Sounds like

some machine out of a science fiction movie. *Everybody to the ornithopter!*" she added in a deep, movie-captain voice. "*The alien cockroaches are attacking!*"

Abby laughed. "They are machines. Machines that fly by flapping wings, trying to imitate how birds fly. It's how man made some of his earliest attempts at flight, although not very successfully in most instances. I need the information for the new exhibit. But I can't imagine how it got into a file on—" Abby peered at the folder. "—blue-footed boobies."

Ida did not inquire why she had a file on blue-footed boobies, a tropical bird that had certainly never inhabited the San Juan Islands of the Northwest. Abby wasn't certain why she had the file, either, except that as an ornithologist, she was interested in any and all creatures in the bird world.

"I'm glad you found what you were looking for. Now how about that coffee and roll to celebrate?"

Abby could almost taste the cinnamon-covered pastry. She seldom indulged, and she did love those rolls. But finding the scrap of paper didn't change the fact that the office still looked as if a paper storm had swept through it. Resolutely she said, "Maybe later."

Ida went back to the public area of the museum, and Abby tackled the clutter. First she filed the stack of folders in their proper places in the filing cabinet, making note even as she did so that she could ask Hugo about getting another filing cabinet. She briskly separated letters that needed to be answered, and filed or deep-sixed the others. She cleaned out the pigeonholes and organized the ballpoint pens and markers that seemed to have multiplied at an alarming rate.

Drawers next, three on each side. She worked her way from top to bottom, gathering a nice sense of satisfaction as the overflow moved from desk to wastepaper basket. The bottom drawer stuck. She yanked and pulled, but the drawer would come no farther than halfway. She finally got down on her knees trying to see what was holding it.

*I hope no one walks in now*, she thought. She was not exactly posed in a dignified position, almost standing on her head trying to see what the problem was. There! A crumpled piece of paper caught alongside the drawer. She tried to pull the paper free but managed only to scrape a knuckle, break a fingernail and rip the paper.

Okay, she'd just have to remove the entire drawer. Working carefully so as not to scratch anything on the lovely old desk, she lifted and eased the drawer fractionally from side to side as she pulled on it.

When the drawer was out, she set it on the floor beside her swivel chair and smoothed the paper that had been the culprit. It might at least have been something important, she grumbled as she rubbed the scraped knuckle, given how much trouble it had caused. But it was only a stray paper with a few lines of computer gibberish printed on it.

She tossed the sheet in the wastepaper basket and started to put the drawer back but then saw that more pieces of paper had collected at the back of the drawer. She reached in to retrieve them, running her hand around the drawer cavity to be sure she'd gotten everything.

Her hand touched something fastened to the underside of the wooden plank that separated this drawer from the one above it. Part of the desk's construction, she thought at first.

No, not part of the construction, she realized as her fingers explored further. Whatever she was touching wasn't wood, and she could feel tape holding it to that section of the desk.

Risking more fingernails, she pulled the tape loose. Now she had hold of something, although she couldn't tell what, because the other end of the *something* was still attached to the desk with more tape.

She dragged that tape free also and looked curiously at the object she had pulled out of the recessed space. It had an oblong, flat shape, and was wrapped in what appeared to be an ordinary paper sack.

She used scissors to cut the tape and sack loose. Now what she was looking at was an oblong box—a rather fancy box— diagonally striped with silver and blue.

*How odd.* Carefully she opened the flat box. And caught her breath in astonishment at what she saw there.

# Chapter Two

IT WAS A NECKLACE, AN incredibly beautiful necklace. A blue stone surrounded by a border of smaller, clear stones hung pendant style from a thick, twisted strand of tiny stones, the central stone so large and vividly blue that it looked almost unreal—as if the bluest sea and the brightest sunshine had somehow been captured and cut into facets exploding with dazzling points of blue light.

Abby blinked. What in the world was this doing in her desk? How had it gotten here? Who did it belong to?

The design of the necklace dramatized the beauty of the blue stone, the smaller stones forming a glittering frame that emphasized its size and color. The blue stone had incredible depth, like looking into a bottomless sea on a clear day. Although the smaller stones surrounding it weren't all that small, Abby realized, except in comparison to the spectacular centerpiece.

"I forgot to bring your mail in earlier and there are several letters—" Ida broke off as she set the letters on Abby's desk and spotted the necklace. "What is *that*?"

"I'm not sure. I just found it hidden in the desk."

"You must have a secret admirer! It's gorgeous." Ida peered closer. "A very wealthy admirer, I'd say."

"Ida, I do not have a secret admirer."

"That's why a secret admirer is *secret*," Ida said with a teasing smile. "You don't know about him."

Abby laughed at Ida's vivid imagination. Ida wanted to be a writer, and she seemed to have the creative imagination for it. Then Abby spotted something she hadn't noticed before, so stunned was she by the dazzling necklace. She picked up the small card tucked in at the bottom of the box.

"Someone may have a secret admirer, but it isn't me. The card says 'To Claudia.'"

Ida came around the desk to study the card with her. It was a heavy, cream-colored paper of the type used for expensive engraved cards or announcements, but this brief message was handwritten. A bold, authoritative handwriting, Abby thought, the letters oversized and forceful. She turned the card over to see if the back side disclosed anything more informative. It didn't.

"So who's Claudia?" Ida asked. "And why is someone leaving an expensive necklace for her in your desk?"

"I have no idea. Maybe Hugo will know. I'll go ask him."

"Watch out for him," Ida warned as she headed out the door of Abby's office. "I think he may be in a bad mood."

Abby replaced the lid on the box. She did not hesitate about carrying it down the hallway to Hugo's office. Hugo was a reserved person, not generally demonstrative, but he was not given to surly bad moods.

She was surprised, however, to find Hugo's door closed. His office door, like her own, always stood open, accessible and welcoming. She raised her hand to knock, then hesitated when she heard his voice inside. She hadn't seen anyone go down the hallway toward his office, so he must be on the phone and it must be a very private conversation to warrant a closed door. His words were indistinct through the heavy wood, but she lowered her hand and stepped back anyway, not wanting to eavesdrop even accidentally.

She turned, intending to return to her own office and talk to Hugo later, but his door suddenly opened behind her.

"Abby! I didn't know you were out here."

From the way he looked at her, Abby had the awkward feeling he thought she may have overheard some of his phone conversation. She hadn't, but she felt a twinge of guilt just for standing there looking as if she may have.

"I've only been here a second," she said hastily. "I just wanted to show you something, but it can wait."

"No, that's fine," he said heartily. "I was headed down to your office anyway. I wanted to tell you I won't be in the office for a couple of days. I'm going over to Seattle and will be staying there overnight. I may have lunch at the Space Needle. And I haven't been down to the Pike Place Market for some time. Can I bring you anything?"

Abby gave her boss and friend a quick, surprised appraisal.

He looked the same as always: thick, silver-white hair and matching mustache, tall, straight-backed figure trim and regal, tailored pants and sports jacket immaculate. Ida had suggested he might not be feeling well, but Abby saw no sign of that. But something seemed different . . .

He stepped back and motioned toward the door to his office. "Come in! Let's take a look at what you have to show me."

That was what was different, Abby thought. That too-hearty joviality, a joviality that sounded suspiciously phony. It also wasn't like him to take time off from the museum for an overnight stay in Seattle. Or to be so chatty about irrelevant details. Ida was right. Something was going on here.

She wanted to ask what. She and Hugo were good friends. They respected each other both personally and professionally. They shared a love of nature and the Lord and a good knock-knock or lightbulb joke. Sometimes she'd even thought there might be a spark of something deeper between them. But they didn't have the kind of relationship that encouraged intimate questions.

So what she said instead was, "I found something odd in my desk. I thought you should see it."

Hugo motioned her into a chair. His office was the same size as her own, but his held mementos from his work and travels all over the world. A whale bone he'd found on a Baja beach, a drawing of a moose done on birch bark by an Alaskan native, a photo of him with a group of Maasai tribesmen in Africa.

He circled his desk and sat in his own swivel chair, fingertips together. "Now what's this you've found?" His alert attention expressed interest, but, like the heartiness, she sensed a certain falseness about it. He gave a small, surreptitious glance toward the digital clock on his desk.

"Really, if you're busy or have a problem—"

"No, no." This time he looked at his watch. "I have an appointment this afternoon, but I have plenty of time now. Everything's fine."

She set the box on his desk and removed the lid without comment. They both stared at the necklace, and Abby felt another jolt of shock at the amazing size and beauty of the blue gem. Hugo looked astonished.

"You found this *where?*" he asked.

"In my desk." Abby explained about the stuck drawer and where she'd found the necklace. "The box was wrapped in a paper sack, apparently so the tape wouldn't damage the box. I can't imagine how it got there."

"Neither can I."

"It looks valuable," Abby added.

Hugo picked up the card. "'To Claudia,'" he read. He turned the card over, as she had, but the blank back side gave him no more information than it had her. "How very strange. Have we ever had a Claudia working here?"

Abby did a small double take. She hadn't been working at the conservatory and museum all that long, and Hugo was certainly more likely than she to know if a Claudia had ever worked there. Another indication that he was indeed distracted about something.

"Not that I know of," Abby said without commenting on the strangeness of his asking this question. "Although she may have been before my time, of course. But if the person who hid the box had intended it as a gift, the person named Claudia wouldn't necessarily be someone here at the museum."

Hugo nodded. "Because the person may simply have been hiding the necklace for safekeeping until he could give it to this Claudia." He hesitated, as if momentarily reluctant to touch the dazzling necklace, then carefully removed it from the velvet-lined box. It hung gracefully from his fingers, the blue stone sparkling in the light from the window, the flexible strand of smaller stones glittering like a thousand tiny lights. "So why didn't this person come back and get it?"

"Yes, that's so odd. Especially since it looks quite valuable," Abby repeated.

"A sapphire, perhaps? Although . . ." Hugo tilted his head, his expression speculative.

"The smaller stones look as if they could be diamonds," Abby offered. She smiled. "Not that I'm all that knowledgeable about gems."

"Neither am I, but they do look like diamonds," Hugo agreed. "And it's a beautifully crafted piece of jewelry, that's for certain. Wonderful workmanship and remarkable styling, very distinctive. But . . ."

"But?"

"If it was really a valuable piece of jewelry, which it certainly would be if the blue stone was a sapphire and the other stones real diamonds, surely someone would have come to retrieve it. He—"

"Or she," Abby interjected.

Hugo nodded. "Yes, or she. But surely he or she wouldn't hide it in the desk and then just abandon or forget it if it was valuable."

"Although it seems odd someone hasn't come looking for it even if it *isn't* highly valuable. It's a beautiful piece of jewelry. Claudia must have been someone special to this person."

"Still, I think it's much more likely an excellent piece of costume jewelry. The clear stones are probably cubic zirconia or some other material rather than real diamonds, and the blue stone is most likely glass or some other material rather than real sapphire."

Hugo set the necklace back in the box. His gesture was dismissive, as if this was the extent of his involvement. Abby was surprised. She'd expected him to be as excited and curious as she was about this strange find. He obviously had other things on his mind.

"What should we do with it?" she asked.

"We should try to find the owner, of course. Perhaps you could talk to Sergeant Cobb at the sheriff's substation. He might have a report about a missing necklace."

"Perhaps even a stolen one," Abby suggested thoughtfully.

Hugo looked surprised at that suggestion, but he nodded.

"Yes, I suppose that's a possibility. Again, Sergeant Cobb may have information. And there must be rules and regulations about what has to be done with found objects and how to locate an owner. Or you might talk to Gordon Siebert down at the jewelry store. Perhaps the necklace was purchased there and he'd recognize it. He has some excellent costume jewelry along with real gems."

Hugo's phone rang, and with the intuitive knowledge that he didn't want to answer it while she was present, Abby hastily stood up.

Hugo pushed the box toward her with one hand and reached for the phone with the other. "Would you close the door on your way out, please?"

Abby must have looked startled at his abruptness, because he gave her an apologetic smile. "I'm sorry. I didn't mean to sound so rude. I'm just a little . . . preoccupied about something that's come up."

"Is there anything I can do to help?"

"Thanks, no."

Abby picked up the box and closed Hugo's door behind her. Back in her own office she shut her eyes for a moment and offered a quick prayer for whatever was troubling Hugo. In spite of his protestations that everything was fine, she was certain something was definitely wrong.

Then she opened the box and studied the necklace, again amazed at its dazzling beauty. If it were a beautiful blue *feather* the situation would be different, she thought wryly. She'd have it classified and identified in no time. But gems were far out of her area of expertise.

Okay, Hugo had suggested she contact Sergeant Cobb, so that's what she would do. She always thought of the officer as Henry rather than the more formal Sergeant Cobb. He was often at the house she and her sister Mary shared, and she and Henry had worked together occasionally to resolve various situations on the island. In old-fashioned terms, Henry was "courting" Mary, although she doubted Mary thought of the relationship in exactly that way. She dialed the substation's number.

"Sergeant Cobb, please," she told the woman who answered, a woman new to the office whom she didn't know.

"I'm sorry. Sergeant Cobb is out on a call right now. I'm afraid he won't be back for some time, but I can reach him if it's an emergency."

"No, no emergency. I'll talk to him later." He might, in fact, be coming to the house for dinner. Abby decided she could show him the necklace and talk to him then.

She tucked the silver and blue box in a newly organized drawer, swiveled the chair to face her computer and got back to work. It took some time on the Internet, but she finally located the out-of-print book on ornithopters at a used book site and ordered it. Then she read and answered her e-mail, worked on a grant application and dusted the rocks and shells on a wall shelf.

But all the time what her mind was really on was that

necklace in her drawer. Who had so carefully hidden it in the desk? Who was Claudia? Why had no one ever come to retrieve the necklace?

On impulse she made a quick decision. The wall clock showed a few minutes past four o'clock. She hadn't seen Hugo leave, but he could have gone out the back door. She found a plastic sack, tucked the box into it and grabbed her jacket from the coatrack in the corner. With a glance at the rain now falling outside her office window, she also picked up her red umbrella gaily emblazoned with hummingbirds, a gift from Mary.

On her way out, Ida called to her from the reception desk. "Did you find out anything more from Mr. Baron about the necklace?"

The museum was almost empty. Only one couple stood beside the Mount Saint Helens exhibit of volcanic activity. Yet they turned when Ida spoke, as if the word *necklace* had sparked their interest.

Abby stepped closer to the desk before answering Ida's question. "No. Hugo had never seen it before and has no idea who Claudia is."

"How strange. I could ask around at the café and see if anyone knows someone by that name."

"No, please don't," Abby said quickly. She wasn't certain exactly why, except that the box in the plastic sack at her side seemed to be growing more mysterious by the minute. She thought a moment, then backtracked. "What I mean is, yes, it would be fine to ask about a Claudia. Do that. We need to know if there's someone around here by that name. But I think it would be better if the necklace wasn't mentioned to anyone just yet. Okay?"

"Oh well, sure, if you don't want me to." Ida sounded puzzled but offered no argument. "I suppose someone who doesn't really own the necklace might try to claim it if they heard about it."

Actually, Abby hadn't thought through her reasoning on not mentioning the necklace to anyone, but Ida had made an excellent point. "Exactly," she said. "We don't want to get a lot of gossip and speculation started."

Ida smiled, a lively spark in her eyes. "Speculation and gossip about a secret admirer leaving a beautiful, expensive gift in your desk?"

"The gift is for someone named *Claudia*. That's why you're going to find out if anyone knows a Claudia on the island."

Ida smiled and waved the name off as a technicality. Abby wanted to be annoyed with her, but she couldn't. Ida's parents had died when she was only seventeen. Now, at twenty-four, she was a sweet young woman, an enthusiastic new Christian and a good worker. So instead Abby offered a tease of her own. "I'm sure people would be much more interested in hearing about a budding romance between a certain young woman here at the museum and a certain young man at the hardware store, than in some older woman's nonexistent secret admirer."

"You wouldn't tell—" A blush quickly followed Ida's gasp at the mention of her tentative relationship with Aaron

Holloway, grandson of the longtime owner of Holloway's Hardware. He'd been interested in her for quite some time now, but only recently had she showed signs of returning that interest, and she was still being a bit secretive about it. Although Ida should know by now, Abby thought, that secrets seldom lasted long on Sparrow Island.

"Wouldn't I?" Abby teased further.

"Okay," Ida agreed, "It's probably a good idea not to mention the necklace or a secret admirer to anyone."

Abby smiled at the unspoken agreement within Ida's statement. Ida wouldn't mention the necklace or secret admirer; Abby wouldn't mention anything about Ida and Aaron's budding relationship.

"Will you be coming back today?" Ida asked.

"Probably not. Although if I have time after I run this errand, I may come back to the lab in the conservatory building. I need to do some cleanup work there too."

Abby opened her umbrella as she dashed from the museum steps to her car. The rain wasn't a heavy downpour, but it had a here-to-stay feel. The weather had been wonderful all fall, remarkably warm and clear, but it looked as if winter rains might be settling in now. Wind had blown most of the colorful leaves off the big maple in the landscaped area in front of the museum. Abby didn't mind the change in weather. She loved the fresh scent of rain mixed with whiffs of cedar and fir, and the salt, fish and seaweed tang of sea, the cozy crackle of a fireplace and a cup of hot chocolate on a

18

rainy evening. The wind had picked up, and the ever-change-able sea off Sparrow Island was storm-gray now, rough with whitecaps. She could hear waves crashing against the rocky shore beyond the trees.

She passed her parents' farm on the drive into Green Harbor, but she didn't see anyone outside. Good. Better that her father was puttering in the barn or the house instead of working outside on this rainy day. Even at eighty-two, George Stanton often had to be reminded to slow down, reminders that he usually cheerfully ignored.

Traffic in town was unexpectedly busy for a weekday afternoon, and Abby had to park around the corner from Siebert's Jewelry. She held the box close to her body as she hurried through the rain to the recessed entryway. She paused to close her umbrella before pushing open the elaborately carved door with an oval window of etched glass.

Inside, there were no customers. A woman she didn't know was industriously polishing a glass display case with a cloth.

The heavy carpet underfoot discreetly muffled footsteps. The display cases were brightly lit from within, but the track lighting overhead was muted except for small spotlights on targeted items. Fresh bouquets of flowers—no doubt from Island Blooms, her sister Mary's flower shop—stood on two counters. Gems sparkled everywhere—rings, necklaces, bracelets and pins—and mirrors behind the glass-front cabinets mounted on the walls reflected dazzling colors.

Gordon Siebert, a tall, slender, sixtyish man with thinning

gray hair, was rearranging items within a central display case. Small rounded glasses gave him a scholarly look, but the goatee and mustache added a surprisingly suave air. He gave her a pleasant smile and walked toward her.

"May I help you?"

The friendly attentiveness pleased Abby. She had been to the store before but never bought anything. She doubted that today she looked as if she were here to buy an expensive diamond ring, but Gordon acted as pleasant and interested as if she were.

"I hope so. Although I'm not here to buy anything," she added hastily not wanting to give a false impression. "I have a piece of jewelry and I'm wondering if it was purchased here."

Abby pulled the box out of the plastic bag and set it on the glass top of a display case. "I'm Abby Stanton, Associate Curator out at the nature conservatory," she added. She held out her hand.

"Yes, I know," he said as he shook it. "My wife keeps telling me the museum has some wonderful exhibits and that the bird walks at the conservatory are most interesting. I'll have to get out there one of these days. Oh, and this is my assistant, Judee Arcuta." He motioned to a young woman polishing a glass case.

The slender blond woman lifted her fingers in a friendly miniwave. Abby nodded back to her and opened the box.

Gordon Siebert peered into the box. Abby had no idea what he was expecting, but the sudden widening of his eyes behind his glasses told her he was surprised.

# Chapter Three

 Do you recognize it?" Abby asked.

"No, no I don't. It wasn't purchased here." Gordon Siebert spoke without a trace of doubt. He glanced up at her, and she had the feeling he was reevaluating her and that he was much more curious than when she first walked in the door. She could almost see questions hovering like comic strip balloons over his head.

Quickly she said, "We're thinking the blue stone may be a sapphire. Although it's more likely just a nice piece of costume jewelry."

Gordon walked over to a shelf below a discreetly concealed cash register and returned with a small object about the size of a remote control. He pushed a button, waited a few moments, then pressed the tip projecting from the instrument against the blue stone. Almost instantly a tiny beep sounded and a small light glowed green.

"What is that?" Abby asked.

"It's a tester." He peered at the instrument with a small frown, as if perhaps considering its reliability.

"It can tell if this is a real sapphire or glass?" Abby prodded when he didn't seem inclined to elaborate.

"This is not a sapphire," he stated with the same conviction with which he'd said the necklace had not been purchased at his store. "But it's certainly not some cheap imitation."

"Then it's . . . ?"

He pressed the tip of the tester against the blue stone again. The beep and green glow repeated. "It's a diamond. The instrument tests thermal conductivity, and diamonds have a much higher thermal conductivity than other gems or imitations."

Abby didn't know much about thermal conductivity, but she did know what she could see. "A *diamond?*" she repeated doubtfully. "But it's blue."

"Diamonds can come in various colors, although the colored stones are much more rare than the clear ones. The blue color comes from tiny amounts of the element boron that were incorporated into the crystal as the diamond was forming."

"God can create beauty in the most unlikely ways, can't He?" Abby marveled.

The jeweler's narrow eyebrows lifted in surprise. "I've never thought of it in exactly that way, but I suppose that's true." He touched the instrument to the blue stone again, as if he still couldn't quite believe what it was telling him. "Definitely a diamond." He sounded awed, and Abby suspected Gordon Siebert did not awe easily.

"And the other stones, the ones that aren't colored?" Abby asked.

Gordon placed the tip of the instrument on each of the clear stones surrounding the central stone. Each time it made the distinctive beep and glowed green. "Diamonds." At random, he touched some of the tiny stones in the entwined strands of the necklace, the ends of the strands joined by a golden clasp. Each one, tiny as it was, also registered positive. "All diamonds."

While Abby was still trying to digest all that, he went to the shelf and returned with two more pieces of equipment. One Abby vaguely recognized as a jeweler's loupe. He held it to his eye and studied the gems. Then he used the other instrument, which had a round face with numbers on it and calipers extending from one side. He placed the calipers on each edge of the blue gem.

"What does that do?" Abby asked.

"It measures the width of a gem in millimeters, which can then be roughly translated into carats. For exact carat weight the gem would have to be removed from the setting and weighed on a scale, but this gives a close approximation." He moved on to a measurement of the smaller, clear diamonds surrounding the blue stone.

"So?" Abby asked.

"The smaller stones around the blue diamond are about a half carat each." He took a deep breath, as if he found it hard to believe what he was going to say next. "The blue diamond itself is approximately twenty-one carats."

Abby gasped. "Twenty-one carats," she echoed faintly. Plus several more carats of uncolored diamonds. Valuable. Very valuable. And, at the moment, all her responsibility. Then a hopeful thought occurred to her. "Perhaps the blue color makes the stone less valuable than a regular diamond?"

Gordon smiled as if that were a naïve question. "Oh no. If anything, a blue diamond is more valuable, because of its rarity. And this one is an exceptionally deep blue color, a 'vivid' blue I'm sure it would be classified. That isn't just a nice term," he added. "It's a specific color classification. The very best for a blue diamond."

He hesitated a moment and then, with what sounded like careful delicacy, as if he were reluctant to pry but too curious not to, asked, "This is a, ah, piece of family jewelry?"

"No, I'm just . . . holding it for someone."

He eyed the card lying in a corner of the box. "Someone named Claudia?"

"We were hoping, if the necklace had been purchased here, that you'd know who Claudia is. Even though the necklace isn't familiar to you, would you happen to know anyone by that name?"

"Let's see . . . I remember a Claudine applying for a job here once. But no, no Claudia."

Abby held back a smile. Gordon Siebert was so curious that even his mustache twitched. At this point, however, she was even more uncertain what to tell him or anyone else. "The necklace must be fairly valuable?"

Unexpectedly, this time Gordon laughed. "'Fairly valuable' is an understatement if I ever heard one. Just offhand,

I'd estimate this necklace is worth, oh, at least three million dollars."

"Th-three million dollars?" Abby stammered, stunned. No wonder he'd been so delicate in his question about whether the necklace was family jewelry. She undoubtedly did not look like someone who would personally own a three-million-dollar necklace. Her blue slacks and jacket were nice enough, but they didn't come from some exclusive boutique, and her blue-bird earrings were more whimsical than valuable.

She peered over her shoulder, half expecting to see an eavesdropping thief or thug creeping up to snatch the necklace, but the only other person in the room was the clerk, Judee, now polishing a mirror.

"It's possibly much more valuable than three million," Gordon added. "Actually, I'm being quite conservative with that figure. I'd have to do a considerably more intensive examination, plus some research on current values of large blue diamonds, to give a more accurate figure. I know that Harrods in London had a large blue diamond set in an elaborate diamond necklace for which they were asking sixteen million."

He carried the necklace over to a microscope set up on one of the counters and peered through the eyepiece at the blue gem. "There are a couple of small flaws, certainly to be expected in a gem this size. They're rather unusually shaped, with a distinctive feathering, but I doubt they would detract much from the value. And the half-carat diamonds are of excellent quality."

"Well." At the moment Abby couldn't think of anything more astute to say.

"Would you like to look?" He stepped back and motioned toward the microscope.

Abby looked. She was familiar enough with the workings of a microscope. She'd studied everything from feathers to bird mites to bird bones with one. But what she saw in the blue diamond was mostly magnified dazzle.

"The styling of the necklace is quite modern, and the way the tiny diamonds are mounted to make a flexible strand is a technique that's come into use only recently. But the cut of the blue diamond is what is called a cushion cut. It's still used, and it's come back in popularity somewhat, but basically it's an old-fashioned cut. It was very popular during the late 1800s."

Gordon smiled, a man who obviously enjoyed his work and was extremely knowledgeable. "It's said that this was a great cut for candlelight. More romantic than modern cuts, which show up better under electric lights."

"And all this means . . . ?"

"My personal opinion is that it means the diamond was originally cut a good many years ago but was reset relatively recently, probably within the last ten years or so. The smaller diamonds are the more modern, round brilliant cut. I don't recognize the styling of the necklace as belonging to any particular designer, and there are no identifying marks on it. But the necklace is definitely not antique, although the blue diamond itself could be considered antique. I hope I'm not just confusing you?"

"No, not at all." At least not about the difference between the stone's being antique and the setting and styling modern. But Abby was more confused than ever about the fact that the necklace had been hidden in her desk. Three million dollars! And no one had ever come looking for it.

"There are a number of very well known blue diamonds," Gordon added. "The Hope Diamond is probably the most famous, somewhere around forty-five carats. It's in the Smithsonian now, but it's supposed to have originally come from the eye of an idol in India. King Louis XIV once owned it, but it later disappeared during the French Revolution. Then it resurfaced and came to be known as the Hope Diamond when an English banker named Henry Thomas Hope owned it."

Abby had been to the Smithsonian, of course, when she lived and worked back east at Cornell University's Lab of Ornithology. But she'd been interested in exhibits of natural history, not gems.

"The history of large, valuable stones is often well documented, then?" she asked.

"Oh yes. Although, for various reasons, they sometimes disappear and the history ends in mystery. King Louis XIV owned another one called The Blue Tavernier, also from India, but it was stolen in the late 1700s and has never been found. And then there's a famous blue diamond called the Wittelsbach. It's had various royal owners, disappeared in the early 1930s and then resurfaced about 1962."

"You're very knowledgeable," Abby commented.

"There's a lot more I don't know than I do know," Gordon said modestly, "but I find the subject of all precious gems fascinating. Blue diamonds have a reputation for being rather bad luck for their owners, although I'm not a believer in such superstitions. But one thing I do know. Although I had a big jewelry store in Tacoma for many years before retiring and coming here—"

"This is retired?" Abby glanced around the well-stocked jewelry store.

Gordon smiled a bit ruefully. "I found I couldn't give it up completely and just sit around watching my wife make quilts." Briskly he went back to what he'd started to say. "In any case, in all those years in the jewelry business in Tacoma, I never saw anything like this necklace. Never."

Abby nodded, still at a loss for words.

"I'd be most interested in anything you could . . . or wanted . . . to tell me about the history of the diamond or the necklace," Gordon added. He paused as if considering what she'd said earlier about holding the necklace for someone else. "I take it you'd prefer not to reveal the owner's name?"

"Actually, ownership at this point is somewhat . . . murky."

That statement brought a lift of Gordon's gray eyebrows, but he discreetly remained silent, waiting for her to continue. Abby glanced around, wondering if the clerk was close enough to overhear. But she was at the far end of the room, still polishing glass. Abby almost told Gordon the circumstances of finding the necklace, but then decided it would be best to keep that information to herself for the time being.

"I'd really like to find out more of the necklace's history myself, if that's possible," she said instead.

"I could make some inquiries. Someone should know something about a stone this large and valuable, especially if it's been reset in the last few years."

"I'd want everything kept confidential."

"Yes, of course. I can keep the inquiries very discreet. There's no need to offer unnecessary details."

"Thank you. I'd appreciate that."

"May I take a photo? It could be helpful for identification purposes when I make the inquiries."

Abby nodded, and he motioned her to follow him to the rear of the room. There he had another piece of equipment. It consisted of a round, white dome, perhaps nine inches high, with an opening that exposed a small, tilting platform.

"This is a digital camera especially set up for photographing jewelry," Gordon explained. "This is the lens up here." He fingered a black object that looked a little like a telescope pointed at the platform. "It projects an image on the screen over there." This time he motioned to a screen similar to her own computer screen. "And then the printed photo comes out over there."

Smoothly the jeweler went through the process he had just described. The image of the necklace appeared on the screen, and a moment later he handed Abby an excellent color photo that showed an enlarged view of the necklace. He then took a separate photo, concentrating on the blue diamond itself.

"The larger size offers more detail and aids identification," he explained.

He printed off several copies of the photos, gave her one of each and carefully handed the necklace back to her.

"You do have a secure place to keep it, don't you?"

Abby realized she hadn't thought that far ahead. She'd assumed the necklace must be fairly valuable, but to her that meant several hundred dollars, a few thousand at most. But *three million*? She'd never before even been in the vicinity of a piece of jewelry worth three million, let alone responsible for such a valuable item.

"No. I . . . I don't," she said finally, halfway beginning to wish she'd never decided to clean out her desk drawers today.

"We have a safe in back." Gordon motioned to a door at the rear of the store, but his expression was troubled. "But I'm afraid, given the value of this necklace, and the liability involved if anything happened . . ."

"Yes, of course, I understand."

"You might want to consider a safe deposit box at the bank."

Abby leaped on the suggestion with relief. "Yes! That's a perfect idea for where to put it until I can talk to Sergeant Cobb." And she and Mary already had a box at the bank.

"Sergeant Cobb?" Gordon repeated, as if that connection raised more questions, and Abby realized she'd said more than she'd intended to.

"I'll go over to the bank right now."

Gordon looked as if he'd definitely like to quiz her, but he was obviously too much of a gentleman to be overly nosy. Instead, with a glance at the clock at the rear of the room, he said, "You'd better hurry. It's almost five o'clock now."

*Yes, hurry,* Abby thought as her gaze also flew to the clock. "Thank you. Thank you so much."

"I'll let you know if my inquiries turn up anything," Gordon said.

Hastily Abby rearranged the necklace in the box and stuffed both box and photographs in the plastic sack. She grabbed her umbrella and hurried to the door, eager to get to the bank with all possible speed.

What she did *not* want, she knew, was to have this three-million-dollar necklace in her personal possession one minute longer than necessary.

# Chapter Four

OUTSIDE, ABBY PAUSED in the recessed entryway to Seibert's Jewelry. Slanting rain hammered the sidewalk now. She struggled to keep the box snugged close to her body while she nervously wrestled the umbrella open.

She reminded herself there was no need for nerves. No one out here on the street knew she was carrying a three-million-dollar necklace in the plastic bag hanging from her wrist. The bag had HOLLOWAY'S HARDWARE written across it and surely looked as if it held a box of nails or a bottle of drain cleaner, and no one was going to mug her for *that*. She couldn't, in fact, recall anyone ever having been mugged on Sparrow Island.

Yet in spite of that reassurance, every nerve in her body felt as if it were standing at attention, like porcupine quills. Except that these quills were jabbing inward, pricking her skin and raising goosebumps, making her mouth feel as if it were full of dry feathers.

Darkness was coming early on this wintry, rainy day. Raindrops haloed the street lights, and headlights already blazed on passing vehicles. She eyed a pickup cruising by with suspicious slowness. Were the occupants sizing her up? They might not know about the three-million-dollar necklace, but they could think she'd just purchased something expensive in the jewelry store . . .

*Enough*, she chided herself. She shook her head, half laughing, half annoyed with herself for these runaway thoughts. And earlier she'd been grumbling that Ida had too vivid an imagination!

She was just about to step onto the sidewalk when she spotted a familiar figure up the street on the opposite side. It was Hugo, carrying his own conservative, dark umbrella. Great! She started to wave and call to him, eager to share what she'd just learned about the necklace, but then she stopped. Hugo was not alone, she realized as she spotted another person on the far side of his tall figure.

Sharing the umbrella with Hugo was Dr. Dana Randolph. At barely five feet tall, dressed in dark slacks and high-heeled boots, the slender, blond woman looked more like a Seattle sophisticate than what she was—the responsible and competent head of the Sparrow Island Medical Center.

Seeing the two of them together puzzled Abby. Back at the museum, Hugo had said he had an appointment later. Was Dr. Randolph the person he meant? Was he ill and not telling anyone? Was that why he'd seemed so preoccupied and distracted? But if that was the situation, wouldn't he have met Dr. Randolph at the clinic, not out here on a rain-swept street?

More likely, Abby decided, he'd just happened to run into her and offered her the shelter of his umbrella.

Yet their heads were bent together as if they were engrossed in an intense and private discussion, and neither of them paid any attention to a couple of passersby on the sidewalk. Abby pressed herself against the door to the jewelry store, umbrella angled in front of her, suddenly reluctant to have them know she'd spotted them together.

If Hugo actually was ill and he'd been on the phone about a medical problem earlier, he obviously didn't want anyone to know about it. She didn't want to embarrass him or herself by intruding on a private discussion with his doctor.

Abby waited until Hugo and Dr. Randolph were well down the street before stepping out to the sidewalk. At the same time, glancing back, she realized Gordon Siebert and his clerk Judee were watching her curiously from inside the store.

They were no doubt wondering why she was acting so furtive and sneaky, she realized in embarrassment. She gave them a self-conscious wave and stepped out briskly, only to realize if she continued going in that direction to reach her car, she might well run into Hugo and the doctor after all.

Okay, she'd circle around the block to reach her car. She grasped the handle of the umbrella firmly and headed in the opposite direction, stepping over a stream of water already flowing along the curb at the corner.

When she got halfway around the block, it occurred to her that since she had no idea where Hugo and Dr. Randolph were headed, she might still run into them. No problem, she told herself firmly. She'd just walk rather than drive over to the bank. It wouldn't take much longer, and she'd be sure to miss them.

When the bank came into view Abby sighed with relief, only to draw up short before the door. There, hanging across the heavy glass door, a sign barred her way: CLOSED. She pushed up the sleeve of her jacket to peer at her watch. Five minutes after five o'clock. She tried the door to be certain. Locked.

She peered hopefully through the heavy glass, thinking she might attract someone's attention. Lights still shone in some back rooms, but no one moved around out front, not even when she rapped lightly on the glass.

Abby turned and looked both ways up and down the street as her nervous apprehension suddenly roared back. For a few minutes she'd concentrated so intently on dodging Hugo and Dr. Randolph that the contents of the plastic bag had slipped her mind. Now it felt as if the box were flashing a neon signal to anyone in the vicinity: *Three-million-dollar necklace here! Just come and grab it!*

She headed for her car almost at a run, encumbered by the plastic bag, her purse, her umbrella and the driving rain. By the time she scooted safely behind the wheel of the car, she felt both foolish and exasperated with herself. If she hadn't been so concerned about dodging Hugo and Dr. Randolph, she'd have reached the bank in plenty of time. And if she hadn't let her imagination run wild about someone snatching the necklace, her palms and back of her blouse wouldn't be soaked with nervous perspiration now.

She now had no choice but to take the necklace home with her for the night. But it had been in her desk for who knew how long, and no one had knocked her on the head to get it, so there was no reason to think someone would do so now. She further brightened with the thought that Henry Cobb might be at the house when she arrived and he'd take the necklace off her hands.

Of much greater importance and concern than the necklace, she reminded herself, was Hugo.

*Could he really have some serious medical problem?* she wondered as she drove toward home. She'd never known him to suffer more than a cold or touch of the flu. But his wife had died of malaria years ago, which she'd contracted when they were in Africa. Could Hugo have some little known tropical ailment that was only now surfacing many years later?

She wished she could ask him, but she knew she had to respect his privacy and wait until, and *if,* he wanted to tell her. She felt an unexpected twinge of regret that he obviously didn't feel he could share something this important and personal with her.

Well, that didn't mean she couldn't talk to the Lord about him, even if she didn't know details. She offered another heartfelt prayer for his healing if he was ill. "And if Dr. Randolph is treating him, I pray for wisdom and good judgment for her too," she added. "Guide her in bringing him back to good health. Amen."

It was going to be a wild night weather-wise, Abby realized as she drove home. Wind buffeted the dark cedars lining the road, and once she had to dodge a fallen branch. Rain pummeled the windshield, and the occasional slap of a windblown, wet leaf on the glass made her flinch. Disappointment hit Abby when she saw that Henry's cruiser was not at the house as she pulled into the driveway. Once in the garage, she hesitated a moment before going on through the laundry room into the kitchen. Should she tell Mary about the necklace?

Yes, of course. But later, not tonight. She didn't want Mary apprehensive and nervous with three million dollars in mysterious jewels there in the house with them.

Inside, the fragrant scent of spicy spaghetti sauce greeted her, and a fire crackled in the fireplace in the living room. Mary was by the sliding glass doors leading to the back deck, leaning over in her wheelchair to dry Finnegan's paws with a towel. The dog's golden coat glistened with raindrops. He gave Abby a welcoming thump of his tail. He was Mary's service dog, helping her with activities she couldn't manage from her wheelchair, but he took a proprietary air toward Abby too.

"Finnegan's been out in the rain?" Abby asked.

"He wanted to go out for his playtime even though it was pouring rain," Mary said. She was in the habit of letting Finnegan out to play for an hour or so every afternoon, time off from his workday to just be a dog and run and dig and play with his ball. The yard wasn't fenced, but he was well trained and never wandered far from the house even when outside alone. She tousled his head affectionately. "He really didn't want to come in even when it got dark."

Abby looked toward the sofa where Mary's cat Blossom was curled into a fluffy white cushion. She laughed. "I don't see Blossom having any such ideas about running around in the rain."

"Right. She looked out the window a couple of hours ago, gave one of those haughty flips of her tail and hasn't moved from that spot on the sofa since."

Blossom, bedraggled and hungry when Mary had first found her a few years ago, had wasted no time taking on airs that proclaimed her royal Persian heritage. It had come as a surprise to both Abby and Mary when Blossom and Finnegan turned out to like each other. The cat was especially fond of washing the dog's silky ears.

"That sauce smells wonderful. Is Henry coming to dinner?" Abby asked hopefully as she shed her damp jacket.

"No, he has a meeting tonight, so it's just you and me."

Ordinarily, Abby would have been delighted. She liked Henry Cobb and never felt his presence intrusive, but Mary had such an active social life with her knitting, crafting and reading groups, plus the flower arranging lessons she taught at Island Blooms, that sometimes it did seem as if she and Mary didn't have much sisterly time together. But tonight she'd really hoped the deputy sheriff would be coming over.

"I thought maybe we could play Monopoly later," Mary added. "I ran across our old board when I was cleaning out my closet earlier today, and stormy nights remind me of Monopoly evenings with Mom and Dad when we were kids."

"Great! I haven't played in years. I'll just run upstairs and change. Want me to make a salad to go with the spaghetti?"

"It's already made. And garlic bread is ready to go under the broiler. With the weather so awful I didn't go over to the flower shop today, so I had plenty of time. I've been working on some greeting cards using those flowers we pressed last summer."

Mary's creative talents with flowers had made Island Blooms well known even beyond Sparrow Island, but her talents were not limited to fresh blooms. She did popular dried arrangements as well. The greeting cards were one of her latest projects.

"I'll be down in a minute, then."

Abby had been discreetly concealing the plastic bag behind her purse so Mary wouldn't notice and ask what she'd bought at the hardware store. The bag bumped her leg as she carried it upstairs. The box weighed only a few ounces, but somehow it had seemed to get larger and heavier and more noticeable ever since she learned the contents were worth three million dollars. Or more.

Upstairs in her bedroom, she looked around for a safe place to stash the box for the night, then reminded herself there was no reason she couldn't just leave it out in plain sight. No one was going to be prowling the house looking for it. She set the plastic bag beside the lamp on her night stand and draped her damp jacket over a chair.

She jumped when a screech from the main road startled her. No doubt just someone braking suddenly on the slick road. Yet the unexpected sound reinforced her feeling that she didn't want the necklace out in plain sight. Just in case.

*Just in case of what?* a small, interior voice questioned suspiciously.

She refused to answer it. Small, interior voices never seemed to ask helpful questions, just annoying ones. But even though the necklace was undoubtedly perfectly safe out in the open, it wouldn't hurt to have it hidden.

After trying several spots in the closet and in a chest of drawers, she finally tucked the box between the mattress and the box spring on her bed. Then she had to laugh at herself. Wasn't that the first place a burglar would look?

She changed into a comfortable pair of faded jeans and an old sweatshirt with a cartoonish version of a hungry-looking vulture eyeing a Volkswagen Bug and the words "Think Big!" emblazoned across the front. Mary was dishing up spaghetti when Abby went down to the kitchen. Abby put the garlic bread under the broiler and poured coffee. When Mary dropped a potholder, Finnegan retrieved it for her without even being asked.

Mary chattered animatedly all through dinner. She hadn't managed the Island Blooms flower shop herself since the accident that had confined her to a wheelchair, but she was still very interested in what was going on with her business. She spoke excitedly of an exceptionally large order of flowers for an upcoming wedding at The Dorset, Sparrow Island's elite resort hotel that was popular with Seattle residents for special events.

"Oh, and I heard someone saw Ida Tolliver and Aaron Holloway renting a couple of horses to go riding together out at the Summit Stables," she added. "Maybe they'll get together yet."

So much for Ida's "secret" about the tentative relationship, Abby thought, smiling to herself.

"And Dad called to say they had an oversupply of eggs now, if we want a couple extra dozen. I thought I might make an angel food cake. I remember you used to love angel food."

"*Mmm*," Abby said. Maybe she should have left the necklace out in the car instead of bringing it into the house.

"Is something wrong?" Mary asked.

Abby jumped. "No. Of course not." She realized she'd lost the train of the conversation. "The spaghetti is delicious."

"You seem rather preoccupied, as if you have something on your mind. Why are you looking at Finnegan like that?" Mary added suddenly.

"I'm not—" Abby broke off as she realized she was watching Finnegan. "I just noticed that he keeps looking toward the sliding glass doors."

As if there might be something . . . or *someone* . . . lurking out there on the deck or in the backyard, though she didn't say that to Mary.

"I didn't let him bring his ball in because it was all wet and squishy. He's probably worried about a raccoon or something making off with it."

Of course. *Put a lid on the runaway imagination*, Abby told herself firmly. What she said aloud was, "I'm busy working on the new 'Bird Flight and Early Human Flight' exhibit for the museum. I'd really like to find a model of an ornithopter to use in it."

Then she had to explain what an ornithopter was, and Mary, who had never quite understood Abby's interest in the bird world, laughed and said, "Sounds like something that would fascinate Bobby."

"It does, doesn't it?" Abby agreed. Bobby McDonald was the ten-year-old son of their next-door neighbors, Sandy and Neil McDonald. He was curious about anything to do with science or nature. A boy who could be as helpful as a third hand, or as unhelpful as a puppy underfoot. "I'll have to tell him about it."

By the time Abby cleared the table and put the dishes in the dishwasher, Mary had the Monopoly board set up on a card table in front of the fireplace.

Abby sat in the upholstered chair by the hearth, determined to concentrate on the game and enjoy her evening with Mary. But just as she landed on a railroad square, a loud thump startled her. "Did you hear that?" she asked uneasily.

"Hear what?"

"That noise. Like . . . something out front."

"Just the wind tossing that old doormat around. We really should get a new one, you know."

Right. The doormat. Not a prowler sneaking around trying to figure out how to get into a house to steal a three-million-dollar necklace.

The game progressed, with Mary rapidly gaining properties and adding houses to them. Abby couldn't seem to concentrate. She kept hearing things. Something rattling in the backyard. A rustle like someone trying to climb the trellis outside the kitchen window. When the phone rang she jumped so hard that she hit the edge of the table, sending Mary's little houses flying in all directions. She had to get down on her hands and knees to round them up while Mary talked on the phone with Candace, her manager at Island Blooms. A few minutes later she made an excuse to dash upstairs because she thought she heard a peculiar noise up there.

When she returned, Mary finally tossed down the dice in exasperation. "Abby, what in the world is wrong with you? You're as jumpy as Blossom when she sees a strange dog. You're making me nervous. And Finnegan too."

Finnegan did indeed seem rather nervous, jumping up every few minutes to wander from the dining room to the sliding glass doors to the front door. Maybe she was making him nervous, Abby acknowledged to herself. Or maybe the storm bothered him. Or maybe, just *maybe*, he was nervous because he knew someone was out there prowling around.

Logically, there was no reason for anyone to be prowling,

Abby reminded herself. Only a few people besides herself knew of the existence of the necklace. Hugo, of course. Ida Tolliver. Gordon Siebert and his clerk. Hugo might also have told Dr. Randolph by now, although that seemed unlikely. Hugo hadn't appeared that interested in the necklace. Yet even if he had told the doctor, neither she nor anyone else on that short list of good people would be prowling around the house with criminal intent.

Yet it was also true that there was someone else who knew of the necklace's existence. The unknown someone who had hidden it in Abby's desk. Could that person somehow have been keeping an eye on his hidden treasure and knew Abby had removed it from the hiding spot today?

"Abby, is something going on that I don't know about?" Mary demanded. She tilted her head speculatively as she studied her sister.

Okay, Mary had a right to know, Abby decided reluctantly. If there was danger, Mary should be aware of it. Silently she went upstairs and returned with the plastic bag. She took out the box and opened it. Mary's reaction of wide-eyed awe was one with which Abby was already becoming familiar.

"Abby, what is this? Where did you get it? It's gorgeous!" With none of Abby's own hesitation about touching the necklace, she picked it up eagerly. In the flickering glow of firelight, the diamonds glittered as if lit from within.

Abby told Mary the full story, from cleaning out her desk

44

to going to Siebert's Jewelry to getting to the bank too late to put the necklace in the safe deposit box. "And that's why I was hoping Henry would be here tonight," she finished. "I keep thinking, valuable as the necklace is, that someone might be willing to do something quite . . . unscrupulous to get it."

"You really think there's danger of someone coming here?" Mary peered around their solidly built home. She sounded doubtful.

"My head says there isn't. My nerves don't seem to be getting the message," Abby admitted.

"The doors are locked. We have Finnegan. I'm not worried." Mary waved a dismissive hand, and her eyes sparkled with a different thought. "What happens if you can't find the owner of the necklace?"

"I don't know. I hadn't thought about that."

"Maybe you'll own it!"

"I'm sure the real owner will turn up. Surely no one's going to simply abandon something this valuable."

"You never know. Maybe the person passed away or has amnesia or something. Such things happen."

Abby could see that having the necklace here in the house definitely wasn't making Mary as edgy as it was her. Mary seemed, in fact, to be rather enjoying the unusual situation.

"Let's try it on!" Mary said.

"Try it on?" Abby repeated doubtfully.

"Why not?" In a moment Mary had figured out the clasp, more complicated than anything in Abby's own small collection of costume jewelry, and held the necklace out to Abby. "Here, fasten it around my neck."

Abby did so, then brought a mirror so Mary could see the results. Mary laughed delightedly at the unlikely sight of the fabulous diamonds against her everyday pink sweater.

"Just the thing for when Henry takes me to dinner at the Springhouse Café! Or you could wear it on bird walks with tourists at the conservatory. Or wouldn't it be fabulous as a collar for Finnegan?"

Abby laughed at Mary's frivolous suggestions, and her own mood suddenly lightened. When Mary suggested Abby try on the necklace, she did. She laughed again. The cartoonish vulture made an even more unlikely backdrop than Mary's sweater for the luxurious diamonds.

Mary picked up the card. "'To Claudia,'" she mused. "I guess no one knows who Claudia is?"

"Not yet."

"Maybe the necklace was meant to be an anniversary present. A fiftieth anniversary." Mary's blue eyes went a little dreamy. "Wouldn't that be romantic?"

"Not if it's a *stolen* gift."

"Who says it's stolen?" Mary demanded.

"No one. But its being in the desk is just so strange. Something just doesn't seem on the up-and-up about it."

"So what are you going to do with it?" Mary asked as she carefully and, Abby thought, with some reluctance, tucked the necklace back in its box.

"Take it to Henry in the morning and see what he thinks."

"Providing we survive the night, of course," Mary said with a teasing twinkle in her blue eyes.

Mary's refusal to be nervous took away some of Abby's lingering apprehension. They played Monopoly until it was time for the late news on TV. Then Mary, yawning, rolled her wheelchair toward her bedroom on the main floor, where everything had been remodeled to accommodate her after the auto accident.

Finnegan would sleep on a rug beside Mary's bed, of course, as he always did, and Blossom would curl up on a favorite chair in Mary's bedroom.

Abby went on up to bed too, taking the necklace with her. She determinedly parked it on the nightstand rather than nervously hiding it away, but it was a long time before she fell asleep.

# Chapter Five

In the morning, Abby called the sheriff's substation before leaving the house, but Sergeant Cobb was at a meeting with other members of the sheriff's department on Lopez Island and wouldn't be in until later. She left a message asking that he call her at the museum as soon as he came in.

She'd been hoping to be rid of the necklace before going to her office. She quickly dismissed the idea of taking the necklace to the safe deposit box because she'd just have to take it out again to show Henry. The only thing left to do was take it to work with her. Wilma Washburn, rather than Ida, was working at the front desk this morning. Abby stuck the box in a desk drawer and locked it, then ignored it as she worked on selecting photographs of birds in flight for the new exhibit.

Rev. James Hale at Little Flock called and asked if Abby could teach the Sunday school class of fourth to sixth graders this coming Sunday. The regular teacher had to go off-island for the weekend. Pastor Jim and Abby had recently decided that her teaching abilities were most useful to the church as a fill-in because, as Pastor Jim said, she was able to relate to any age group and was always willing to do so.

Henry Cobb called about ten o'clock. "I had a message that you wanted to talk to me?"

"I have something here at the museum that I'd like to show you and discuss with you."

"I can come out a little later this morning. Or immediately, if it's an emergency."

Abby hesitated only a moment before saying, "No, no emergency." What she didn't want was a law officer's presence at the museum arousing speculation and curiosity, because word would get around, of course. On Sparrow Island, word often seemed to travel faster than a computer virus whizzing around the Internet. "Would it be okay if I come into the substation instead?"

"Sure, that's fine. I should be here all morning."

"I'll see you in about fifteen minutes, then."

HENRY SPOTTED HER when she entered the substation and waved her past the front desk and into his office. As usual, when he was in uniform, his gun was in official evidence on his hip, along with his handcuffs, baton and other law-enforcement gear. Henry wasn't intimidating to her, but in his brawny, uniformed presence, Abby was always glad she was on the right side of the law.

"Something wrong?" He sounded concerned as she slipped into a chair by his desk. She knew he was thinking of Mary.

"Mary's fine," she assured him. "This isn't about her."

"Good." He leaned back in his swivel chair as if relieved.

She set the box on his desk and opened it.

Henry peered at the contents. He looked curious but not awed. "Very pretty," he commented.

Once more Abby went through the explanation about finding the necklace in her desk, showing it to Hugo and then taking it to Siebert's Jewelry. When she came to the part about Gordon's identification of the gem as a blue diamond and his estimate of the necklace's worth at three million dollars, Henry whistled. He scooted his chair closer to the desk for a better look.

"Three million dollars! No wonder you seem a little jumpy, carrying around something that valuable with you."

Abby hadn't realized her jumpiness was so obvious. "We need to find the rightful owner, of course. But I really don't know how to go about it. Does the sheriff's department investigate this sort of thing?"

"I don't recall any recent report of a lost or stolen necklace, but I'll do some checking. It would seem that with something this valuable, someone would definitely be looking for it."

"Exactly. And in the meantime, until the rightful owner shows up . . . ?"

"Found objects, especially something worth so much, have to be turned over to the authorities, of course."

"I'm relieved to hear that! I planned to put it in our safe deposit box yesterday, until I could contact you, but the bank was closed when I got there. I've been nervous having the necklace in my possession ever since I found out what it's worth." Abby stood up, eager to get back to the museum sans necklace. "So I'll just leave it with you—"

"Hold on. Wait a minute. The sheriff's department has an evidence room with a safe over at Friday Harbor on San Juan Island where we keep important items for prosecution of criminal cases, but I'm not sure about something like this. I'll have to check with Sheriff Dutton."

Henry put in the call to his supervisor, but the sheriff was on another line and Henry had to hold. With a hand over the phone he said to Abby, "You realize, of course, that if the owner doesn't turn up within a specific length of time . . . a year, I think it is, though I'll have to check . . . you can claim the necklace yourself. There's no doubt some official red tape to go through, but I can help."

Abby shook her head. "I wouldn't feel right doing that. Somewhere there's a rightful owner, and he or she should certainly have the necklace. Or perhaps it should go to this Claudia, for whom it was apparently meant as a gift. I don't suppose you know anyone by that name?"

Henry frowned without answering the question. He fingered the card with Claudia's name in bold handwriting on it. "You mean you wouldn't even put in a claim for the necklace?"

"I don't want to try to obtain something that rightfully belongs to someone else."

"That's an admirable attitude, Abby," Henry said, although

he sounded rather less than approving. "But if no owner turns up within the specified time, you should be practical. You need to consider Mary's needs, and this necklace could go a long way toward providing security for both of you."

Abby was a bit taken aback by that comment, which seemed to suggest that Abby's and Mary's financial situation might be precarious. She straightened in the chair and said a bit stiffly, "We get along fine with my salary and what Island Blooms brings in. I don't believe Mary is wanting for anything."

Henry hesitated, frowning again, but finally he gave her a sheepish smile. "I'm sorry. I didn't mean to imply you weren't looking out for Mary's interests. It's just that she's so determined to be independent, and I worry about her sometimes."

He also cared for her, Abby knew, although their relationship was still in a casual dating stage. Henry had been the person who found Mary trapped in her car after it had spun off the road into a ravine when she tried to avoid hitting a deer on a rain-slick island road. The Jaws of Life had been needed to extract her from the crumpled car, and a helicopter was called in to evacuate her to a Seattle hospital. Without Henry, Mary probably wouldn't have survived the accident.

"It was a big change in her life when she lost the use of her legs in the accident. She's still coping with both the physical and emotional aspects of it. Keeping as independent as possible is important to her."

"The accident was a big change for you too," Henry

pointed out. "You left your home and work in New York and moved back here to the island to be with her."

"And we're both doing fine," Abby said firmly.

A voice apparently came over the phone then and Henry swiveled his chair so his back was to Abby while he talked to his superior officer. He put the phone down when he turned to face her again. The overhead light gleamed on the seven-pointed star on his tan shirt.

"Well, Sheriff Dutton thinks your idea about putting the necklace in a safe deposit box is the way to go, although it will have to be a box in the name of the sheriff's department, not your personal box. We can walk over to the bank together and make the arrangements."

"There really isn't any need for me to go along, is there?"

"I think you should." Henry smiled. "That way you know I'm not absconding with the necklace myself. Three million bucks is quite a temptation, you know. I could buy myself a tropical island. Maybe a yacht and a high-powered speedboat to go with it."

"Henry Cobb, you wouldn't abscond with something that didn't belong to you if it were worth thirty million dollars," Abby declared. "You're too honest. And much too good a man for anything like that."

Henry dipped his head in a small bow. "Thanks. I appreciate the vote of confidence." He smiled. "Perhaps you should write that in a note of recommendation to Mary? I think I need all the help I can get."

Abby smiled back. "Any time."

"But I want you along anyway. And I need to give you something that shows you turned the necklace over to me."

He searched through several drawers that looked much like the drawers in Abby's desk before she'd cleaned and reorganized them. Soon he found the form he wanted and made out a receipt showing the date and a description of the item received from her. Abby folded and tucked the form in her purse.

The bank was just down Municipal Street from the substation, a short, pleasant walk on this invigorating morning. Henry carried the necklace, now in a large, official looking envelope with the sheriff's insignia in the corner. A scent of fresh rain still lingered in the air, but the main storm had blown over and a bit of sun peeped out from between the swiftly moving clouds overhead.

At the bank, Henry stepped up to the counter where customers signed in to enter the vault where safe deposit boxes were located. He told the clerk he wanted to rent a box.

While he was doing that, Abby was pleased to note a fresh bouquet of fall chrysanthemums, zinnias and ferns, no doubt from Island Blooms, in a big brass vase farther down the counter. She looked up from the flowers when Steven Jarvis charged out of his office and strode toward them.

Steven's shaved head always momentarily startled Abby. A shaved head was definitely outside the norm for Sparrow Island, even more outside the norm, she suspected, for the manager of a conservative bank. She knew that in Steven's case it was not, however, a rebellion against bank or local standards; the shaved head was simply Steven's way of coping with the fact that he was going prematurely bald. She rather admired his bold stand, and the surprising fact was that the shaved head looked good on him. Under his vigorous direction, the bank had done very well in the past three years.

"Sergeant Cobb," he said heartily. "And Abby Stanton. Good to see both of you. Are you getting everything you need taken care of here?"

He sounded solicitous, and Abby knew he probably was, but she also heard the curiosity and perhaps a bit of concern in his voice. She doubted he rushed out of his office whenever the average client wanted to rent a safe deposit box. He eyed the lumpy, official-looking envelope Henry had set on the counter. *What*, his wary expression asked, *is the top officer in law enforcement on Sparrow Island doing in my bank on what appears to be official business?*

"Nothing wrong, I hope?" Steven added, when Henry bypassed the opportunity to explain why they were there.

"Everything's fine," Abby assured him while Henry went on filling out the application form.

Steven straightened a pad of scratch paper on the counter as he watched Henry sign his name. He replaced a bank pen in its holder. He straightened his tie and eyed the sheriff's department star embroidered on Henry's green jacket. "Official business?" he finally asked, his carefully casual tone failing to conceal his curiosity.

"Yes," Henry answered.

Henry's polite but uninformative manner indicated that was all he intended to say, and Abby saw a twinge of frustration on Steven Jarvis's smooth-shaven face. The clerk handed Henry two keys. Steven glanced at Abby as if assuming she'd get one key. She didn't, of course. The necklace was in the custody of the sheriff's department now, much to her relief.

"I'd like to put something in the box now, please," Henry said, and the clerk pushed a button that gave him access through the small gate in the counter. Henry picked up his envelope and disappeared into the vault with the woman.

Steven eyed Abby as if hoping she'd be more talkative than Henry had been. She was, but not about this official business, since she felt it was up to Henry whether or not he wanted to say what that business was.

"Quite a storm we had last night, wasn't it?" she offered conversationally.

"Storm?" Steven's gaze remained on the door to the vault. "Oh yes. Of course. The storm."

"The rain we had here was probably snow in the mountains, so you'll no doubt be skiing soon."

There was no skiing on Sparrow Island, but Steven's enthusiasm for the sport was well known. Now, however, skiing seemed to be the last thing on his mind. His only comment was a distracted sounding, "*Hmmm.*"

"We'll be opening a new exhibit at the museum before long," Abby went on. "'Bird Flight and Early Human Flight.'"

"That's interesting." Although not, obviously, as interesting to Steven as whatever Sergeant Cobb was doing in his bank.

"Perhaps you'd like to come out and see it," she suggested.

"Right. I'll do that."

Abby doubted he had any idea what he'd agreed to. She smiled and tested him. "Bring your skis."

"Yes, I'll do that." Steven's gaze suddenly focused on her. He frowned, skin on his shaved head pulling tight, as if he realized something about this conversation had gone awry but he wasn't certain just what.

Henry came out of the vault. He was still carrying the official-looking envelope, but it was no longer lumpy.

"Everything okay?" Steven asked, obviously still hoping for information. "Not using the bank for storing pipe bombs or sticks of dynamite for criminal evidence, I hope?" He smiled broadly to indicate he was joking.

"Everything's fine," Henry assured him.

"Well, have a good day," the banker called as Abby and Henry headed for the door. He sounded frustrated.

At the last minute Henry relented and turned back. In a low tone he said to Jarvis, "The sheriff's department has custody of a rather valuable piece of jewelry, which is now in one of your safe deposit boxes. We have full confidence in the bank's security system and know it will be safe here."

Steven Jarvis was smiling again. "You can rest assured of that."

Outside, Abby looked at Henry and smiled. "You rather enjoyed that, didn't you?"

"Enjoyed what?" Henry asked innocently.

"Making Steven Jarvis practically squirm with curiosity before you told him what an officer of the law was doing on official business in his bank."

"Now Abby, do you really think I'd do something like that?" Henry's tone was reproachful, but he laughed and she joined him. "But he was squirming a bit, wasn't he?" He peered at himself in a store window as they walked past. "I wonder how I'd look with a shaved head."

Abby decided it was a rhetorical question and didn't offer a response, which would definitely have been negative. Her car was still at the sheriff's substation, so they walked back together. With the three-million-dollar necklace no longer weighing her down, Abby felt hummingbird light, delightfully free. Although, she had to admit, her curiosity about the necklace and its mysterious owner had decreased not one iota.

"I'll let you know if I find out anything about a missing necklace," Henry said when they parted company at the substation.

"And I'll let you know if I turn up any information about a Claudia." Abby started to ask if Henry would be coming to the house that evening, then remembered Mary would be out. Anyway, it was up to Mary to issue invitations, not her. She knew Mary definitely cared for Henry, but there was that matter of her fierce independence.

The rest of the day went well, though the museum felt rather empty with no more than a handful of people strolling through all day. On reflection though, Abby suspected with a certain chagrin that it was more Hugo's absence than lack of tourists that made the place feel empty for her.

That evening, Abby had the house to herself. Mary had driven to the class she was teaching on flower arranging at Island Blooms. With the van that had been modified for wheelchair use, Mary could go almost anywhere she wanted by herself and didn't have to depend on Abby to chauffeur her around.

Abby settled in the den and turned on her laptop. In minutes she was on the Internet. Gordon Siebert had said that many large and valuable gems had documented histories. With all the information that was available on the Internet, covering almost every conceivable subject, she was hoping to find something helpful.

Putting "blue diamonds" into a search engine turned up a surprising number of Web sites. One site was devoted exclusively to the Hope Diamond. Several sites were selling the gems, sometimes loose, sometimes mounted into glittering rings or necklaces.

The array of items available for purchase on the various sites was quite dazzling. One ring held three blue diamonds, one large central stone and two smaller side stones. A collar type, gold-band necklace held a lone, spectacular blue gem. One piece of blue-diamond jewelry, which rather astonished Abby, was made to be worn as a belly button adornment.

But none of the jewelry—and Abby was certain she was being quite objective in her judgment—was nearly as spectacular and dazzling as the necklace she'd found hidden in her very own desk. Puzzling, so very puzzling.

Then, just when she was about to give up for the night, she stumbled onto a site devoted to specific histories about a number of gems. And there she found information that truly electrified her. Perhaps the diamond necklace hidden in her desk was not only beautiful and valuable, but also famous.

# Chapter Six

ABBY PRINTED OUT THE information and took it to the museum with her in the morning. She was rather late arriving and Hugo's car was already in the parking lot when she pulled into her usual spot. He'd apparently returned to the island on an early ferry. She stopped in her own office just long enough to hang her jacket behind her door and then hurried down to Hugo's office. She had so much to tell him!

His door wasn't closed when she arrived but he hastily shoved some papers into a drawer when she peeked through the open doorway.

"Abby, everything go okay in my absence?"

"Oh yes, fine. No problems."

He smiled. "Well, maybe I'm not as essential around here as I like to think I am, then?"

Hugo sounded cheerful, but again Abby detected that uncharacteristic note of too-hearty joviality. Half a dozen questions poised on the end of her tongue. *Why did you go to Seattle? What did you do there?* But again he obviously didn't want to confide in her, so she laid her receipt from Henry and the computer printout on his desk.

"First, I took the necklace into Siebert's Jewelry. Gordon Siebert had never seen it before. But he identified the center stone as a blue diamond and the clear stones that encircle it as diamonds also. Even the tiny stones in the entwined strands are diamonds. He estimated the necklace's value as at least three million."

Although Hugo had earlier seemed less interested in the necklace than Abby would have expected, these blunt facts got his attention.

"Three million *dollars?*" he repeated. "Are you sure?"

"Three million or *more*. Gordon Siebert said that was a very conservative figure."

"Abby, that's incredible. How could something like that possibly wind up here at the museum?"

Abby had no answer, of course. "So then I took the necklace to Henry . . . Sergeant Cobb . . . at the sheriff's substation. He's going to check for reports of a missing or stolen necklace. For now, he put the necklace in a safe deposit box at the bank." She pushed the receipt Henry had given her for the necklace toward Hugo, but he didn't pick it up.

"And then, because Gordon Siebert said valuable gems often have documented histories, last night I went on the Internet and did some research."

Hugo eyed the computer printout. After the initial shock

of the necklace's worth, his attention seemed to have faded again. He picked up a brass letter opener and toyed with it. "And you found something, I take it?"

"Oh yes. Something quite interesting. You can read it for yourself—"

"Maybe you can just give me the gist of it?"

Abby wasn't truly surprised, given his dismissive attitude the day she'd found the necklace, but she was still puzzled. It just wasn't like Hugo to be so . . . what? Not bored, but certainly not as intrigued by this mystery as she was.

"I found a site that gave information about a long list of famous gemstones, about twenty of which were blue diamonds. There was much information about some of the stones, all about their size, history and current ownership. But little is known about many of the others. I found one description of a blue diamond that closely matches the one in my desk. It's called the Blue Moon."

"The Blue Moon." Hugo repeated the name as if he found it mildly interesting. "A colorful word picture. Someone had an imagination."

"All of the well-known gems seem to have names, although the origin of the name is often not known."

"So in what way does this Blue Moon match the necklace in your desk?" Hugo didn't sound truly disbelieving, but he did sound as if he needed convincing.

"Gordon Siebert measured the stone and said it was twenty-one carats. The Blue Moon is twenty-one carats. None of the others on the list were that exact carat size. It's large enough to be quite rare."

"But there are probably other blue diamonds that aren't on the list that do weigh twenty-one carats."

"Yes, that's true, of course. Gordon also said this diamond was cut in an older style called a cushion cut. The cut of the twenty-one carat gem on the Web site was not specifically named, but it was originally cut in 1888, when the cushion cut was popular."

"Can't gems be identified by what shows up inside with a microscope? I've heard flaws can be almost like a fingerprint."

"Yes, I think so. Gordon said this one has a couple of small flaws, but the Web site didn't mention the Blue Moon as having any. So that isn't helpful for identification."

"Was there a photo on the Web site?"

"Yes, but it's very old, just a fuzzy black-and-white shot. The diamond was also in a different setting back when the photo was taken, one of those old-fashioned, fussy styles. Not particularly attractive, actually, and not nearly as spectacular as the current setting."

"So the photo itself can't actually be used to identify the necklace."

"True."

"Abby, I'm not trying to be some grumpy spoilsport here, but it just seems so unlikely that a diamond with a name and a three-million-dollar value could turn up here. This is the kind of thing that happens in a Gothic novel. Maiden trapped in crumbling castle finds famous gem lost for a century, saves the family estate from the greedy, mortgage-foreclosing villain. It just doesn't seem likely here on Sparrow Island, and comparable size and cut of the diamond itself really aren't much to go on."

"I suppose my imagination could be running away with me," Abby admitted. It had certainly done so at the house when she imagined prowlers everywhere, stomping on the front steps and climbing the rose trellis. "But it *is* a twenty-one carat blue diamond. No imagination about that. And it is worth an exorbitant amount of money."

He eyed her for a moment. "Actually, although you have been known to have an active imagination on an occasion or two, I think you're quite well grounded in reality, not given to wild speculations. Scientific people usually are sensible. I've also never known you to be short on good sense." He paused, and for a moment she thought he was going to plunge into a different subject entirely. Instead he shifted in his chair and said, "I don't suppose there was an owner's name on the Internet?"

"No. The raw diamond was supposed to have been discovered in India in the 1880s. It was cut in France and had several owners, a king and various noblemen among them. But at some point about the time of World War II it disappeared, although whether it was stolen or sold to someone who wanted to remain anonymous is unclear. There are rumors that it's here in the States now, probably reset, but the owner is unknown."

"Well, in any case, the gem's history probably doesn't matter now that the sheriff's department is handling the situation. It's out of our hands." There again was that dismissive attitude, which seemed so unlike Hugo. Ordinarily he'd be as eager as she to find out more about the blue diamond and locate its owner.

"Would you like to see the photo I got off the Internet?"

He hesitated, and she suspected he'd rather get back to those papers he'd stuffed in his desk drawer, but he finally said, "Yes, please. You're doing a great job of gathering information here."

She rifled through the computer printout on the desk until she found the paper she was looking for. Hugo studied it only briefly before handing it, along with Henry's receipt, back to her.

Hugo glanced up and saw Abby watching him with concern. "Abby, I'm sorry. I don't mean to disappoint you by being rather blasé about this. Finding an incredibly valuable necklace with an unknown owner here in the museum is exciting and intriguing. It's just that I have some things on my mind."

Now he sounded more like the old familiar Hugo, a man always sensitive to the needs of people around him, a man whom she knew had helped more than one young Sparrow Islander to a college education, a man who'd given her the bluebird earrings she wore today.

"If it's anything you want to talk about, I'd be glad to listen," Abby offered. "Or if I can do anything to help . . . ?"

He looked at her, head tilted, worry lines cut between his

thick white eyebrows, and for a moment she again thought he was going to tell her something. That he *wanted* to confide in her. Then, although he didn't physically move, she sensed him backing off again.

"What else did this Web site have to say about our mysterious diamond?" he asked.

She, too, slipped back into the impersonal. "The Blue Moon comes with a superstition. A curse, actually," she said lightly.

"What kind of curse?"

"The original owner in India was beheaded, reason unknown. An owner in France was believed murdered by a lady friend, although nothing was ever proved. A later owner, a wealthy woman whose family was a big name in the wine-making business, lost everything when some disease destroyed their vineyard."

"Sounds as if an owner of the Blue Moon had better watch his back. And not let his insurance lapse."

"It's kind of an all-purpose curse and may strike a whole area rather than an individual person. Most of a town in France where it was once kept burned to the ground. And a lodge in the Alps where a woman wore the diamond to a ball was buried in an avalanche a few weeks later, although, fortunately, no one was in the lodge at the time. Some disease hit another area where the stone was in residence. The Web site didn't say so, but if my knowledge of history is correct, the disease hit various other places as well."

"Well, this does sound like one big, evil-tempered diamond. How was it supposed to have acquired this curse?"

"That wasn't explained. The beheading gave it a rather gruesome start, of course."

"Does this mean this curse is now going to affect the museum because the diamond was here for a while? And we're doomed to have, what? A flood, a fire, an earthquake?"

"An invasion of mice perhaps. I've spotted a couple in my office."

Hugo laughed at Abby's frivolous possibility. "You don't take the curse seriously, I can see."

"No, I don't. God is in control, not some inanimate chunk of boron-contaminated carbon," Abby said firmly.

Hugo lifted his white eyebrows at that inelegant description of the valuable blue diamond. "No jewelry company is going to hire you to write their ad copy," he observed. "Not with that kind of attitude. You're too truthful."

"Diamonds are a form of carbon," Abby elaborated. "Gordon Siebert said the color of a blue diamond comes from a tiny amount of boron mixed with the carbon. So when you get down to basics, that's all this valuable diamond is, a chunk of carbon contaminated with boron."

"Put that way, it certainly sounds harmless. Not that I'd believe in something as foolish as a curse under any circumstances."

"I do feel this really may be the Blue Moon. Not on a scientific basis, because what was on the Internet isn't true proof, of course. I just . . . feel it." She also felt a faint flush rise to her cheeks because the feeling was so very unscientific, so very much just a feeling. Not how she usually approached a problem or situation.

Hugo lifted those expressive white eyebrows again. "Woman's intuition?"

Abby smiled. "I guess that's as good as anything to call it."

"Good enough for me."

Abby turned to go when a new thought occurred to her. She felt a fresh tingle of excitement. Why hadn't she thought of this before? "We have no idea how long the necklace had been hidden in the desk, and the desk is an antique. Maybe the necklace was put in there long before you brought the desk to the museum!"

"That's true. Actually, I think that makes more sense than the possibility someone hid the necklace in the desk during the time it's been in your office."

"Where did the desk come from?"

He answered without hesitation. "I bought it right after you first agreed to become Associate Curator for the conservatory, and I was getting the new office ready for you. From Donna Morgan at Bayside Souvenirs."

"Are you sure?" Abby asked. "I didn't know Bayside ever carried any furniture. I thought it was all knickknack type souvenirs, coffee mugs, kites, wind chimes, that kind of thing."

"It was in the back room, not part of her regular stock. I'd been planning to go over to Seattle to look in office or antique stores for something appropriate, and then I heard Donna had this antique desk for sale so I stopped by to ask her about it. Actually, even though she had it for sale, she was rather ambivalent about letting it go, as I recall."

"I'll check with her and see what I can find out."

"Okay. Only . . . be careful."

"Be careful?" Abby repeated, surprised. "What's there to be careful about?"

"Nothing, I suppose. It's just that this situation with the necklace is very peculiar. With something this valuable, who knows who might be involved or what might happen?"

# Chapter Seven

Abby didn't expect any activity at the museum on this drizzly day, but after her talk with Hugo a lively tour group from Scotland showed up and wanted a guided bird walk through the conservatory woods. It turned out, in spite of the drizzle and dripping trees, to be a surprisingly successful walk. An eagle perched regally atop the dead snag of an old cedar, almost as if posing so everyone could admire and take his photo. Blue jays were in noisy abundance, and she even spotted a colorful ring-necked pheasant on the ground. Several people in the tour wanted their photos taken with Abby.

The group trooped through the museum afterward and bought what looked to Abby like enough postcards for all their known relatives back home.

Later, when she was back to work on the new exhibit, organizing a display of feathers along with information on how the different types affected flight, Hugo stuck his head into the workroom. "No effect from the curse yet?"

"I haven't even seen another mouse."

"Good. Maybe we're safe then." He gave her a jaunty wink.

Abby was pleased to see that Hugo's usual good humor had returned, although she wondered if he wasn't putting on a cheerful face for her benefit. Hugo was not usually a winking man.

Abby looked at her watch and was surprised to see that it was already almost 1:30. "I think I'll run into town for lunch, okay?"

"Sure." He hesitated, and for a moment Abby thought he was going to issue another warning about being careful. But all he did was smile and say, "Just don't let Donna talk you into buying a flock of her glow-in-the-dark frogs. She's already donated a bunch of them to Dr. Randolph to give to kids at the medical center."

Hugo obviously guessed she intended to use her lunch hour for a trip to Bayside Souvenirs. "I'll be careful."

"About getting stuck with a lifetime supply of frogs?"

She smiled too. "About everything. I'll be close to the Springhouse Café, so I'll probably stop there for a sandwich."

Once in town, she had no difficulty finding a parking space right in front of Bayside Souvenirs. Traffic was light today. Touristy items filled the windows, everything from Sparrow Island T-shirts to big ceramic platters with topographical maps of the San Juan Islands. And yes, floppy-footed frogs of rubbery green plastic that looked as if they indeed might glow in the dark.

The shop was empty of customers at the moment, but Donna, fortyish, slim, blond and bubbly, was rushing around restocking shelves. "Have you run into those tourists from

Scotland? They came in here and bought everything in sight! There are going to be Sparrow Island T-shirts all over Scotland."

Before Abby could even respond to that greeting, Donna rushed over and gave her an enthusiastic hug. "What are you doing in here today? Oh, you're looking wonderful! I love those bluebird earrings. How about some woodpecker salt and pepper shakers? And aren't my frogs fantastic?"

Abby laughed. Donna's enthusiasm for her merchandise almost made her want to scoop up a purchase, even though the last thing she needed was salt and pepper woodpeckers. Or floppy frogs, which peeked from nooks everywhere. "Today I'm just after information."

"Information?" Donna's bubbles turned to surprise. She was wearing a green paisley smock over dark slacks and a turtleneck, blond tendrils escaping from a haphazard topknot tied with a green ribbon. "What could I possibly know that you don't?"

"It's about the desk in my office in the museum. Hugo says he bought it from you."

"Oh yes, I remember that desk well! Those beautiful walnut burl inserts and all those compartments and pigeonholes." She clasped her hands together as if enraptured by the memory. "And those lovely dangling wooden drawer pulls with the brass tips."

Hugo had definitely not made a mistake about having purchased the desk from Donna, then. Her description was exact, right down to the brass on the drawer pulls.

"I bought the desk with the intention of keeping it for myself," Donna explained. "I had it here at the store just until I could get rid of an old metal desk at home to make room for it. But I rather quickly realized I'd paid more than I could afford for it and decided to sell it. I mentioned that to several people, but then, by the time Mr. Baron showed up asking about it, I'd become attached to it and decided not to sell after all."

Donna smiled at Abby's bemused expression as she listened to this rather convoluted explanation of her relationship with the desk.

"But then you did decide to sell the desk to him after all?"

"He wanted you to have something really special, I think. He mentioned you specifically, and I just decided such a handsome old desk really deserved to be in some place like a museum rather than stuffed in a corner of my living room."

"So where did *you* get the desk?"

"It was in an estate auction right here on the island. Remember that guy out on Wayfarer Point Road who died of a heart attack, and then his widow had some professional out-fit come in and hold a big auction? It's that big yellow house with all the rock work out front."

"I know the house. I think some people named Duranger own it now. They don't live there full time, but they've come to the museum a couple of times."

"Maybe the heart attack was before you came back to the island. Although it couldn't have been much before. I don't remember how much time there was between the man's death and the auction. Although I do remember it was about the time I had the new sign put on the front of the store here . . ." She cocked her head as if trying to withdraw the information from some memory bank.

Abby tried not to get impatient with Donna's irrelevant details, but she prodded gently to hurry her along. "And so—?"

"And so I went out to the auction, fell in love with the desk and bought it. I wanted to bid on a beautiful old étagère too, but after buying the desk I couldn't afford it. The prices were *exorbitant*. And you know how it is when you're bidding on something. You wind up going way higher than you intended. Buyers came from Seattle and Portland and everywhere. It was quite an event."

"You checked the desk over thoroughly when you bought it?"

Donna gave Abby a look that suggested she thought that an odd question. "I suppose. Although I don't really remember. Are you thinking it *isn't* an antique, maybe just a rip-off copy?"

"Oh no, nothing like that. Definitely antique. A beautiful antique. I'm just wondering . . . You didn't find anything in it?"

"Maybe a couple of old pencils and some paper clips. But no stash of hundred dollar bills or family jewels or anything like that, unfortunately."

Abby knew Donna's mention of "family jewels" was just chatter, but its closeness to the possible truth jolted her anyway. "You didn't hide anything in it yourself?"

"Me? No. Of course not. Why? Did you find something in it?" Donna's green eyes lit up with interest.

Abby detoured that question with one of her own. "Do you know anyone named Claudia?"

"Here on the island?"

"Possibly. Although not necessarily."

"I have a cousin named Claudia down in California. But I don't know any Claudia here on the island. Abby," Donna chided with a small frown, "you're acting very mysterious. What's this all about? Did you find something in the desk?"

Abby again detoured the question. "Do you have any idea how I might go about contacting whoever formerly owned the desk? The widow I guess it would be. Is she still on the island?"

"I'm sure she isn't. I don't think she even attended the auction. Too painful, I suppose. She'd lost her husband, and then to have to get rid of her home and all her beautiful furniture and antiques too. I'd certainly have been sad to see them go if I were her."

"Do you remember this woman's name?"

"Oh sure. It was kind of unusual. It's—" Donna broke off, frowned and caught her lower lip between her teeth, as if that might help her think. Apparently it didn't. "Well, isn't that frustrating? The name is right up there in my head, but I can't quite grab it. But I can look it up, though I'll have to go into last year's records to do it."

Abby's first inclination was to say, Oh, I don't want to put you to all that bother. But on second thought she smiled encouragingly and said, "Could you?" She really wanted that name.

Donna headed for a green curtain strung across a door to her supply room and office in back. "This may take a few minutes. If anyone comes in, push those glow-in-the-dark frogs, would you? I can't believe how many I let that salesman talk me into buying." Donna's disappearance behind the curtain was followed by several unidentified clunks and thumps, then a small crash as if something fell over, but she didn't stop talking. "Do you suppose the fact that he was so good-looking had anything to do with it? I'll have to sell a frog to every tourist who visits Sparrow Island in the next six months to get rid of them all."

"You can do it," Abby said. She'd once heard someone say that Donna could sell hair spray to a bald man. Although it appeared she may have met her equal in the floppy frog salesman.

Donna returned triumphantly waving a scrap of paper. "Here it is. Her name was Liberty Washington. Isn't that odd? But kind of pretty too. Though it's hard to imagine a mother yelling, 'Liberty, you get that smirk off your face right this minute!'"

Abby shook her head. Talking to Donna was like trying to carry on a conversation with a small tornado. "Do you have an address?"

"No, but you might be able to go through the auction company to get it. I wrote their name down, too, along with a phone number in Woodinville that was on the sales slip." She pointed to a second name on the scrap as she handed it to Abby.

"Donna, thank you so much. You've been a big help." She tucked the scrap of paper in her purse.

Donna tapped Abby on the front of the shoulder. "What I want to know is, a big help with *what*?"

"A . . . problem. A small problem," Abby added quickly, not wanting to whet Donna's curiosity. "And I do believe I'll buy one of those glow-in-the-dark frogs."

Bobby McDonald would get a kick out of it. She pulled out her wallet and handed Donna a ten. If she hoped the sale would distract Donna's curiosity, she was mistaken.

"That beautiful old desk. Something mysterious in it. A mysterious woman named Claudia," Donna mused as she tilted her head before counting the change into Abby's hand. When Abby didn't offer any explanation, Donna said, "I know! You found some mysterious document hidden in the desk. A will, perhaps, maybe relating to someone named Claudia? Or maybe a long-lost pirate's map. Although it seems unlikely a pirate would be named Claudia."

Abby laughed and didn't bother to deny Donna's wild speculations. "And here I thought I could keep it a secret," she teased.

"Haven't I earned the right to know what this is all about, being so helpful and all?" Donna wheedled as she dropped the frog in a plastic bag.

"Later," Abby promised. "For right now it's kind of a, oh, confidential matter." Given the value of the necklace, Abby was now more certain than ever that the information shouldn't be scattered indiscriminately or people really would be coming out of the woodwork to claim the necklace. And given Donna's chatterbox personality, she wasn't the person to whom to tell secrets.

"Okay, I'll just have to be patient then." Donna gave a melodramatic, put-upon sigh. "Although patience has never been one of my virtues, I'm afraid."

"Oh, Abby, tell Mr. Baron that if he ever decides to sell the desk, I'd love to buy it back. I have a different apartment now, one with more space."

"I doubt he'll ever want to sell."

"Probably not. Oh, hey, I heard a bit of interesting gossip about Mr. Baron and a certain attractive woman yesterday!"

Donna's comment made Abby instantly uncomfortable. She tried to avoid listening to gossip and did her best not to pass it on. She didn't want to pay any attention to it now and this particular hint of gossip made her especially uncomfortable. Were people talking about some relationship between her and Hugo? "Oh?" she said warily.

"He's been seen several times with Dr. Randolph, you know." Donna nodded significantly. "They were at Winifred's together a few evenings ago. People are saying there may be a big romance brewing."

Abby was so dumbfounded that she simply stared. *Hugo and Dr. Randolph*? Could that possibly be? Words popped out before she had a chance to think and stop them. "But she's half his age!"

"Well, she is much younger," Donna conceded. "But she's not *half* his age, I'm sure. And men have never let an age difference stop them." She wrinkled her nose. "I should know, considering that my marriage broke up over a *college* girl."

Hugo and Dr. Randolph together at Winifred's, certainly the most elegant and expensive restaurant on the island. Abby was astonished. The restaurant was popular with people staying at the Dorset, and tourists who had money to spare, and the food was excellent. But it was the kind of place Sparrow Island locals reserved mostly for special occasions. She and Henry had taken Mary there for her birthday.

"Not that I'm suggesting Mr. Baron is anything like my ex-husband, of course." Donna shook her head vehemently. "No way. Actually I think this is rather nice for both of them, don't you? Mr. Baron is a wonderful person and he's been alone for years, hasn't he?"

"Yes, I . . . I believe he has."

A blooming relationship between Hugo and attractive and personable Dr. Randolph would explain several things. Hugo's odd air of distraction. A man in love often was distracted. The phone calls he was keeping so private. Perhaps even the trip over to Seattle. Could he and Dr. Randolph have slipped off for a getaway day together? No wonder he wasn't interested in something so minor as a blue diamond necklace! His mind was on Dana Randolph.

"Of course Dr. Randolph has been seeing that other guy, the one with some kind of business over on Lopez." Donna chattered on. Apparently she was well up on all the local gossip. "But that's probably all over now, with Mr. Baron in the picture. He's just the most *distinguished* looking man, don't you think?"

Interior embarrassment suddenly flooded through Abby. She'd been afraid it was she and Hugo people were gossiping about, which assumed that *she* was the "attractive woman" Donna had mentioned. Abby had never considered herself an egotistical person, but this certainly smacked of egotism. And right this moment, in her slacks and sensible shoes, she felt totally dowdy. She also felt a flush of embarrassment rising to her cheeks.

Donna didn't seem to notice. "And Dr. Randolph is a wonderful person too. When I came down with the flu last year, she really *cared*. I wasn't just a medical chart to her. They'll make a wonderful couple."

Abby nodded dumbly and hurriedly headed for the door.

"Hey, you forgot your frog!" Donna called.

Abby grabbed the plastic bag with the frog in it and fled to her car. She just sat there without turning the key. Hugo and Dr. Randolph. After the first shock, the idea of the two of them being attracted to each other wasn't all that startling. Why wouldn't they be attracted to each other? Hugo was a vital and handsome man, well-traveled, knowledgeable, thoughtful and kind. To say nothing of wealthy. Dr. Randolph was slim and beautiful, intelligent and competent, a descendant of the Randolphs who had founded Green Harbor.

Abby suddenly realized that Donna was watching her curiously from the glass door of the store. She hastily pretended to be searching for something in her purse, then started the car and headed back toward the museum.

*Okay*, she scolded herself sternly, *why are you acting like some adolescent girl who expected to be asked to the high school prom and wasn't?*

Well, if she was honest with herself, she had to admit that was about how she felt. Yet she shouldn't feel that way, she told herself firmly. She and Hugo had been to dinner a few times, although these dinners certainly were not *dates*. And they'd gone hiking and bird-watching on several of the islands together. They also seemed to have many interests in common, but theirs was basically a working relationship.

*So what's the problem here?* the interior voice that often asked annoying questions inquired.

The problem, Abby decided uneasily as she poked warily at her subconscious, was that deep down it had always seemed as if there might be a stronger connection between Hugo and herself than just a working relationship. Maybe even a spark of something special between them.

Now she had to wonder if secretly she'd been hoping for more, a hope that would never be realized if Hugo was involved with Dr. Randolph.

Was the real problem here that she was muddling around in plain, old-fashioned *jealousy*?

*Oh no, certainly not* that *unlovely emotion*, she thought, horrified with herself. But if not outright jealousy, she had to admit there was at least *something* here that she didn't want to feel.

*Lord, keep me away from that*, she prayed fervently as she passed the Stanton Farm. She managed a smile and wave at the hired farmhand, Samuel Arbogast, who was out front working on a stretch of fence brought down by a branch in the rainstorm two days ago.

She should, in fact, be happy about this. Finding out that Hugo's uncharacteristic behavior the last few days was due to a romantic involvement rather than some serious illness was *good* news. Had he perhaps felt self-conscious about the relationship, perhaps concerned that Abby would disapprove? Was that why he'd acted troubled as well as distracted?

*Help me to be truly happy for both of them*, she added in prayer.

Back at the museum parking lot, she realized that in her foolish turmoil about Hugo and Dr. Randolph she'd forgotten all about picking up a sandwich at the Springhouse Café.

Never mind. She didn't feel very hungry now anyway.

# Chapter Eight

ABBY'S PHONE WAS RINGING when she walked into her office. She slipped out of her jacket as she picked it up.

"The Nature Museum. Abby Stanton speaking."

"Hi, Abby. Henry here. I just wanted to give you a report on the necklace. Actually, I'm afraid it's more of a non-report."

"You haven't found out anything?"

"Absolutely nothing. There are state and national reports on everything from missing people to stolen boats and stolen vehicles, and, locally, even a flock of stolen pink flamingo yard ornaments on one of the islands."

"But no missing or stolen blue diamond necklaces?"

"No. And that does seem so strange. More than strange. Baffling actually. Wouldn't you be raising a ruckus if your three-million-dollar necklace was missing?"

"Maybe, to the owner, the necklace *isn't* missing," Abby speculated thoughtfully. "Maybe he or she hid it in the desk for safekeeping and believes it's still safely hidden there."

"Just waiting for Claudia's birthday or Christmas or whenever to dig it out and give it to her?" Henry sounded interested but skeptical. "Possible, I suppose. But who would do that? Why would someone pick your desk in the museum to hide something in? And how could they do it without someone seeing? Does anyone come in after hours?"

"There's the cleaning crew. They're here a couple evenings a week. And sometimes Rick DeBow the handyman comes in to repair something. Although I can't imagine any of those people planning to give someone a three-million-dollar necklace as a gift."

"It's possible there's some crime involved here that we don't yet know about."

"I also can't imagine any of those people having a connection with some big crime. I think they're all completely trustworthy."

"I have inquiries in with the state patrol and the FBI, and I'll try to contact some insurance companies to see if they've had any claims on such a necklace. That's doubtful, though, since it hasn't been reported lost or stolen." He paused, his tone different when he added, "Abby, I think you need to be careful."

The same warning Hugo had given, but given by a law officer, it had even greater impact. "Why is that?"

"What happens if this unknown person suddenly discovers the necklace is now missing from the desk? Who does he suspect has it? You, of course, since it's your desk. And who does he come after?"

The obvious answer: *Abby*. She decided to sidestep those questions, however, or she'd be back hearing sounds in the night and finding her nerves skittering like exploding popcorn. "Actually, I picked up some information that makes me think we should be looking in a different direction for the owner of the necklace and Claudia's identity. In a direction not connected with the museum."

"Oh? Been sleuthing again, have you?"

"I suppose you could call it that," Abby admitted. She related the background of the desk as she'd heard it from Donna Morgan. "So what I'm thinking is that the necklace may have been in the desk before either Donna or the museum acquired it. Although probably not longer than a few years, since Gordon Siebert said the setting was modern and that the technique used for mounting the tiny diamonds to make a flexible strand has come into use only recently."

"*Hmmm.* That's interesting. I remember the man who suffered the heart attack. As I recall, they medevaced him over to Harborview Medical Center in Seattle, but it was too late. We had a rash of rather unpleasant things happen about that time," Henry reflected. "Him, dying from a heart attack, another guy getting killed not long before that in a hang-gliding accident off Mt. Ortiz, and then a boat accident out near the lighthouse. All before you arrived on the island, I guess."

"I'm thinking I could contact the auction company and see if they're willing to give me a phone number or address for this Liberty Washington who sold the desk at auction. Unless you have some objection, of course."

"None at all. It isn't as if this is a criminal case, and, even though the necklace may be worth a bundle, the department has limited resources for investigating this sort of thing if no crime is involved."

"I'll give locating Liberty Washington a try, then."

"Although I can't think the widow would be much help. She certainly would have removed the necklace before she sold the desk, if she'd known anything about it."

"But maybe she'll know something helpful. The name of another previous owner, perhaps. I'll try anyway."

"You're a stubborn and persistent woman, Abby Stanton," Henry said. She could tell there was a smile in his voice when he added, "But I guess it runs in the family, doesn't it? Mary can be stubborn too."

"Which is a very good thing for her. She wouldn't have made the kind of recovery from her accident that she has if she wasn't stubborn and persistent."

"Very true," he agreed. "Well," Henry now said briskly, "you let me know if you get anywhere with Liberty Washington and I'll let you know if I come across anything. By the way, Mary and I are going to try pizza at the Springhouse Café this evening. It's new on their menu. Would you like to come along?"

Abby knew he'd probably rather be alone with Mary, but he was a considerate and good-hearted man and often invited

Abby to join them. Abby also knew gregarious Mary wouldn't mind her coming along; Mary's attitude in most situations was the more the merrier. For tonight, however, Abby declined.

It wasn't until she'd hung up the phone that she realized she hadn't passed along the information she'd found on the Internet about the Blue Moon. On second thought she decided that, at this point, it was probably irrelevant. She had no proof the diamond in the safe deposit box was the Blue Moon. She just had that persistent feeling.

SHE INTENDED TO CONTACT the auction company in Woodinville later that afternoon, but she forgot all about it when she got immersed in looking up information for a professor at a British Columbia university who called with questions about an unusual type of plover recently spotted in his area. She remembered the call on the way home and went to the phone immediately after walking in through the garage and calling to Mary, "Hi, it's me. I'm home."

"I'm in the bedroom. The craft group was canceled tonight, so I'm having dinner with Henry. He was supposed to be here about six o'clock, but he just called to say he'd be a little late. I decided to change my sweater."

Abby smiled to herself. Mary wasn't a fussbudget about her appearance, but she was very fashion conscious and never wanted to settle for looking less than her very best.

Abby dug out the phone number Donna had given her and dialed. She'd been afraid it was so late in the day that the business office would be closed, but the information she received was more dismaying than that.

Coming into the kitchen, Mary asked, "Something wrong?"

Abby briefly explained about who she was trying to call and why. "But now I've just found out that the number has been disconnected."

"You could try Information."

Abby did, but Information had no information to offer.

"I'll try the Internet a little later. But it sounds as if the company has gone out of business."

"How about the Chamber of Commerce?" Mary suggested. "They might know if the company moved somewhere else or changed its name."

"I never thought of that. Good idea!"

Mary pushed up the sleeve of her emerald green sweater and looked at her watch. "Although it's probably too late today."

"It's no emergency, of course. But talking to Liberty Washington seems, at the moment, like our only possible lead to whoever owns the necklace." Abby inspected her sister more closely. "You know, stunning isn't a word that is often in my vocabulary, but that's how you look tonight. Stunning."

It was true. The outfit was casual enough for pizza at the Café, but the brilliant green of the sweater and her matching earrings emphasized the silver gleam of Mary's hair. In spite of her inability to walk, Mary's figure was still trim and lovely.

Mary smiled her appreciation for the compliment. "Thank you."

"Be on the watch for any stray Claudias," Abby called after Henry arrived and the two of them were leaving for dinner.

Abby fixed herself a quick soup-and-salad supper and then got on the Internet to look for a Web site listing the auction company. Nothing. Neither did she have any success locating Liberty Washington. In total, it was a thoroughly frustrating evening.

IN THE BUSY TOURIST SEASON the museum and conservatory were usually open on Saturdays, but now that the rains had come and tourist activity was down to a dribble, Abby's Saturdays were free. This Saturday, she and Mary both slept a little later than usual, and Mary drove into town for breakfast with some friends. Abby caught up on e-mail correspondence with people back east and did one of her least favorite tasks, vacuuming. She studied the lesson for the class she'd be teaching the fourth- through sixth-graders the following day.

For lunch, she ate pizza leftovers Mary had brought home from her dinner with Henry the night before. Quite tasty, even warmed over. The phone rang as she was putting her plate in the dishwasher.

"Hi, Abby. This is Bobby," a young voice said.

"Hello, Bobby," Abby said. "What are you up to today?"

"I was wondering if you'd like to go walk on the beach. I looked at the tide book and there's lots of time yet. The tide's going way out, and we might be able to get clear out to that funny rock up there by the bend on Wayfarer Point Road."

"I think that's a wonderful idea, Bobby. How about if I stop by your house, and then we'll drive up and park at one of the turnout viewpoints on the road?"

"Awesome!"

Abby smiled, pleased that he could consider a beach hike with a friend her age as "awesome."

"Oh, and I have a little something for you."

"You do? *Okay!*" She could hear the anticipation in his voice.

Abby dressed warmly in slacks, a turtleneck and a heavy jacket. Clouds and rain had given way to bright sun, but a brisk wind whipped the sea into a glitter of whitecapped froth. South of the beach, she saw that the small dock on the Wetherbees' place was empty now. Old Lars Wetherbee must already have put his little boat into storage for the winter. When she turned into the McDonald driveway, Bobby dashed out to meet her. His mother, Sandy, who taught at the high school, followed, arms wrapped around herself against the wind.

"*Brrr.* You guys sure you want to do this?"

"I'm up for it if Bobby is."

"Stop in for hot chocolate on your way back, then."

Bobby slid into the passenger's seat of Abby's car. He offered her a stick of gum. Abby accepted gravely, although she never chewed gum except when she was with Bobby. She wondered if he'd ask what she had for him but wasn't surprised when he didn't. Bobby's parents had brought him up to be too well mannered for that. She could see him peering around the car hopefully, however. She didn't keep him in suspense. She brought out the floppy green frog and tossed it to him.

"It's supposed to glow in the dark," she explained. "Although I didn't check last night to see if it really does."

"Hey, this is great! There are some deep-sea creatures that glow in the dark, you know," he said, ever the scientist. "But I've never heard of frogs that do."

"I doubt this one was designed with scientific accuracy in mind."

Then, reverting from young scientist to small boy again, Bobby enthusiastically hopped the floppy frog across his legs and the dashboard and up the window. He giggled. "It feels kind of like Jell-O that escaped from the bowl."

Abby parked at a turnout on Wayfarer Point Road. They carefully made their way down a short, steep trail to the beach. A wide stretch of rocky beach stretched in both directions now, but at high tide the very spot on which they stood would be under water. Piles of driftwood stumps and logs lined the upper edge of the beach, indicating that storm tides sometimes rose even higher than the average high tides. Strands of greenish kelp littered the rocks, and Abby remembered how once, when she was a little girl, she used a long strand to spell out the letters of her name. Now she spotted the sleek, dark heads of two seals swimming only a hundred feet from shore. She pointed them out to Bobby, and they watched until the seals gave a final flip and disappeared.

"I'm glad God made seals," Bobby announced.

Walking on the beach with Bobby was always an interesting experience. Every shell, rock, feather and scrap of driftwood had to be examined, every bulb of kelp squished or popped. Gulls swooped and squawked overhead, and once a blue heron flew by, wings flapping with languid grace, long legs trailing behind.

Abby offered to carry Bobby's plastic bag of treasures as it grew heavier, but he'd soon collected another bag almost as heavy.

They talked about everything from what was going on at Bobby's school to information he'd found on the Internet about underwater volcanoes to the fact that he'd grown three-quarters of an inch in the last six months. She told him about the new exhibit and was astonished when *ornithopter* turned out to be not a new word to him at all. He knew exactly what an ornithopter was.

"You can buy models on the Internet to put together. Some of them are powered with a rubber band. If I make one, will you put it in your exhibit?" he asked.

"Indeed I will. Sounds like a great idea."

Abby hadn't thought about the house that had formerly belonged to Liberty Washington until she spotted it high up on the far side of Wayfarer Point Road. She suddenly wondered if the current owners might know how to reach the widow and made a mental note to herself to check that out.

Their progress was slow, but Abby and Bobby did make it to the "funny rock" near the big curve in the island. They both clambered up its rough but slippery sides, stopping along the way to inspect every clinging starfish and mussel, of course. Afterward, they shared hot chocolate at the McDonald house. Sandy wrinkled her nose and declared they both smelled as if they'd been wallowing in a boatload of fish.

Abby sniffed the jacket hanging on the back of her chair. Yes, she had to admit, it did have a certain fishy aroma.

"But maybe it's like that old saying 'Beauty is in the eyes of the beholder,'" Sandy added. "Only in this case it might be, 'Fragrance is in the nose of the smeller.'"

Bobby, ever the charmer said, "You're beautiful, Mom. And you smell good too."

Abby and Sandy just looked at each other and laughed, and Sandy gave her son a hug.

THAT NIGHT, Abby woke suddenly. She jerked upright in bed, muscles rigid as she realized the phone on her nightstand was ringing. Middle-of-the-night phone calls were not usually harbingers of good news. Her parents? She snatched up the phone. "Hello?"

"It does, Abby, it really does! It glows in the dark!"

Abby slumped back against the pillow, smiling in spite of the scare the ringing phone had given her. She didn't have to ask the caller's identity or what he was talking about. "I'm glad to hear that, Bobby. Now go back to bed." She peered at the red numbers on her digital clock. "It's after midnight."

"Did I wake you up? I'm sorry. I thought you'd stay up

late. I will when I grow up. And sometimes I'm going to stay up all night!"

"I'm sure you will." *Just don't call me in the middle of the night and scare the wits out of me*, Abby thought. Finnegan was up now too, apparently wakened by the phone. He padded upstairs to Abby's bedroom, checking things out. She gave him a pat on the head when he stuck his nose over the edge of the bed.

"Oh and, Abby, I sent for an ornithopter on the Internet tonight. It should be here in three days."

"That's great. Now go back to bed."

"Okay. See you in Sunday school tomorrow. I studied the lesson. I have some questions to ask."

Abby would have to look over the lesson again before she and Mary drove into Little Flock the following morning. It wasn't easy keeping ahead of Bobby McDonald!

BY MONDAY AFTERNOON Abby hadn't heard anything from Gordon Siebert. She decided to leave the museum a little early and drop by the jewelry store to get his opinion on what she'd picked up on the Internet about the Blue Moon.

A customer was looking at rings when she arrived and Gordon appeared to be working alone in the store today. She wandered around admiring the displays. One glass cabinet caught her attention. Everything in it was blue, the hues varying from stones of a clear, light blue to the opaque blue of turquoise. Scattered among the pieces were raw chunks of a blue mineral and even peacock feathers with iridescent blue "eyes."

Gordon came over after the customer made a purchase and departed. "After you were in, I got to thinking about all the blues the world of gems has to offer, so Judee and I put this display together. You might say it's in honor of your necklace, although I'm not telling anyone that, of course." His smile was conspiratorial.

"Good. I want to keep the necklace confidential for a while yet."

"There's even one blue diamond," Gordon said, pointing to a ring with a tiny but vividly blue stone. "Nothing to compare with that blue diamond of yours, however."

"It's not—" Abby automatically started to deny ownership, but she had the sudden feeling Gordon might be artfully fishing for information. So instead she broke off and commented on the display. "It's a beautiful display. Very creatively done."

"Judee's good at that. She brought in the peacock feathers. The blue chunks of mineral I already had. They're azurite, which is a hydrous copper carbonate."

He went on to identify the varying blue tones of sapphires, the rich blue of a necklace made of beads of lapis lazuli, and the light blue of aquamarines.

"Aquamarine is the birthstone for those born in March, if you're interested in that sort of thing." Gordon laughed. "Birthstone jewelry is always popular and sells very well. I've always suspected the birthstone thing was invented by some enterprising salesman so he could sell more jewelry."

Interesting, but not why Abby had come here. "You haven't found out anything about the necklace?"

"Not a thing. Which is puzzling. Someone should know something because that's a spectacular stone and I'm certain it's been reset in the last few years—though it may have been done far out of this area, of course. On the east coast, or even overseas."

"Could it have been done in a . . ." Abby trailed off, not certain what word to use. She didn't want to imply that a criminal element could be involved here. Yet a criminal element might be exactly what they were dealing with. Hiding a three-million-dollar necklace in an old desk was not exactly on the up-and-up.

"The resetting could have been done by some individual outside the general commercial jewelry business," Gordon suggested, the rather generic answer suggesting he knew what she was getting at. More bluntly he added, "If the gem were stolen that's exactly the kind of person who would be involved in resetting it."

Abby pulled the computer printout out of her purse. "I found this on the Internet. I wanted to see what you thought."

Gordon Siebert read the material about the Blue Moon with brow-furrowed intensity, occasionally tapping his mustache with a forefinger.

"I'm wondering if there's any chance the blue diamond I showed you could actually be the Blue Moon described here. The size is identical, and its ownership and location have apparently been unknown for some years."

Gordon spread the papers on the glass display case and studied the black-and-white photograph of the gem in its old-fashioned setting. "Hard to say from this. But I definitely wouldn't rule out the possibility. The size certainly matches, and twenty-one carat blue diamonds are not exactly commonplace. What a find this would be if it actually is the Blue Moon!"

Was Abby hoping it was? She wasn't certain.

"What we need, of course, is a photo or diagram of the interior of the Blue Moon so I can compare it with your diamond. But the technology wasn't available to do such photography until recent years, so it may never have been done."

"Do you have the equipment to do it now?"

"No, unfortunately I don't. I let it go when I sold the business over in Tacoma. But an accurate diagram done by hand can be just as helpful and is in some ways preferable because you can get more of a three-dimensional effect. It's possible such a diagram was done sometime, but I don't know how we'd ever locate it."

He read further then and laughed. "And a curse! How exciting. I hope you're being careful of safes falling out of windows, hostile bird life, greedy jewel thieves, etcetera?"

"I'm not concerned." Although his mention of greedy jewel thieves echoed Hugo and Henry's warnings about being careful. "I don't believe in superstitious curses."

"I don't either," Gordon agreed. "But I do hope you've put the necklace somewhere secure for safekeeping?"

"Sergeant Cobb rented a safe deposit box at the bank. I'm sure it's safe there."

Gordon jumped on that, his gaze lifting with interest. "Oh, so the authorities are definitely involved, then?" He hesitated and then with a sideways tilt of his head, added, "Would it be too, ah, indiscreet of me to inquire if the necklace is the item found in your desk at the museum?"

"*What?*" Abby gasped, astonished. "Where did you hear something was found in the desk?"

"Judee said something about it, although I didn't ask where she'd heard it. The necklace wasn't mentioned, but with what I knew about the necklace, I just put two and two together. And I'm keeping my conclusions totally confidential," he assured her.

Abby knew where the information must have come from. She hadn't actually told Donna Morgan she'd found something in the desk, but basic honesty had kept her from fabricating a denial to Donna's speculations. Now, uncomfortably clutching her purse, she said, "Thank you. I appreciate that. We don't want finding the real owner complicated by a flood of phony claims."

"I can understand that. May I keep this?" he asked, lifting the computer printout off the glass counter. "It's fascinating information and may be helpful in my inquiries. Again, keeping everything discreet and confidential."

Abby managed a smile. "You keep all this confidential, and I'll keep your comment about the economic factor in birthstones confidential."

He also smiled. "It's a deal."

# Chapter Nine

THAT EVENING WHILE MARY was at her knitting group, Abby tried to call the Durangers, the current owners of the house in which Liberty Washington and her husband had once lived. She let the phone ring a dozen times, but neither a live person nor an answering machine picked up, which wasn't surprising, of course. When the weather turned bad, the population of Sparrow Island tended to drop as people scurried back to the mainland for the winter, even though statistics showed the San Juan Islands had considerably less total precipitation per year than Seattle. Many people did return for an occasional weekend, but it was possible the Durangers wouldn't be back until spring.

By the following morning, the wind had dropped to an occasional gust, but dark clouds now hung low over the island. They obscured not only the island's highest point, Mt. Ortiz, but Arrowhead Hill as well. In some places even the treetops disappeared into the misty fog as Abby drove through Green Harbor. She turned up the heater in her car.

Rain had begun by the time she parked outside the museum, but Abby never found rain depressing, as some people said they did. Everything was so wonderfully green and fresh. Hugo's car wasn't in the parking lot yet, but he passed her open office door a few minutes later.

"Hugo, when you have a free minute, would you let me know?" she called. "I need to talk to you about some details on the new exhibit." Although she was uncertain how to do it, she hoped she could work in an assurance that he needn't feel uncomfortable around her about a romantic involvement with Dr. Randolph.

Unexpectedly Hugo turned into her office right then. "No time like the present," he said.

Abby hastily dug out her diagrams and plans. This exhibit was to be glass enclosed and not a hands-on type of exhibit. She showed him the layout she had in mind and also mentioned that Bobby McDonald might be supplying a model of an ornithopter.

"It's probably not going to be a totally professional job, even though Bobby is extremely competent for his age," she said. "But I think that's okay, because some of the early attempts at flying with wing movements like a bird's were definitely on the primitive side."

"Sounds good to me. I think something about hang gliding or parasailing should be included, since they also use the lifting power of air to stay afloat."

"Good idea." She jotted down a note.

"I'm sorry I'm not as involved with this project as I should be. I've been distracted by a personal matter. In fact, I'll probably be spending another day over in Seattle."

Another getaway day with Dana Randolph? Abby tried to think of some tactful way to let Hugo know that he didn't have to hide the romance from her. She didn't want to come off sounding nosy about the relationship, but she did want him to know she cared and wanted the two of them to be happy.

"Hugo, I, uh, realize that something's been troubling you lately. And I just want you to know that I care and I'm concerned, and you can count on me to help anyway I can."

Abby couldn't think how she could possibly help in his romance with Dr. Randolph, unless it was to make certain other people knew she didn't disapprove. And to keep to herself those unattractive moments of disappointment and jealousy she'd experienced.

"Thank you, Abby. I appreciate that. It's been a difficult time and your caring means a great deal to me." He absent-mindedly picked up a paper clip on her desk and twisted it into a new shape. "I've taken it to the Lord, of course."

"That's good. I have too."

"You have?" He looked surprised. "But how did you know? Dr. Randolph surely didn't tell you. That would be a violation of professional ethics, and Dr. Randolph would never—"

He sounded upset, then broke off as he realized Abby was looking at him with a bewildered expression.

"Dr. Randolph didn't tell me anything, but there is talk around town."

"Talk around *town?*" Hugo repeated. "Abby, what are we talking about here?"

"You and Dr. Randolph," she said.

Hugo gave a small groan and then laughed and shook his head. "Don't tell me you've heard that rumor that's going around." He peered at her across the desk, his eyebrows lifted into an inquiring line. "Yes, you have heard it, haven't you?"

"Rumor?" she repeated warily.

"The ridiculous and totally unfounded rumor that Dr. Randolph and I are engaged in some torrid romance."

"You're not?"

"Of course not!"

"But you and Dr. Randolph had dinner together at Winifred's, didn't you?"

"Oh well, yes, that's true." Hugo nodded. "But it had nothing to do with romance. Mitch called while I was waiting to see Dr. Randolph—"

"Mitch?" Abby interrupted. She was feeling as if she needed a program to keep all the players straight here.

"Mitch Ziegler, the man Dr. Randolph's been seeing for some time. He's in insurance, I think. Over on Lopez. I've never met him." Hugo waved his hand dismissively. "Anyway, they had reservations at Winifred's, but some emergency came up at Mitch's office and he couldn't make it. He called while I was in her office. Dr. Randolph said they'd already asked the chef to make a special scallop and crab dish they both like, and it was a shame to let that go to waste. So then, quite impulsively, I think, she asked if I'd like to go with her. Which I did. That's where apparently half the town saw us and jumped to the foolish conclusion that we are seeing each other," he added with a palms-up lift of his hands.

"But I saw you together too. Walking down the street together, looking very engrossed in each other," Abby blurted before she could stop herself.

He tapped the paper clip on the desk, his unfocused gaze squinting at the window and drizzling rain. "I don't remember . . . Oh yes, I do. It was that day it rained so hard, wasn't it?"

"Yes, it was raining. You were, *um*, sharing an umbrella, in fact."

"I don't remember seeing you."

"I was across the street, just coming out of Siebert's Jewelry." *Hiding behind my own umbrella so you wouldn't see me.*

"I had an appointment at the medical clinic for X-rays late that afternoon and then I ran into Dr. Randolph as we were both leaving the building. She had forgotten her umbrella at home. We both had errands to run, so I shared mine with her and we walked downtown together. And what we were talking about was a new surgical technique she'd read about, which I have to admit I did find engrossing."

"Surgical technique?" Abby repeated, feeling she'd somehow lost the focus of this conversation. "X-rays?"

"I have prostate cancer," he said bluntly.

Abby's hand flew to her mouth as she gasped. "Oh *no* . . ."

"Dr. Randolph was reasonably certain I have it, but she wanted me to consult a specialist in Seattle. That's why I was there overnight, to have a biopsy."

"Oh." Abby repeated. She felt dazed and a little ill herself because of the guilt that suddenly deluged her. *Cancer. A trip to Seattle to see a specialist for a biopsy. And I'd foolishly thought—*

Hugo leaned forward in the chair. "Surely you didn't really think I was involved in some big romance with Dr. Randolph, did you?" He sounded as if he couldn't decide whether to be astonished or amused.

"I'm sorry, Hugo. It didn't seem an unreasonable possibility."

For a moment she thought he might be angry that she had so misinterpreted the situation, but instead he laughed with his usual good humor. Then his expression turned serious as he studied her thoughtfully. "And you were willing to do whatever you could to help?"

"Of course. You deserve happiness and a full life. If you could find it with Dr. Randolph, I wanted to be supportive."

"You're a good woman, Abby." He nodded as if affirming something he'd always known but perhaps hadn't fully appreciated. "And a generous one too."

"For a short time I did have a twinge of, oh, something other than supportive feelings," Abby admitted, wanting to be honest without going into embarrassing details. "Now I'm just so terribly sorry that you're facing *this*. Was the specialist in Seattle helpful?"

"He confirmed Dr. Randolph's diagnosis. For the time being I'm on medication, but it may go beyond that. There are various options for treatment, of course. Surgery, radiation, the implantation of radioactive seeds, chemotherapy. I can't say that I'm looking forward to any of them. I just hope the medication does the job and nothing else will be necessary. One blessing is that the cancer hasn't spread beyond the local area. Dr. Randolph caught it early."

"She's a fine doctor. I have every confidence in her."

"So do I, as well as in the specialist she sent me to. I just hope she doesn't hear that ridiculous rumor. Can you imagine what she'll think? She'll be horrified."

"I doubt she'll be horrified," Abby said. "But if you're concerned, perhaps you should tell her about the rumor yourself. Then if she does hear it, it won't come as such a shock."

Hugo blinked, as if that straightforward approach hadn't occurred to him. Then he smiled and nodded. "You're right, of course. That's exactly what I'll do. You're a smart woman, Abby. About people as well as birds and science. You see beneath the surface."

"Thank you."

"I should have confided in you from the very first. But sometimes men have this stubborn pride." He lifted his big shoulders as if bemused by his own actions. "I should have known, given the way you've taken Mary's accident in stride and all you've done for her, that I could count on you."

"*Is* there anything I can do, Hugo?" She searched her mind

for possibilities, knowing full well he wasn't apt to come up with something himself even though he'd now confided in her.

"I can handle whatever needs to be done here at the conservatory and museum if you're hospitalized or need recovery time," she went on, "so you needn't worry about that. I can be with you at the hospital. I can provide transportation to and from the hospital, or around here, whatever you need. I'm not the world's greatest cook . . . Mary does most of the cooking at our house now . . . but I can come to your place and see that you don't go hungry."

"Thanks, Abby, I appreciate this more than you can know."

"Or if there's something else I haven't thought of?"

"Actually, at this point, I have no idea how things will work out or what kind of help, if any, I may need. For now it's just a matter of taking my medication and twiddling my thumbs until the experts decide what, if anything, comes next."

Not easy for a man of action like Hugo, Abby knew.

"Just talking with you and not trying to carry it around by myself is a big help," he added.

"Are you in physical pain?" she asked with concern.

"No. Physically I feel fine. But up here—" He tapped his temple. "Up here I don't do as well. I suppose some of it is that I keep remembering that prostate cancer was what ended my father's life."

"I'm sorry, Hugo. I didn't know that."

"And, looking back, although no one ever mentioned it at

the time, I'm reasonably certain now that my grandfather also had prostate cancer."

No wonder he'd been so distracted and troubled. "I wish you'd told me," she said softly.

"I wish I had too. I'd have made things easier for myself." His smile was rueful. "I'm afraid it took me a while even to take it to the Lord. Behaving like what some young people would no doubt call a stubborn old geezer."

Abby smiled. Hugo may have taken on a few years and he could be a bit stubborn, but he was a long way from geezerhood.

"From what I've heard, the cure rate for prostate cancer is now quite high when it's caught early. Treatment is much more advanced than it was back when your father and grandfather died."

"I'm counting on that."

"And prayer never hurts."

"I'm counting on that too." He stood up, looked at the twisted paper clip in his hand as if he didn't know where it had come from and tossed it at the waste basket. He headed for the door, then stopped and turned, a mischievous twinkle in his usually dignified blue eyes. "Actually, I'm quite flattered that you thought there even could be a romance between the beautiful young doctor and me."

"I won't comment because you might get a swelled head," Abby teased.

Hugo laughed again and turned back to the door, head

shaking back and forth, although she didn't know if that was bemusement at the rumors or at what she'd just said.

ABBY TRIED TO CALL the Durangers on both Tuesday and Wednesday evenings. Again no response. No news from Henry, either. Nothing from Gordon Siebert. Sometimes it felt as if the necklace had simply materialized out of thin air and somehow attached itself to her desk. One matter did get resolved, although it was unrelated to the necklace. Thursday morning Hugo stopped by her office.

"I did what you suggested and mentioned that rumor to Dr. Randolph."

"Had she heard it?"

"No, not yet anyway."

"What was her reaction? Was she upset?"

"Not at all. She just laughed and said she was flattered that anyone might think that."

"That sounds like Dr. Randolph," Abby said.

"Well, flattered as I am by the rumor, if you hear it again, just stomp on it, okay? Really squash it."

"I'll do that."

ABBY SETTLED INTO HER OFFICE and worked solidly throughout the morning. When she finally took a break and went out to see if the museum had any visitors today, she realized Ida Tolliver was at the front desk this afternoon. She was surprised. Ida usually peeked in to say hi when she arrived.

"Hi, Ida. I didn't know you were here. I spotted you at Little Flock on Sunday but didn't get a chance to talk to you. Have you heard about a Claudia?"

"Not so far." Ida briskly walked over to straighten brochures and postcards on the rack, her back to Abby.

The situation regarding Claudia and the necklace was certainly consistent, Abby thought with frustration.

"Well, keep your ears open," she said finally.

"Something may turn up now that *everyone* knows," Ida said.

A definite tartness in Ida's tone made Abby look at her sharply. She realized that Ida was acting rather miffed. "Everyone knows what?"

"About your desk. About the necklace. About the *curse*, and even I didn't know about that." Hands on hips, Ida flashed her an accusing look.

"Ida, what are you talking about?"

"You warned *me* not to tell anyone about the necklace and I haven't said a word, not a single word to anyone. But *you've* been blabbing all over town about it! You could at least have told me about the curse."

The accusation about blabbing was such a gross inaccuracy that Abby was momentarily indignant. But a mental picture of herself running around town and "blabbing" to people on every street corner struck her as funny, and she laughed even as she tried to figure out what had prompted the accusation.

"Can you be more specific about my blabbing?" Abby inquired. "'Everyone' is whom?"

"Well, maybe I shouldn't have called it blabbing. You're not a blabber. I'm sorry," Ida apologized. She tucked a strand of blond hair behind her ear. "It's just that everyone does seem to know. One of the other waitresses told me. She said the necklace even has a name. The Blue Moon."

"Actually, a blue diamond, not an entire necklace, is named that. But we haven't determined that the diamond in the necklace I found is definitely the Blue Moon. It's merely an interesting possibility."

"But if it is the Blue Moon, it has this curse on it right? People have died strangely. Whole towns have been wiped out."

"Ida Tolliver, do you actually believe such a thing is possible?" Abby demanded, hands on her hips.

Ida slid a brochure back into its proper slot. "Well, no, I guess I don't," she said slowly, as if she was perhaps only now straightening this out in her head. "It's more like a superstition than a Christian belief, isn't it?"

"It's definitely not Christian."

"I'll point that out to Aaron."

Abby groaned. "Aaron knows about this too? You told him?"

"I didn't tell him." Ida sounded defensive. "He'd already heard it. I told you, everyone knows. And some people are scared."

"Scared? Of what?"

"Julie, that's the friend who works with me at the café, had a copy of something that told all about a whole town where the diamond was kept for a while that burned down. Although I don't think that's going to keep her from calling you. She said her grandmother used to have a blue necklace, but no one knows what became of it and she thinks this one you found might be it. Julie's nice. She works double shifts sometimes, trying to pay off some medical bills from when she had an ear operation."

Abby felt leaden. Just what she'd feared. That the true owner's identity would get lost in a tangle of phony claims. People might be afraid of a curse, but the prospect of three million dollars tended to embolden even the apprehensive.

She marched back to her office, looked up a number and dialed. Gordon Siebert's suave voice answered.

"Siebert's Jewelry. May I help you?"

"This is Abby Stanton. I've just heard there are all sorts of rumors and gossip flying around town about my having a valuable necklace with a curse on it in my possession and that the ownership on it is up for grabs."

There was a moment of startled silence and then Gordon said stiffly, and with an almost palpable hauteur, "And you think I am behind these rumors?"

"As far as I know, you're the only person outside Sergeant Cobb and Hugo Baron who originally knew about this." A second thought reminded her that not even Sergeant Cobb knew about the supposed curse. "There are apparently even copies of that computer printout I gave you floating around."

"I assure you I haven't said a word, and the computer printout is still in my desk where I put it after you left. In fact I'll check, just to prove it to you."

Silence, as he put her on hold. He returned a few moments later.

"I have the computer printout you left with me right here in my hand. I haven't, as yet, even had an opportunity to contact other jewelers concerning it."

"I see. And do you have a copy machine?"

Another silence, one that seemed to hum with tension until Gordon said stiffly, but with considerably less hauteur, "I'll have to get back to you on this."

# Chapter Ten

THE FIRST CALL CAME THE following evening. Abby, Mary and Henry were at the dining room table eating dinner and discussing what Abby had found on the Internet about the Blue Moon and its curse when the phone rang. Abby got up from the table to answer it.

"Hi. Um, my name is Marcy Bailor?" The young voice sounded nervous and the name came out more question than statement. "Is this, uh, Mrs. Stanton?"

"Yes, this is Dr. Stanton," Abby said. "May I help you?"

"The thing is, my boyfriend had a necklace he was going to give me and he . . . he worked for those people who lived out on Wayfarer Point Road? And he put the necklace in the desk there, just so it would be, you know, safe for a while, and then the man died, and Patrick didn't know what became of the desk or the necklace. And now I guess you've found it? It's really valuable. It belonged to his mother—" She broke off as a whispered voice said something behind her. "I mean, his grandmother. Anyway, I want to get it back."

The story was so obviously phony, so awkwardly contrived that Abby would have laughed if she hadn't been so startled by the audacity of it.

"Are you Ida's friend from the café?"

"No, I don't know anyone named Ida." She paused. "But maybe I do and I just don't remember her name . . ." The woman sounded as if she were willing to jump in either direction to help her case.

"I think you should talk to Sergeant Cobb from the sheriff's department about this. He happens to be right here. Hold on a minute please."

Abby carried the cordless phone into the dining room and handed it to Henry. "A young woman claims she owns the necklace," she whispered.

Henry took the phone. "Sergeant Cobb here, San Juan County Sheriff's Department." He waited a minute, then pulled the phone away from his ear. "No one there."

The three exchanged glances. Mary laughed first. "Maybe she wasn't so eager to tell her story to the strong *ear* of the law," she suggested.

Abby laughed too. "Especially when she was having a hard time keeping her story straight." She shook her head and related the details of what the woman had told her. "Did she really think I was just going to hand the necklace over to her?"

Henry had laughed with them, but his tone turned unexpectedly somber when he said, "You may be surprised what we'll run into with a three-million-dollar necklace involved. I've already warned you, Abby." He targeted her with a pointed forefinger. "But I think you *both* need to be careful."

"Surely you don't think there's anything to that curse nonsense," Abby protested.

"No, of course not. But I think there are way too many greedy people in this world who may do more than make phone calls. Again, you both need to be careful."

"But why me?" Mary sounded surprised and a bit miffed. "What's any of this got to do with me?"

"With that much money at stake, who knows how the mind of someone who wants that necklace may work?" Henry said, still somber. "And Abby, if you get any more calls when I'm not around, just refer them to me at the station."

THE NEXT CALL CAME Sunday afternoon, a few minutes after Abby returned from an invigorating hike on the trail around Cedar Grove Lake. Mary and Henry had taken the ferry over to visit friends of his on Lopez. Mary hadn't taken Finnegan along today, and Abby had just turned him outside for his daily playtime.

The call started out much as the other one had, although the young woman didn't sound quite so nervous.

"You don't know me," she began, "but my name is Julie Richards. I work with Ida at the Springhouse Café and I heard you found a necklace in an old desk."

"Yes, Ida mentioned that you might call."

"I think it may be a necklace that belonged to my grand-mother. It disappeared here on the island years ago."

"If you want to make a claim for the necklace, you'll have to go through the sheriff's department. They're handling it."

"The sheriff's department?" The woman sounded taken back by the fact that there would be legal formalities involved, but she agreed readily enough. "Oh well, okay. I can do that."

Curiosity made Abby ask, "Do you have any idea how your grandmother's necklace could have gotten into the desk?"

"No. I don't. No idea at all. It's puzzling."

Abby appreciated the fact that the woman wasn't making up some outlandish story to explain the necklace's being in the desk. She had the impression that this woman, unlike the ear-lier one, actually believed the found necklace might be her grandmother's. "Could you describe your grandmother's necklace?"

"Yes, I can! I called my mother over in Redmond and asked her. She remembers Grandma wearing it when they lived here on the island. It had a gold chain, not a fine chain, but one with big, chunky links. Mom said the links had an almost sharp feeling. And the blue stone was big, really big, with a bunch of smaller blue stones around it."

"I'm sorry, but I'm afraid that description doesn't match the necklace I found at all." Nor did it match the photo of the necklace in the old setting that Abby had seen on the Internet. Abby found herself oddly disappointed. Wouldn't it have been nice if the valuable necklace really had belonged to this hard-working and apparently sincere young woman?

"Oh well, okay then. I guess I won't bother talking to the sheriff's department. Thanks." The woman unexpectedly laughed. "I guess in a way I'm kind of relieved. I know the necklace you found is supposed to have some big unlucky curse on it, and I have enough troubles without *that*."

AT THE MUSEUM the following morning, a Claudia actually showed up. She was tall and slim, black pants and spike heels accentuating her height. An abundance of red hair floated around her narrow face. Gold hoop earrings flashed at her ears.

The woman tossed a driver's license on Abby's desk. "I'm Claudia Seaver. I understand you have a necklace that belongs to me."

Abby picked up the Oregon license, which gave the name Claudia Seaver with an address in Portland, Oregon. The photo matched the face of the woman standing in front of her desk. If Hugo were in the office today, she'd call down to his office and ask him to sit in on this, but he'd had to make another trip to Seattle for more tests.

"This is my husband, Winston," the woman went on in an imperious tone. She gestured toward the big, beefy man in a suede jacket beside her. *If this woman had a scepter, she'd be waving it*, Abby thought. "We're staying at the Rosario resort over on Orcas Island for a couple of weeks and we heard about the necklace."

"You heard about the necklace over on Orcas?" Abby repeated, astonished. Before Abby could get in another word, the woman launched into her version of the necklace's history.

"My ex-husband and I never actually lived here on Sparrow Island, but we vacationed here several times. Our marriage had been in trouble for some time, and the last time we were here, it came to a breaking point and we split up." She tugged lightly on one of the gold hoop earrings.

Since Claudia had obviously already acquired a new husband, Abby didn't know whether to express sympathy about the breakup with the former husband or not. She discreetly murmured a noncommittal, "I see."

"I had an old necklace that my grandmother had given me before she died a long time ago. I'd assumed the big stone in it was really just a chunk of blue glass and never thought of the necklace as having anything other than sentimental value. Anyway, I couldn't find the necklace in my luggage when I got home, and I realized Jack must have taken it with him when he walked out. We were staying at The Dorset," she added.

"Did you report the necklace as missing at that time?"

"No. I was unhappy about losing it, of course, because it had been my grandmother's. But since I thought it was just old costume jewelry, there didn't seem to be any point in reporting it." Now she smoothed a finger across an eyebrow. "I didn't realize until yesterday how valuable it is."

"I wonder why your former husband would bother taking it, if you didn't know at that time it was valuable?"

She leaned forward. "One of two reasons, I think. Either he took it just to hurt me because it was my grandmother's and I valued it for that reason, or maybe he already knew it was really very valuable. He was sneaky. For all I know, he could have secretly had it appraised."

Abby mentally reviewed the story. It had a certain ring of plausibility, and the woman's eyes flashed angrily as she spoke of her ex-husband's motivation. Yet the woman's nervous gestures suggested she wasn't at ease telling the story.

"I understand you found the necklace here in the museum?" The woman glanced around warily and Abby realized the rumors she'd heard must not have included information about the desk as the hiding place.

"Would you have any idea how it got here?" Abby asked.

The woman hesitated and Abby had the impression this might be a weak point in her story. "Well, uh, no, I guess not."

"I see. And could you describe the necklace for me?"

"Of course." Without hesitation the woman launched into a detailed description of the necklace. A description that exactly matched the appearance of the necklace in that old black-and-white photo Abby had downloaded off the Internet, not the current modern setting. If photocopies had been made at Siebert's jewelry, Abby thought, they were apparently flying from island to island as if self-propelled.

"How long has it been since you saw the necklace?" Abby inquired, careful to give no hint that her suspicions were mounting.

The woman glanced at her husband. Abby wondered how long they'd been married. "A couple of years, I guess."

It was possible that the blue diamond had been reset and hidden in Abby's desk during that time, although she definitely had her doubts. "You'll have to talk to Sergeant—"

The husband, who had been silent until now, suddenly broke in. "We're willing to pay a substantial reward for the return of the necklace, of course."

The woman eyed Abby's tailored blue jacket and sensible shoes. Abby saw her shrewd gaze mentally price-tagging them as if evaluating how much of a "reward" it would take. "We'd be very fair," she said.

"I see. Well, you'll have to discuss that and all other details with Sergeant Cobb at the county sheriff's department. You can find him at the substation on Municipal Street in Green Harbor. The sheriff's department is handling all claims for the necklace."

"*All* claims?" The woman's eyes flashed in alarm. She and the beefy husband exchanged glances. "But it's *my* necklace. No one else has a right to claim it. I'm entitled to it."

"Sergeant Cobb will give you every opportunity to prove that, I'm sure."

The tall man leaned forward, palms on top of Abby's desk. "It's cursed, you know," he warned. "If anyone has the necklace in their possession and isn't entitled to it, something very bad is going to happen to that person."

It wasn't exactly a threat, but neither was it a have-a-nice-day kind of statement.

Abby stood up. She was considerably shorter than both the Seavers, but she herded them toward the door with authority. "Thank you for your interest," she said in as polite a tone as she could muster.

"We're on our way to the sheriff's department now," the husband said. As if this were a last-chance warning, he added, "You'll never see a cent of reward money if we have to do that."

"Fine," Abby said. "Tell Sergeant Cobb I sent you. He'll also be able to tell you if making a false claim is a form of attempted theft, a misdemeanor or a felony."

She didn't know that making a false claim was a crime, of course, but neither did she know that it wasn't. And she was almost certain now that this was a false claim. Especially when the couple exchanged worried glances as they went out her office door.

Perhaps she should start writing these stories down, Abby mused as she looked out the window and watched the couple cross the parking lot to a small motor home. She could title the collection of stories *Granny and the Three-Million-Dollar Necklace*, since a grandmother seemed to play a prominent part in these stories. Or, considering the quality of tales she was getting so far, perhaps it should be *Granny and the Three-Million-Dollar Boondoggle*.

WHEN THE PHONE RANG AGAIN a few hours later, Abby almost hated to answer it. Another phony claimant with a grandma story? But this was a boat owner down at the marina saying he'd just seen a seagull entangled in some fishing line near the dock and someone had told him to call her.

"I'll be there in a few minutes," Abby said instantly. "Where can I find the bird?"

"It's near the south end of the dock. It's pretty well tangled up, but I didn't have any luck trying to catch it myself."

She ran over to her lab in the conservatory building and exchanged her good clothes for a sweatshirt and an old pair of cargo type pants with pockets for everything. She didn't have her usual birding vest here, and she hastily stuck a pocket knife, small scissors and basic medications in the pockets so she'd have them with her whenever she managed to catch the seagull. She realized she probably looked more like a beach bum than an ornithologist as she grabbed a net and headed for her car. But she didn't mind if she could save a bird's life.

Considerably fewer boats were tied up at the long dock at this time of year than during the busy tourist season, but it was by no means deserted. Tie ropes creaked, and small waves, gentle in this protected area, lapped against the moored boats. Rigging on the tall mast of a sailboat clattered and clanked. She ran to the south end of the dock and stood listening, trying to catch sounds of distress above the usual squawks and shrieks of circling gulls. She found the gull a few minutes later sloshing helplessly against the dock.

It took a few tries, but she finally scooped the bird up in the net. She then knelt right there on the dock to work on it.

The lines had tangled the bird's feet together, incapacitated a wing and even wound around the bird's neck.

She'd thought the bird was probably too weak to protest her rescue work, but it set up a noisy squawk and flailed its free wing. She ignored the bird's protestations and the drenching with seawater from the flapping wing and quickly used the small scissors to cut through the strong nylon fishing lines.

She was relieved as she removed the fishing lines to find the bird didn't appear badly injured. She held the bird gently between her knees and dabbed antibiotic ointment on cuts on the leathery yellow legs and under the bird's wing. She debated taking the bird back to the lab for care but decided to give it a chance on its own. Care in a human facility, even good, conscientious care, tended to be traumatic for any wild creature. But if it couldn't fly, she'd definitely take it in.

Carefully she released the bird on the dock and stepped back. It took a few unsteady steps, gave her an indignant look as if somehow this were all her fault, and then lifted its wings in wobbly but determined flight. Abby smiled. She didn't mind the lack of gratitude. She was just glad of the successful outcome.

Abby was now surprised to realize she'd had an audience of half a dozen people watching her work. They applauded as the bird flew and landed on one of the tall wooden pilings supporting the dock. She carefully gathered the scraps of fishing line and took them to a trash can on the dock for disposal.

She felt cheerful as she drove back to the conservatory to change clothes, gratified by the success of the rescue venture. Helping one of God's creatures in distress always lifted her spirits.

The upbeat feeling lasted until some fifteen minutes later when Ida led two people into her office.

# Chapter Eleven

Judee has something to tell you," Gordon Siebert said. He planted his feet in a spread stance and crossed his hands behind him with an almost military formality.

Abby hadn't given Judee more than a passing glance at the jewelry store, just enough to notice that she was a slender blonde and rather attractive. Definitely an energetic glass polisher. Now she also noted that the woman was thirtyish, perhaps a bit too slender, as if she may have lost weight recently. She was attractively dressed in brown slacks and a gold cable-knit sweater, her hair in a neat, short style, but a hint of dark shadows lay beneath her eyes. The woman's gaze targeted the floor, her eyes not meeting Abby's.

"Yes, Judee?" Abby finally said encouragingly. The woman looked thoroughly miserable, as if she'd like to crawl under the desk and hide.

"I . . . I want to apologize," Judee said. She squared her shoulders, as if trying to give herself courage. "I did something I shouldn't have and I'm very sorry."

Abby glanced at Gordon Siebert. The harsh line of his mouth looked as if it had been carved from a rocky cliff on Mount Ortiz. "Something concerning the necklace?"

Judee nodded. "I didn't say anything to anyone about it that first time you came in. I didn't even get a good look at it. But I could tell Mr. Siebert was really impressed, and I heard him telling you it was worth three million dollars and should be in a safe deposit box. And I heard the name Claudia mentioned."

No comment from Gordon Siebert. He obviously intended to let Judee struggle through this on her own.

"Then I heard from somewhere else that you'd found something in an old desk here at the museum. This one, I guess."

Judee inspected Abby's desk with a small spark of interest, as if wondering where in it the necklace had been found. "It . . . it's a really pretty desk."

"Yes, this was where I found the necklace," Abby said.

"Anyway, I was at a meeting with some people—"

"What kind of meeting?" Abby cut in. Probably sounding more suspicious than she intended, she realized a moment later.

"It's a singles group. My husband divorced me a few months ago, when we were living over in Kent. I . . . I was having a hard time and some friends invited me to come stay over here until I kind of got my life back together. So I changed the spelling of my name to J-u-d-e-e so it wouldn't be so ordinary, and moved here. Then Mr. Siebert gave me a job."

Abby didn't need to ask about the divorce. The weight loss suggested that Judee had been devastated by it. And if going to Judee from what had probably been Judy to begin with helped strengthen her confidence, Abby saw no harm in it.

"Just get to the point," Gordon snapped.

Judee avoided looking at him. Her gaze jerked hopefully to Abby a couple of times, but mostly she simply looked at the floor.

"Anyway, I've been going to this singles group. Sometimes it's an actual meeting but mostly it's just a few people getting together at the Springhouse Café to sit around and drink coffee and talk. A few people are there almost every evening. But I never seemed to fit in. I'm always thinking, if my husband dumped me, why would anyone else want me? One guy acted kind of interested, but he never asked me out."

Gordon rolled his eyes. "Please just tell Dr. Stanton what you did."

Which Judee had been sidestepping as she tried to work up her courage, probably because she was so ashamed of what she'd done, Abby suspected. No wonder Judee had dark shadows under her eyes. "Would you like a glass of water, Judee?" she asked encouragingly.

"No, but thank you." Judee made an appreciative attempt at a small smile. "Anyway, they were all talking one night about this mysterious something being found in a desk here at the museum and your name was mentioned. And all of a sudden I realized I knew what that something was. So I . . . I told them that it was an incredibly beautiful blue diamond necklace, worth at least three million dollars. For the first time they acted as if they actually knew I was alive. But a few minutes later they were mostly scoffing, as if they thought I was just making it all up trying to impress them. So the next day I photocopied those papers you'd brought in about the Blue Moon, and I passed them around to prove I wasn't fibbing or exaggerating or anything." She swallowed and then admitted regretfully. "Although I guess I was trying to impress them."

"How many copies did you make?"

"I don't know. Several. Everyone wanted one."

Judee's head hung at a hopeless angle and her eyes now focused somewhere in the middle of Abby's desk. "I . . . I'm really sorry. I didn't mean any harm doing what I did, but it was the wrong thing to do anyway."

"You've damaged the reputation of the store," Gordon said stiffly. "Possibly irreparably."

That sounded a bit melodramatic to Abby. She doubted people were going to be standing outside the store picketing it because of this. "I don't think—"

"Our transactions are always most discreet and confidential," Gordon cut in.

"I'm sorry," Judee repeated miserably.

Abby couldn't help also feeling sorry for the young woman. The divorce had obviously left her feeling worthless and insecure, her self-esteem as tangled in loneliness and discouragement as that gull had been tangled in fishing line. That didn't justify trying to win herself the attention and popularity she was missing, but Abby could understand what had led her to do it.

A thought occurred to Abby. "Did you also give your friends a copy of the photographs Gordon took of the actual necklace?"

Judee momentarily brightened. "No, I didn't." Then her shoulders slumped, and she apparently opted for honesty rather than try to make Abby think she'd made at least one good decision. "I couldn't find them or I probably would have."

"I'd put them in a different place," Gordon said. He lifted his arms and folded them across his chest.

"But you did mention the name Claudia to these people?" Abby asked.

Another unhappy nod.

In spite of the unpleasant situation, Abby couldn't help asking, "And did anyone know someone by that name?"

"No. But one guy said, 'For three million bucks, *I'll* be Claudia.' Then he asked if anyone wanted to lend him a wig and some high heels and a dress. And we all laughed."

Abby smiled too, but Gordon remained stiff-faced.

"Several people have already contacted me about the necklace," Abby said. "So far the claims have been obviously phony and I'm relieved that no one seems to know what the necklace actually looks like. But all this information out there about the diamond and the so-called curse does complicate matters."

"I'm sorry," Judee repeated once more.

Gordon added his own formal apology. "I am also sorry about all this. Nothing like this has ever happened before either here or at my former business in Tacoma." He gave the young woman with bowed head an unhappy look, then turned back to Abby. "Judee is no longer in my employment, of course, so I hope you will continue to consider Siebert's Jewelry for all your jewelry needs."

He didn't actually bow, but somehow a faint movement of his upper body gave the impression that he did. Abby smiled, thinking just how minimal her "jewelry needs" were.

"I don't really think it's necessary that Judee lose her job," Abby said carefully. She didn't want to condone what Judee had done, but neither did she want Gordon treating the error in judgment as if it were an earth-shattering disaster. "It isn't as if her indiscretion actually caused the necklace to be stolen or damaged. I'm sure she's learned a strong lesson about keeping store business confidential."

Gordon hesitated and for a moment Abby thought he was going to relent. But then he shook his head. "The matter is closed." He wheeled and headed for the door.

"Again, I'm so sorry," Judee said after he disappeared. "But I guess I've already said that a dozen times and it doesn't really make any difference, does it? As my mother used to say, 'What's done is done.'"

"It makes a difference to me, because I'm sure you mean it."

"Thanks." Judee started out the door, then hesitated a moment. Tentatively she asked, "Do you think there's anything to the, uh, curse?"

"I think it's foolishness. Right up there with worrying about black cats crossing in front of you and avoiding cracks in the sidewalk so you won't break your mother's back."

Judee smiled bleakly and fingered the ridge of collarbone under her sweater. "I guess that's probably right. Superstitions are silly. Although . . ."

"Although?"

"I never touched the necklace. I was just *around* it, you know, and look what happened to me. Fired from my job. And now my friend Barb says it would be best if I leave the island. They don't think I should live with them anymore."

"Oh, Judee, I'm sorry—"

"It's okay. I have only myself to blame, not some dumb curse. Anyway, I'm leaving the island later today. Thanks for not jumping all over me. I appreciate your kindness."

"I think it does more good to pray for people, not jump on them."

Judee gave her a wan smile. "Thanks."

And Abby did offer a prayer as the young woman stumbled toward the door. Ida came in a minute later, curiosity over-riding her earlier short-lived annoyance with Abby.

"What was that all about?"

Abby gave her a condensed version of what had just taken place in her office. With Ida being one of the few people who had actually seen the necklace, Abby ended with a warning. "So I think it's especially important now that not a word gets out about what the necklace actually looks like."

Ida smiled. "No blabbing?"

"No blabbing. Although it's probably a good thing Judee included the old photo along with the other information she spread around. It serves as a kind of barometer of honesty. Anyone who tries to claim the necklace using a description based on that photo can almost surely be classified as a phony."

ABBY THOUGHT THE DAY'S unpleasantries were over. First the phony Claudia, then the tense meeting with Gordon Siebert and Judee. Surely the day could only get better from this point onward.

She was mistaken.

The phone on her desk rang again a few minutes later. The museum had several incoming lines, with separate listings for Hugo, Abby and the front desk. Abby answered it the way she always did. "The Nature Museum. Abby Stanton speaking."

"Get rid of it, lady," a deep voice said.

"Get rid of what?" Abby repeated, startled, her mind momentarily blank.

"The necklace," the man said impatiently. "No one wants it here. It's dangerous. Get rid of it."

"Dangerous? You mean because of—" Abby broke off. No, she was not going to say the ridiculous word and reinforce this nonsense about a curse. "I would point out to you that the necklace has apparently been on the island for a considerable length of time and no calamities have yet occurred. I believe everyone is quite safe. Who is this?" she demanded.

He ignored the question and repeated, "Get rid of it, lady. It's evil. Deadly."

The phone went dead.

# Chapter Twelve

THE NEXT TWO DAYS were blessedly free of strange calls of any variety. No more relatives of grannies who'd misplaced their valuable necklaces. No more harsh voices warning dire consequences if the necklace wasn't removed from the island immediately.

As Mary had earlier suggested, Abby put in a call from the office to the Woodinville Chamber of Commerce to see if they knew anything about an auction company located in that area. She did receive helpful information, although it was helpful only in that it told her she could quit trying to find the company. A woman who answered the phone said the auction company had disbanded when the owner died a few months ago. No trail to Liberty Washington led along that dead-end path.

She tried nightly to call the people in the yellow house, but always got the same empty ringing.

Life in general, however, seemed to be settling back to normal. She started setting up the feather section of the new exhibit. Hugo reported that the specialist in Seattle was still keeping him on medication, hoping that would be all the treatment he'd require. Bobby called and said the ornithopter kit had arrived and he was putting it together, though he'd like to get a bigger one. Henry reported that so far no one had come to the substation to make an actual claim on the necklace, although he'd had a couple of cautious calls.

One bit of information, the fact that the necklace was now resting in a safe deposit box at the bank, apparently hadn't yet made it into the rumor pipeline. Blessings on Steven Jarvis, Abby thought, for keeping what he knew confidential.

Perhaps, Abby thought hopefully, the whole uproar around the necklace would die down now and she could quietly go about finding the rightful owner.

Then a call came when Abby was home alone on Wednesday evening. Mary had gone out with her friends after attending Wednesday night Bible study at Little Flock Church. Abby had begged off, wanting to spend a quiet evening at home. The phone rang and Abby removed Blossom from her lap and put down the mystery she was reading. Here at home she answered with a simple hello.

"I'd like to speak to Abigail Stanton, please." A male voice. She immediately knew this was not someone she knew personally.

"This is Abigail," she stated warily.

"My name is Jules Gamino. I'm calling from Friday Harbor over on San Juan Island. I've just run into information about a valuable necklace that I've been trying to locate for some time now. I understand you've found it."

Abby's first thought was, *Here we go again. Another grandma story.* Her second thought was about the necklace itself: *If you've been trying so hard to locate it, Mr. Gamino, why didn't Henry find some report of that in the official records?* She put that thought into a direct question. "And have you reported to the authorities that the necklace is missing?"

"No, it isn't that kind of 'missing.' You might call it a business matter. I was, how should I put it? Manipulated? Deceived? The blunt truth is that I was cheated out of the necklace by someone I trusted."

This was, at least, a story with a fresh angle. Although she was as skeptical of it as she'd been of all the other calls. "Your grandma perhaps?" she asked tartly.

"My grandmother?" the man repeated blankly. "No, of course not. Why would you think my grandmother had anything to do with this? My grandmother wouldn't cheat anyone."

Abby, feeling guilty and mildly chastised for her frivolous remark, didn't elaborate. "Never mind." She started to tell him to contact Sergeant Cobb, then changed her mind. If this was another fraud, perhaps she could eliminate him right now rather than letting him take up Henry's time. "Could you describe the necklace for me, please?"

"No, that's one of the frustrating parts about this. I never actually saw the necklace. It was just part of this business deal. But I do know that the main stone in it was a very large blue diamond with an old-fashioned cut."

His refusal to describe the necklace surprised Abby, as did his reference to an old-fashioned cut. On quick consideration, however, she decided the man was probably just protecting himself, shrewdly eliminating the possibility of offering a wrong description. Did he know enough about diamonds that he'd been able to identify the cut from that old black-and-white photograph that he had no doubt seen?

It was also remotely possible, she had to admit, that he was telling the truth and did have an honest claim on the necklace. Somewhere there was a rightful owner, of course. Perhaps this Jules Gamino was that person.

Carefully she tossed out a small line of bait to see if it snagged anything. "We have reason to believe the necklace was intended as a gift for someone."

"Oh? Who?"

Apparently that part of the traveling rumors hadn't made it to him, but if he didn't already know the name Claudia, she wasn't going to supply it. "Perhaps you could tell me."

"Look, let's not play games. The necklace is rightfully mine and I want it. This so-called friend of mine who ripped me off had no right to give it to anyone."

Okay, Abby decided, it was time to turn this over to Henry and the sheriff's department and let them sort it out. Out of curiosity, however, she let herself ask one more question. "You've heard about the curse?"

"Oh sure. Big deal," he scoffed. "I've had plenty of miserable things happen in my life without ever having laid a finger on that necklace, so I doubt my luck's going to get any worse when I do get hold of it. Now, let's arrange a—" He broke off as if he'd just thought of something. "You're entitled to a reward, of course. Ten percent . . . no, let's be fair. How does fifteen percent sound to you?"

All these generous people and their rewards! Although perhaps *bribes* would be a better word.

"Actually, I should tell you that the necklace is no longer in my possession, so I can't—"

"So where is it?" he cut in. The gloss of smooth politeness had suddenly vanished, his tone now sharp as a lawyer's cross-examination.

"I'm not at liberty to disclose that information. You'll have to talk to Sergeant Cobb. He's the officer in charge at the local sheriff's substation in Green Harbor. He's handling all claims concerning the necklace."

"Claims? How many claims are there? Let me tell you, if anyone but me is making a claim, they're trying to con you."

"You'll have to talk to Sergeant Cobb."

There was silence as the man apparently digested that bit of information. Abby doubted he liked hearing that he'd have to deal with an officer of the law rather than a lone woman whom he thought he could manipulate or intimidate.

"Surely you didn't think I'd keep such a valuable item just lying around my home or office?" she suggested lightly.

"If you turned that necklace over to the authorities, Ms. Stanton, you're not nearly as intelligent as I thought you were."

The statement startled Abby. "Why do you say that?"

"Because items disappear when they're in police custody. Drugs that are supposed to be evidence in a trial come up missing. So do guns, which sometimes show up later on the black market and then back in the hands of criminals. Cops aren't saints, you know. They're as tempted as anyone else by the chance to make a quick buck."

"I can assure you that Sergeant Cobb's integrity is above question. He is absolutely honest. I'd trust him with my life. The necklace is safe in—"

Abby stopped herself, realizing just in time that in her anger with this man's ugly accusations she'd almost slipped and revealed the location of the necklace. She carefully finished the statement with generic vagueness. "The necklace is in a safe place."

The man's breathing made an audible rasp in the silence that followed, as if he were waiting for her to slip again. Unexpectedly he broke the silence with rough laughter.

"Playing it cool, huh? Okay, I can understand that. Probably a smart move. I'll be over in Green Harbor by Friday. I'll contact you then."

"No! Please don't. There's no need to—" But Abby was protesting to a dial tone. Jules Gamino had hung up.

Abby mentioned the unsettling phone call to Mary when she returned home that evening. Mary didn't find it particularly disturbing since the man hadn't actually threatened anything, but she was still fidgeting about the call when she sat down at her desk in her office the following morning. She couldn't pinpoint anything more disturbing about Jules Gamino's call than any of the other contacts. His tone had sharpened a couple of times, but, as Mary had pointed out, he hadn't made any actual threats.

Finally, realizing that all she was getting done was ruining a perfectly good sheet of paper with nervous doodles, she dialed Henry at the substation and reported the incident to him.

"I know he didn't make any actual threats, but there's something about the man that kind of twangs my nerves," Abby admitted. "Some undercurrent I can't pinpoint, but it keeps tugging at me."

"Maybe it's the fact that he says he's going to contact you again. He sounds as if he doesn't intend to give up."

"His laugh didn't help. It was kind of sly." Almost as if he considered Abby to be in an unspoken conspiracy with him and she was "playing it smart" so as to get the biggest reward money possible out of the necklace. "Of course, it's probably unfair to be suspicious of someone just because you don't like his laugh," she added. But she hadn't liked the man's attack on the honesty and trustworthiness of law enforcement officers either.

"I don't suppose he said what kind of business dealings this necklace was supposed to have been a part of?" Henry asked.

"I didn't think to ask."

"I doubt he'd have told you anyway, if any such dealings ever actually existed. It may be just another wild story." Static from a police radio scratched somewhere in the background. All the deputies had radios to keep in touch with the substation. "Hold on a minute, will you?"

Henry put her on hold while he took care of official business, but he was laughing when he came back. "Small uproar over at The Dorset. Unbeknownst to the management, a guest brought in a pet ferret. Another guest became quite irate when it got loose and ran up his pant leg. A rather rude shouting match followed and a deputy had to intervene. But all is well now and everyone is having hot mocha lattes, compliments of the management."

Somehow the small interruption soothed her nerves and helped put everything into perspective. Not all law enforcement was deadly serious and dangerous, and she needed to keep that outlook on the necklace situation. The claimants, including Jules Gamino, were probably all more imaginative than dangerous.

"Right. Now," Henry said, obviously trying to stop chuckling and get back to serious business, "about this latest caller of yours—"

"If he contacts me again, I can try to find out what kind of business dealings he was supposedly involved in that concerned the necklace."

"No, don't bother. I doubt you could believe anything he says anyway. If he contacts you again, just refuse to talk to him," Henry advised. "Tell him he'll have to talk to me. Then hang up."

# Chapter Thirteen

B$_{Y}$ SATURDAY EVENING, Abby was beginning to think she wouldn't hear from Jules Gamino again after all. He'd said he'd be on Sparrow Island by Friday, and now Saturday was almost gone. Perhaps he'd decided he didn't want to tangle with the law. Or a less comforting thought: Maybe it was just the weather that had delayed him.

A new storm had blown in on Friday with gusts of wind and rain. By Saturday morning, the water around the island was so rough the Coast Guard had issued a small-craft warning, and only the indefatigable ferries were still plowing through the big waves.

Whatever the reason Abby hadn't heard from Jules Gamino again, she was relieved. One call did come Saturday afternoon. Abby picked up the phone gingerly when it rang, readying herself to be firm and abrupt, but the caller was only cheerful Janet Heinz, secretary at Little Flock Church, saying they'd decided on an impromptu potluck the following day after church.

"Pastor Jim, Patricia and I thought it would be a good way to celebrate the weather. Places all over the Northwest have been hit by drought, and here we are with enough rain to make people think we perhaps ought to start stockpiling lumber to build an ark."

"A potluck sounds like a fine idea."

"Bring whatever you'd like," Janet added. "Somehow it all seems to balance out."

This was one of the many things Abby appreciated about Little Flock. People in this congregation had a definite "if life hands you lemons, make lemonade" attitude. And thank the Lord for the lemons while you're at it.

George Stanton had brought over three dozen fresh brown eggs, so Abby settled on deviled eggs for her contribution. Mary went fancier and whipped up a white cake complete with a picture of the church done in vanilla cream frosting on a chocolate background.

"I don't know. It needs something," Mary mused as she eyed her creation, spatula in hand.

"People?" Abby asked.

"Yes! People. That's exactly what it needs." And she proceeded to add in a half dozen little frosting figures around the church—because it was the people who really made Little Flock special, as they both knew.

ABBY ENJOYED THE BOUNTIFUL POTLUCK Sunday afternoon, a fitting follow-up to Pastor Jim's morning message on "Feeding on the Word."

The downpour of rain certainly didn't seem to affect anyone's spirits. Chatter and laughter filled the church's recreation room during the meal.

Abby's mother had made good use of the abundant supply of eggs in a tasty potato salad with bits of colorful pimento for decoration. Candace Grover, Mary's manager at Island Blooms, had brought along her boyfriend from Seattle, lawyer Bradford Collins, and was introducing him around. Abby spotted Aaron Holloway and Ida. They hadn't been together during the morning service, but they were sitting together to share the meal.

Singing followed the potluck. Hugo was there, his deep baritone coming in strong on the men's section of a praise chorus divided into parts. Afterward there was general socializing as small groups formed and reformed, people flowing genially from one cluster to another. Abby was talking with Sandy McDonald about Bobby's ornithopter project, when a gruff male voice interrupted.

"Abby, what's this I heard about you finding a valuable necklace that was hidden away for a long time? Something that had belonged to your grandmother?" The speaker was short, stocky Frank Holloway, longtime owner of the local hardware store. He wasn't overweight, but today, after the big meal, the buttons on his snug vest were certainly being put to the test.

Abby wasn't surprised by the reference to the necklace, considering all the information bouncing around the islands, but she was surprised that it came from the usually taciturn Frank. It must mean he was really curious. She was also startled by this totally erroneous connection with her grandmother. Where had *that* come from?

"I hadn't heard anything about that," Sandy said, looking interested. "Is this the grandmother on your father's side—" She glanced toward George Stanton, who was standing near the coffeemaker and laughing with Pastor Jim about something. "—or your mother's?"

"Is your grandmother the one who's supposed to have put a curse on the necklace?" Aaron Holloway, Frank's grandson asked eagerly as he came up to join the conversation. "It's said that something terrible will happen to anyone who owns it or touches it or something. Right?"

Ida flicked Aaron with her napkin, an annoyed expression on her face. "Aaron, you know as well as I do that that's ridiculous. And even if such a thing as putting a curse on something were possible, which it *isn't*, Abby's grandmother certainly wouldn't do it."

"What I heard is that anywhere the necklace is, that place may be in for trouble, and not just a few people," Al Minsky, well known as the best mechanic on the island, put in. Abby saw him surreptitiously run the thumbnail of his left hand under the thumbnail of his right. Al's hands were always scrupulously clean, but he sometimes acted as if he were afraid he may have missed a bit of grease on his hands or under his fingernails. "Not that I believe that kind of superstitious stuff. Makes about as much sense as that movie with the haunted car running people down all by itself. But there was supposed to be an entire town in India or somewhere that was completely wiped out by a big earthquake while the necklace was there."

"Where in the world did you hear that?" Abby asked. None of the material off the Internet had mentioned an earthquake.

"Somebody told me. I don't remember . . . Oh yeah, it was probably Ed Willoughby at the drugstore when I was waiting to get a prescription filled for Eileen. There's a bug going around school, you know, and she caught it, so I was in there."

"I heard the desk was at Bayside Souvenirs for a while," Margaret Blackstock, secretary to the principal at Green Harbor School, chimed in. She picked up the glasses hanging by a chain around her neck and placed them on her nose so she could peer at Abby. "And have you heard what happened to Donna Morgan? She fell in her back room there at the store a couple days ago and did something to her neck. I certainly can't believe the necklace had anything to do with that, but apparently Donna does."

The little group around Abby had suddenly grown, and everyone was looking at her for information and explanations. Abby knew rumors expanded and twisted like weeds as they traveled from person to person, and here was dismaying proof of that. These rumors had, in fact, not only grown and twisted, they'd turned into a giant, jungle-sized weed of misinformation.

This was also an unhappy reminder that even though most people professed disbelief in the power of a curse, there was still an uneasy smidgen of "Could there be something to this?"

simmering under that disbelief. She realized she'd unintentionally played a part in all this by including the computer printout about the curse in with the information she'd given to Gordon Siebert, which Judee had then distributed. It was time to set things straight.

"Okay, everybody, with all these inflated rumors going around, I need to clarify some things here and now." Abby raised her voice to include everyone who had gathered around. "I did find a necklace in my desk at the museum. A very beautiful necklace, and apparently quite valuable."

"I heard it's worth thirty million dollars!" Janet Heinz said. "Wish we could look in some cubbyhole here at the church and find something worth thirty million dollars. Think of all the good we could do with it! But all I ever find are lost gloves and scarves."

"When I heard about Abby's finding this fancy necklace in her desk, I dug around in mine at school," Margaret Blackstock said. "I found four pennies and a package of bubble gum so hard it broke when I dropped it."

People laughed at this, including Abby. But all she could think was, *Thirty million dollars, ten times the estimate Gordon Siebert had made on the necklace's value!* With rumors raising the value like an overinflated balloon, the number of greedy pretenders rushing to claim the necklace just might sink the island.

"The necklace is indeed valuable, but I think that figure is considerably exaggerated. The stone in it may or may not be a blue diamond known as the Blue Moon that apparently disappeared some years ago. It's certainly not been proven yet." Thinking what other rumors needed to be squelched, Abby added, "Neither the necklace nor the desk in which it was found ever belonged to either of my grandmothers. We're still trying to locate the former owner of the desk. And the necklace has been turned over to the authorities until the rightful owner can be located."

"Don't you get to keep it if the owner doesn't turn up? You'll be the richest person on Sparrow Island!" someone called, although Abby didn't look quickly enough to see who.

"I'm sure the rightful owner will be found," she said firmly. "And it doesn't take a fancy necklace to make me rich in everything that's important. Now, about this so-called curse. I'm very sorry to hear about Donna Morgan's accident, but the necklace had nothing to do with it."

"Right. If you've ever seen the mess in that back room of hers, it's a wonder she didn't fall over something a long time ago and *break* her neck," someone agreed, and there were muffled chuckles.

"This information about the so-called curse came off an Internet Web site, and I think we all know that, although there is a lot of valuable information on the Internet, there is also much misinformation," Abby stated.

Aaron lifted his hand. "But bad things apparently have happened to various people and places in connection with that blue diamond."

"Bad things happen to people and places everywhere all the time," Abby said bluntly. "They're a fact of life. If people start looking, sometimes they see connections where none exist. In any case, there is one important point to remember here: God is in control, not some inanimate object. We have nothing to fear from a necklace."

Hugo, standing near the edge of the group, lifted his hands in applause. "Well said, Abby." A spattering of further applause followed.

That seemed to create a natural end to the conversation. People started gathering up their leftovers to take home. Hugo wound through the crowd to Abby's side while she was putting her empty deviled egg dish in a plastic bag.

"Would you believe that I even got a call at home from someone saying that I, as your supervisor, should insist that you take the necklace off the island immediately, even if it did belong to your grandmother." He shook his head in disbelief both at the demand and the erroneous connection with Abby's grandmother.

"Someone you know?"

"I asked, but the person wouldn't give a name, except to say that as a tourist she was very nervous about staying on an island where that necklace was located."

"She? It was a *he* who called me with the same demand. I hope we don't have some sort of paranoid conspiracy going on here."

"I want to think they're just misguided people with paranoid delusions and too much time on their hands. But sometimes people like that can be real troublemakers."

Abby nodded. "The truth about my finding the necklace in the desk is incredible enough, and then to have the facts so embroidered and twisted is almost scary. I'm going to call Donna Morgan and see if I can nip her little story in the bud."

"Good idea. I'll talk to Ed Willoughby at the drugstore too. I have to go in tomorrow for another prescription. I doubt he really believed any of what he was passing along to Al. He's a sensible guy. But he does like to talk. He seems to feel obligated to pass along whatever he hears." Hugo glanced up as a tallish, thin man with bushy brown hair approached. "William, hello! Good to see you. I didn't realize you were here today."

"I've been keeping out of sight. That's what a good news-paperman does, you know. Stays in the background." He nod-ded knowingly. "That's how he hears all sorts of interesting things people might not say if they knew he was listening. Things they'd rather he didn't know. And I heard lots of inter-esting things today."

William Jansen had become a newspaperman fairly late in life, after having spent his younger years as the CEO of his family's diaper manufacturing business in Chicago. Abby had never seen anything wrong with that background, but she'd heard he was a bit touchy about it and no one ever mentioned it to his face. He was an excellent, conscientious newspaper-man, although big news was scarce on the island, so he tended to make the most of any tiny incident.

Now he eyed Abby as if calculating how big a story she might provide. Abby was thankful when Hugo spoke up first.

"Sure, we have some news for you. Abby is working on a new exhibit for the museum, 'Bird Flight and Early Human Flight.' And Ida Tolliver has recently come to work for us part time."

William was not detoured by Hugo's diversionary tactics. "And Abby found a valuable necklace in her desk at the museum. She admits that herself."

"Surely you're not thinking about publishing anything about that," Hugo protested. "We're already getting too many calls from people trying to claim the necklace with some phony story. And I think you'd really be doing the community a disservice to print anything about that foolish curse."

"I have no intention of printing unconfirmed rumors or irresponsible gossip." William, sounding affronted, straightened his narrow back. "But there are facts here. The finding of the necklace is a fact, a newsworthy fact."

"Yes, I suppose it is," Abby agreed reluctantly. "But it's not necessarily a fact that the stone in the necklace is the one called the Blue Moon. That's merely an interesting possibility. And the curse connected with the Blue Moon, which may or may not be the blue diamond I found," she emphasized again, "is strictly a matter of unfortunate coincidences strung together by overactive imaginations."

"We'd really appreciate it if you could hold off for a while," Hugo added. "Abby is working on locating the real owner, and she promises to tell you everything if she finds that owner. Right, Abby?"

"Right."

"An owner possibly named Claudine or Clarissa?" William said with a sly tilt of his head that suggested he knew more than they thought he knew, and wanted them to know that.

Abby couldn't help laughing. The rumor mill had churned out a new payload of misinformation.

Hugo glanced at Abby for confirmation, then said to William, "We'll tell you one small bit of information, if you promise to keep the whole thing under your hat for a while."

William hesitated, as if weighing the possibility of a good news story now against a better one later. Finally he nodded, and Abby knew that meant they could count on him not to add fuel to the blaze of rumors.

"We're trying to find someone named *Claudia*," Abby said, purposely lowering her tone to a confidential level. "There's a definite connection between the necklace and someone with that name. You're in a position to know a lot of people, so if you come across anything to do with someone named Claudia, we'd appreciate your letting us know."

William nodded as if pleased to be taken into their confidence. "I can do that. But this is news," he warned. "And I'm not going to hold off printing it for long."

ABBY AND MARY WERE HEADING out to the van, Finnegan using his strength to help Mary's wheelchair over some rough places in the parking lot, when Abby heard someone calling. She turned to see Sandy McDonald running to catch up with them.

"I'm sorry to bother you, but could you keep Bobby for the rest of the afternoon? Neil is working today, which is why he isn't here, of course. And now the nursing home in Seattle just called—" She lifted the cell phone still in her hand. "—so I need to make a quick run over there to check on Dad."

"I hope it's nothing serious?" Abby asked, concerned. Sandy's father had been in a nursing home for some time now. She and Neil were paying much of the cost of his care there, not easy for a couple also trying to save for their son's college education.

"I don't think it's serious. But he was recently moved to a different room in the nursing home. A better room, actually, but he's having some problems adjusting. I think I just need to go over and reassure him."

"Bobby's always welcome to stay with us," Mary assured her.

Abby echoed the sentiment and added, "We'll put him to work." She lifted a palm and looked skyward. A few anemic patches of blue now showed between the clouds. "The rain's stopped, at least for a while, and the weeds are growing like, well, weeds around the house." Bobby had now run up to join them and she asked him, "How about it? Are you up for helping me pull weeds today?"

Bobby grinned and lifted and bent his arm to show what might, by a big stretch of the imagination, be the beginning of a muscle. "Look at that," he proclaimed. "I can pull the biggest weed in your yard."

BOBBY CHANGED INTO some old gray sweatpants and a shirt at the McDonald house. After Abby had also changed into work clothes, they tackled weeds in one of the flower beds. Mary let Finnegan come out with them for his daily play and exercise time. Even Blossom, after haughtily checking the weather from the sliding glass doors, deigned to come outside. She wandered through the wet grass, pausing to lift and shake her paws after every few steps. After a few minutes she chose to return to the deck and fastidiously clean her feet while Finnegan, unmindful of the wet, romped and played happily.

Weeds pulled easily from the soft ground. Bobby said he was still working on the ornithopter model, but he wanted to order another bigger one that he thought would be better for the exhibit. Abby had to laugh. Typical Bobby, the young perfectionist. Mary came out to join them for a while, then went back inside to call her daughter in Florida.

Abby and Bobby talked as they worked, subject matter wide ranging, as usual. From the question of whether a worm accidentally chopped in two turned into two whole new worms, to a discussion of why God made mosquitoes and cockroaches, and would Abby make a trip to Mars if she had the chance. "I would!" Bobby declared enthusiastically.

After an hour or so, the knees of Abby's old jeans were muddy and soaked through, and her shoes were caked with mud too. Bobby's mud wasn't limited to knees and shoes. Abby hadn't actually seen him roll in the dirt, but he certainly looked as if he had. Mud everywhere, from nose to toes.

"Okay, shower time." Abby stood up and stretched muscles and joints that seemed to have stiffened into temporary cricks.

"We're going to give Finnegan a shower?" Bobby asked eagerly in what Abby suspected could be a deliberate misinterpretation of her words. "Awesome!"

Abby laughed. "No, the shower is for you. It's only Finnegan's feet that are dirty."

Bobby looked down as if he hadn't realized until then that he was dirty at all. She thought for a moment he might protest. But he glanced at Abby, apparently decided he already knew the answer to *that* question, and just said, "Then can we watch Animal Planet afterward?"

Abby walked over to the McDonald house with Bobby so he could pick up more clean clothes. They both left their muddy shoes outside when they returned to the house. Upstairs, Bobby's shower wasn't necessarily the world's shortest, but he was in and out before Abby got the tangles brushed out of her hair. The murmur of Mary's voice drifted up the stairs as Abby came out of her own shower. Mary and her daughter always talked at least weekly, and at least once a month they shared a really long marathon chat. This was apparently one of those times.

Bobby was just closing the front door when Abby came downstairs in a comfortable long skirt and sweater. Finnegan, not in his working harness or cape on this relaxed afternoon, was with Bobby.

"Was someone at the door?" Abby asked, surprised.

"It was some guy on a bicycle. He wanted to know if he

was on the right road to the lighthouse. I told him this was the right road, all right, but it was a long ways to get there."

The San Juans hosted quite a number of bicyclists in good weather. Touring the islands by bicycle was an activity popular with the more athletic-minded tourists. Yet this was an unlikely day for it. Abby suddenly felt uneasy about the bicyclist. She dashed to the window, but he'd already reached the main road and she could see only the top of a hat as he turned north. That direction would take him to the lighthouse, but . . .

Abby turned to her sister. "Did you see him?"

Mary put a hand over the phone. "No. Nancy was telling me about this terrible rash little Nicholas has, so when the doorbell rang I just told Bobby to answer it."

Abby knew people in some areas wouldn't send a child to answer an unknown caller at the door. Here on Sparrow Island, however, people seldom gave a thought to the dangers that concerned people in big cities. And certainly nothing had happened. Bobby was safe and sound, looking totally unconcerned. Still, Abby felt uneasy.

"It wasn't someone you knew?" she asked Bobby.

"Nope. Never seen him before."

"That's all he wanted, just to know if he was on the right road to the lighthouse? He didn't ask about anything else?"

"You mean like the necklace? Mom and Dad were talking about that. So were some of the kids at school."

To hear that rumors about the necklace had invaded even the school was not welcome news, but Abby didn't want to make an issue of it. So all she said was, "But he didn't say anything about that?"

"No."

"What did he look like?"

"He was kind of, uh, well, scruffy looking."

"Scruffy looking how?"

"I don't know if it was a funny looking beard or he just hadn't shaved for a few days, but he sure looked like he needed a shave. Dad would never go around looking like that. I think his hair was dark, maybe even black. But I couldn't see much of it because he was wearing a hat, and he had it all scrunched down over his ears. Kind of a dirty ol' hat. But he seemed nice enough," Bobby added hastily. His folks had taught him not to judge by appearances. "Finnegan came to the door with me, and the man said he was a nice looking dog and asked if he was mine."

"What did you tell him?"

Bobby looked puzzled, as if he wondered if Abby thought he might lie about the dog's ownership. "I said no, that he was Mary's service dog, and he helped her do things because she's in a wheelchair. And that you and Mary always said he was a real part of the family now, that you couldn't get along without him. Even if he did sometimes like to dig holes in the backyard when he was out there playing."

Bobby apparently saw something in Abby's expression that made him ask apprehensively, "Did I do something wrong?"

"Oh no. Of course not. And you're right. Finnegan is a real part of the family."

"I didn't like one thing about that guy. When he asked me about Finnegan, he said 'This your dog, son?' I don't like someone I don't even know calling me *son*. He's not my dad."

Abby tousled Bobby's hair. "I'm sure he didn't mean any harm."

"I don't think he's going to make it to the lighthouse," Bobby added.

Mary was off the phone by now. "Why not?"

"Because he sounded, you know, kind of wheezy. Like when you've had a bad cold or cough or something. It's a long ways to pedal a bike all the way to the lighthouse and it gets pretty steep in places too."

Abby nodded agreement, but she was thinking something else. *Wheezy.* Which might be a different way of describing that audible rasp she'd heard in Jules Gamino's breathing when she was on the phone with him.

Had Jules Gamino, pretending to be an innocent bicyclist, come right here to the house? And if so, why? What was he up to?

# Chapter Fourteen

HENRY CALLED MARY THAT evening just to chat, since he hadn't been able to come over for church. Abby tapped Mary on the shoulder when it sounded as if the conversation was coming to a close.

"Tell him I'd like to talk to him for a minute," she whispered. "About our visitor."

Mary continued the conversation for a few more minutes, then said to Henry, "We had a rather odd person come to the door today. Abby wants to talk to you about him." She handed the cordless phone to Abby.

"What kind of odd person?" Henry asked without preliminaries, his tone instantly alert. "What did he want?"

Abby started to tell him what she knew, but Bobby suddenly appeared at her side. He'd been sitting cross-legged in front of the fireplace eating a grilled cheese sandwich.

Now he held out his hand for the phone. "I can tell him."

Abby hesitated. She didn't want to pull Bobby into this. But, unfortunately, the fact that he was the only one who'd actually seen and talked to the man had already pulled him in. "Here's Bobby. He's the one with firsthand experience."

She listened as Bobby gave Henry a competent description of the man and what he'd said, including how he'd sounded wheezy. He added one item he'd forgotten to mention to Abby earlier: the man was wearing sunglasses.

Abby's suspicions instantly jumped a notch. Sunglasses with more rain threatening to fall any moment?

"So, what do you think?" Abby asked Henry when Bobby returned the phone to her.

"I don't want to get paranoid here. The guy could be exactly what he said he was, a bicyclist looking for the lighthouse. I've seen people pedaling out in the rain and insisting they were enjoying themselves even when it looked to me like they had to be miserable."

"To each his own, I guess."

"Right. And some people think it looks cool to wear sunglasses anytime, even at midnight. So he wasn't necessarily trying to use them as a disguise."

"So you don't think there's anything to be concerned about?"

Brief silence before Henry finally said reluctantly, "I wish I could say that, but I'm not sure I can."

"Bobby said he sounded wheezy." Now Abby came out with her concern. "I don't think I mentioned it before, but that Jules Gamino who called me also sounded very wheezy, kind of raspy when he spoke."

"You think it could be the same person?"

"I don't know. A wheeze isn't much to go on. But the whole thing just strikes me as suspicious. I'm wondering if Gamino thought I lived alone, but when he came to the door and saw other people he decided to remain anonymous."

"Could be. Although he may not have intended to identify himself to you today. He knows you have no idea what he looks like. So he may have been checking you out."

"That could be right."

"The thing is," Henry went on, "I can't pick up a guy just because he looks scruffy and sounds wheezy and wears sunglasses at unlikely times. None of that is a crime, and he hasn't done anything actually threatening or illegal. But until we get this all settled, neither of you open the door to anyone unless you know the person. Okay?"

"Okay."

"Like I said, I can't pick the guy up on what we have here, but I'll run his name through official channels and keep an eye out for him. You'd think criminals would be particularly careful not to attract the law, but they're always doing it. Running red lights, using defective taillights, getting in fights, things like that. That's often how criminals get caught, rather than some fancy detective work. Maybe I'll spot him doing something."

"Although this guy probably isn't going to commit any big traffic infractions on a bicycle," Abby observed.

"True. But I'll keep an eye out. If I spot him, I can just stop him for a friendly chat. I think we can be reasonably certain, whether or not he's up to something, that he isn't a Sparrow Island resident."

Abby had already come to that conclusion. "He must have brought the bicycle to the island with him," she reflected thoughtfully, "because the bicycle rental place down by the ferry slip is closed for the season."

"Right. Good thinking. He may have brought it in a pickup or van, of course, and no one would notice. But if he was riding it, someone working on the ferry may remember him because there aren't many bicyclists this time of year. I'll check with them."

"It's kind of hard to think of some dangerous criminal tooling around on a bicycle," Abby said. "It seems so, well, out of character."

"True," Henry agreed. "But it could be a really smart move on his part. A bicycle doesn't tend to arouse suspicions, and there's no car license number for anyone to catch. And a bicycle is easy to stash out of sight."

"But, unless he takes a late ferry out tonight, he has to stay somewhere on the island. There's The Dorset, of course, although, from how Bobby described him, he'd certainly stand out among their clientele. The Chois' bed-and-breakfast is still open, and maybe a couple of others are too."

"He could be camping out, but he'd have to be pretty rough and tough to be doing that in this weather. But I'll check the usual places."

"Thanks, Henry. I appreciate this. I don't want to be a worrywart."

"Like I said earlier, *both* of you need to be careful. Maybe we'd better make that *all* of you. You might mention this to Bobby's folks too. Although don't alarm them. From what I hear, there are already enough people on the island alarmed about the 'curse' factor with the necklace. We don't want to raise more fears. One thing I'll definitely do is send a patrol car out your way more often."

When Sandy came to pick Bobby up that evening, Abby did mention the visitor and Henry's warning. Sandy had already reported that her father was fine, just a bit agitated in the new setting.

"I don't think there's any danger," Abby added when Bobby was out of earshot. "Bobby is in no way connected with the necklace, and this guy didn't try to do anything today. But be careful anyway, okay?"

Sandy nodded. "Are you sure you two are okay?"

"We're fine," Mary assured her. "Anyone tries to do anything here, we'll zap him with our can of Raid. I read somewhere that a spray of it in the eyes is very effective."

Sandy laughed. "Okay. I know how self-sufficient you two are. But call anytime if you need help and Neil will come right over."

"Thanks. We hope it doesn't come to that though," said Abby.

THE NEXT MORNING on her way to the museum, Abby remembered that she'd intended to call Donna Morgan but had gotten sidetracked. On impulse she decided to go by the souvenir shop and talk to her in person. Donna was just turning the sign on the door from CLOSED to OPEN when Abby pulled up to the curb. She could see that the brace around Donna's neck made it difficult for her to turn her head.

"I heard you'd hurt your neck so I just thought I'd stop in and see how you're doing," Abby said when she stepped inside.

"Oh, thanks, Abby. I appreciate that. It's nothing serious, just a strain. But with this neck brace on I have trouble even tying my shoelaces. And my neck hurts too, but I can't afford to close the store down and take time off. Though I might as well, considering how slow business has been the last few days."

Donna sounded morose and grumpy, not at all like her usual bubbly self.

"I could take an afternoon off and come in to help out so you could have some time off. How about tomorrow afternoon?"

"Oh no, that's okay. Thanks anyway. I can manage." Donna said it so hastily, that Abby was momentarily taken aback. "I just hope this is all that happens," Donna added.

"Why would anything more happen?" Abby asked, but then she knew exactly what Donna was going to say even before she spoke.

"Because it was the necklace that did it, don't you think? It was right here in my store so now this happened. But maybe this isn't enough, maybe there's something worse coming."

Now Abby realized why Donna would rather not have her on

the premises. Abby, having had even closer contact with the necklace than Donna had, might bring calamity to the store with her.

"Donna, the necklace is just a thing. It can't cause something bad to happen. It can't cause anything to happen. No more than . . . than one of those silly glow-in-the-dark frogs can." An oversupply of which were still peeking out from various shelves.

Donna ignored the frog comparison. "Tell that to the people in the town that burned down over in England or wherever it was," she retorted.

Abby ignored this new contortion of the rumor that had now moved the fire calamity to England. "Donna, have you ever strained your neck or been injured before?"

Donna ran a finger along the ridge of her nose. "I broke my nose when I fell with my bike when I was a kid. There's still a bump. If I ever get enough money together, I'll get it fixed. But that was my own dumb fault. I was pretending I was like that guy who jumped all those cars on his motorcycle, and I tried to jump my bike over—"

Donna stopped short as if suddenly realizing what Abby was getting at, that this wrenched neck was no more caused by the necklace than the broken nose had been. She glanced toward the back room. The green curtain was pulled aside and Abby could see into the room. It looked like a combined maze and obstacle course. A desk, boxes, files, tools and junk. A disaster waiting to happen.

Donna looked thoughtful as she fingered the stiff brace

around her neck, as if she was considering Abby's argument, but then she said, "This is different. The necklace really did have something to do with this."

Abby tried a few more points of logic, but Donna wasn't convinced. Abby left feeling thoroughly frustrated.

THE PHONE WAS RINGING when Abby reached her office. She stared at it, dreading picking it up. Given the way things were going, who knew who it might be? Another Claudia or Jules Gamino again? Then, not one to avoid hard situations, she steeled herself and picked it up it. "The Nature Museum. Abby Stanton speaking."

To her delight, the call had nothing to do with blue diamonds, necklaces or irrational superstitions. The caller was a former colleague from Cornell wanting to, as he put it, "pick her brain" about possible exceptions to normal feather coloring in a certain species of woodpecker. They had an enjoyable discussion both on a professional and personal level.

So when the phone rang again later, she picked it up without really considering who the caller might be. "The Nature Museum. Abby Stanton speaking."

"Abby!" the male voice said heartily. "I didn't know that's the name you go by. I must apologize for calling you Abigail before. It's probably a name you hate and never use."

A slight wheeze identified the caller as Jules Gamino, acting as if they were old buddies. "I'm fine with Abigail. But I'm really quite busy this morning—"

"I won't take much of your time. Sorry I didn't contact you earlier like I said I would, but I just got to the island this morning. This is Jules, by the way. Jules Gamino."

*Just got to the island this morning.* Abby doubted that, since she strongly suspected he was the man who had come by the house on a bicycle. But there didn't seem much point in challenging the statement, so she let it go.

"I told you before, Mr. Gamino," she said briskly, "you'll have to talk to Sergeant Cobb at the sheriff's substation in Green Harbor about anything concerning the necklace."

"Oh, I don't think that's necessary," he said easily. "We can do this quite simply. You just get the necklace out of safekeeping, wherever you have it, and I'll see that somewhere down the line you get your share."

"Mr. Gamino, I have no interest in receiving any share in the necklace's value. And you will have to talk to Sergeant Cobb." A hint of challenge crept into her voice when she added, "And I'm sure you'll have to provide some proof of ownership. Can you do that?"

"I told you, it was part of a private business transaction. A trade actually. My so-called friend got the necklace and I got nothing. He just up and disappeared with it." Gamino was beginning to sound impatient.

"So what you're telling me is that you don't have any proof of ownership?"

"You don't need to . . . All you . . . is . . . rightfully mine. And . . . want you . . . get it . . ."

His voice had been coming through clearly, but it suddenly started to break up, cutting off some of the words as if a giant scissors was slashing through them. Abby was puzzled for a moment, then realized this must mean he was talking on a cell phone. Cell phone transmission was spotty on most of the islands. Sometimes they worked great, but other times they were about as effective as yelling from one tin can to another. Gamino had apparently been standing in a good transmission area when he started but had now moved away from it. By car? Bicycle? There was also a faint sound she couldn't quite identify in the background, a little like Blossom's purr when it was in high gear, except with a rougher undertone.

"I'm sorry, Mr. Gamino, but as I've told you repeatedly, I don't have the necklace. I turned it over to the authorities." She wondered if her voice was breaking up as badly as his. Once more she repeated the bottom line. "Please understand, you'll have to talk to Sergeant Cobb."

"No. You understand *this*," he growled, all pretense of joviality gone now. "The necklace . . . mine. No intention . . . dealing with . . . sheriff's . . ."

"The only way you can make a legal claim for the necklace is through Sergeant Cobb. I can't get it for you."

"Then it looks as if I'll have to come up with a way to convince you that you *can* get it for me. And soon."

The warning, even with the inconsistency of island cell phone transmission, came through loud and clear.

# Chapter Fifteen

ABBY REPORTED GAMINO'S call to both Hugo and Henry, along with the man's claim that he'd just arrived on the island. Both were as skeptical of that as Abby was. They, too, thought he was the man on the bicycle.

Henry said he'd contacted the ferry operators, but no one recalled seeing anyone arrive by bicycle recently. Neither was anyone with the description of their bicycle visitor registered at The Dorset, the campgrounds or the bed-and-breakfasts.

Abby tried to keep her mind off Gamino and spent the rest of the morning working on the new exhibit, with only one interruption. Another Claudia showed up, this one young and stylish in low-cut jeans and a tight, stretchy blouse under a denim jacket. She claimed the necklace was hers because it was a family heirloom. She offered a detailed description of the necklace, exactly the same as the photo on the Internet, which immediately raised Abby's suspicions about the authenticity of her story.

"The problem is that my grandfather developed

Alzheimer's and couldn't remember where he put the neck-lace," the young woman said. "He was always hiding stuff, like his pills. He'd pretend to take them, but then my mother would find them hidden in his socks or under the mattress."

"I see."

"And I don't know how you got it, but this desk where you found the necklace is the one my grandparents used to own," she'd added with a triumphant toss of her considerable mane of gold-streaked hair. Some claimants seemed to know about the desk, some didn't. "Grandpa made it and I know it's where he'd hide the necklace."

Abby had a strong urge to laugh. She restrained herself, but she couldn't help her curiosity. The very brashness of some of these stories intrigued her.

"How do you suppose the desk came to be here on Sparrow Island?" she inquired politely.

The woman had a quick answer. "A renter stole a bunch of Grandpa's stuff. He must have sold it to somebody here."

Abby considered and decided that on a scale of one to five, this story rated three stars for imagination but only one star for probability. She referred the woman to Sergeant Cobb. "Claudia," like the claimants before her, turned wary when she realized she'd have to deal with an officer of the law.

"Well, I'll think about that," she muttered. "Probably no point in it. They'll figure some way to cheat me out of it."

"No one's going to cheat you if you're telling the truth and the necklace really is yours," Abby said gently.

Soon after the woman left, Mary called Abby from Island Blooms and asked if she'd like to meet for lunch at the Springhouse Café. Abby agreed readily and drove into town a few minutes later.

The day, with the island's sometimes capricious changes of weather at this time of year, had turned quite pleasant, unexpectedly springlike for a late fall day. Boats dotted the calm water, rather like mushrooms sprouting in a field after the rain. Mary was in good spirits after a morning at the flower shop, which had included taking a big order for flowers for a Tacoma couple's fiftieth wedding anniversary celebration at The Dorset.

Abby knew Mary must regret that her own marriage would never reach fifty years because of her husband Jacob's death, but she also knew Mary had come to terms with the loss and was always thankful for God's other blessings.

Now, after placing their orders for the quiche that was the special of the day, Mary was laughing as she said, "And one of my students stopped in to pick up yellow roses for a flower arrangement she's doing for her sister. For a while I had my doubts about this woman's ever getting the hang of flower arranging. She brought in some 'pretty leaves' to use in an arrangement a while back, and they turned out to be poison oak."

"Oh no!"

"But she's doing great now. She had some nice wild vines to go with the roses. So, how was your morning?"

Abby grimaced and filled Mary in on the details of her unpleasant call from Gamino. Abby then tried to lighten the mood with a "Claudia" story. "Another Claudia with a wild claim for the necklace showed up. She said her grandfather made my desk. At least this story didn't involve a grandma." She glanced at her watch. "I want to try calling those people in the yellow house during the daytime about the woman they bought their house from. I don't suppose there's any more chance of them answering their phone in the daytime than in the evening, but I thought I'd give it a try."

"Why not right now?" Mary suggested. She reached for the embroidered denim bag hanging on the arm of her wheelchair and pulled out her cell phone. She held it up invitingly. "No time like the present, and all that."

"Why not?" Abby agreed. Abby excused herself so her call would not disturb the other diners. Standing outside the café she punched in the numbers, by now having memorized them from other times she'd tried to call. To her surprise, someone picked up on the second ring.

"Oh, Mrs.—" Abby hadn't been prepared for an answer, and her mind went momentarily blank. What was their name? Dowinger? No, Duranger. Yes, that was it. "Mrs. Duranger?"

"Yes?"

"I've been trying to call you for several days now, but—"

"Oh, we left for the season a couple of weeks ago. We just came back this morning. We wouldn't be here now except that Ward forgot and left some important papers here, and we had to come back for them. All the way from Palm Springs, can you imagine that?" she added, sounding exasperated.

"I'm sorry to bother you. This is a neighbor here on the island, Abby Stanton. I'm trying to locate the woman who formerly owned your house, Liberty Washington. I'd thought I might be able to go through the company that auctioned off the contents, but they're out of business. I'm hoping you can give me some information about her."

"I'm afraid not. We don't have an address or phone number."

"What about the real estate company that handled the sale?"

"I can give you their name, but I doubt they'd tell you anything. Everything is so confidential now, you know. Although I do recall something about her moving down to Oregon, one of those little towns on the Columbia River. I don't remember the name." Mrs. Duranger's voice faded as she apparently turned her head to snap at someone, probably the unfortunate Ward, who was definitely in the doghouse for his forgetfulness. "Don't bother looking in that drawer. I've already looked there."

"Thank you, Mrs. Duranger," Abby said hastily. "This information is very helpful and may be just what I need to locate her."

"Now if someone could just help *us*. I'd like to get started back to Palm Springs this afternoon." Mrs. Duranger clicked the phone without saying good-bye.

"Helpful?" Mary asked as Abby handed the cell phone back to her. She tucked it back in the denim bag.

"Yes indeed. I'd looked at the Web site with phone listings on the Internet, but I'd only looked in Washington. Now I'll expand the search to Oregon. And thanks for the suggestion about calling them now." Abby reached across the table to pat Mary's hand to emphasize her thanks. "A couple more hours and I might have missed them completely."

"I'm on my way home after lunch. How about if I do it?"

"You?"

"I'd love to. I'm starting rather late in life, but maybe I can be a sleuth too!"

Abby smiled. "To add to your many other talents."

MARY HANDED ABBY A SLIP OF PAPER as soon as she got home that day. "Liberty Washington's phone number. She lives in The Dalles, Oregon. It's a small town right on the Columbia River."

"Mary, this is great! Thank you."

"Actually, it wasn't all that difficult to find," Mary admitted. "I've been trying to figure out a way to find a Claudia using the Internet, but there's no getting around it, you have to have more than a first name."

"Maybe Liberty Washington will provide that."

That wasn't going to happen today, however, Abby realized in frustration when she immediately tried the number her sister had located. She received no answer then nor on two more attempts later that evening.

But the following evening met with success. With the

phone to her ear, Abby gave her sister a thumbs-up sign when someone picked up the phone.

"Hello."

The voice startled her because it was male.

"I'm trying to reach Liberty Washington."

"I just brought her home a few minutes ago. May I tell her who's calling?"

"My name is Abby Stanton. I've never met Mrs. Washington, but I live on Sparrow Island. She also lived here at one time, I believe."

"Okay, hold on. Mom," he called, "do you want to talk to someone from Sparrow Island?" Abby couldn't hear the answer, but a moment later he said, "She'll be here in a minute."

There was a small clunk as he put the phone down. It took some time for it to be picked up again.

"This is Liberty Washington. I'm sorry to be so slow. I broke my hip a while back and I have to use a walker to get around." The pleasant, soft-spoken voice gave Abby a quick mental picture of a genteel older woman with silver hair and a kind smile. "I've never had one of those cordless phones, but I surely need one now. I could just carry it around with me."

"They can be very handy," Abby agreed. She was pleased to realize that Liberty Washington was apparently the chatty type. "What I'm calling about is a desk that came from the house you sold here on the island. A very handsome desk, solid walnut with decorative walnut burl inserts. But if you're busy I can call back later?"

"Oh no, this is fine. My son was just leaving. Excuse me a moment." There was silence as she apparently put her hand over the receiver to say good-bye to her son. She came back sounding eager to chat. "Oh my, yes, I remember that desk. It was in the guest room. One of my favorite pieces. I hated to let all those lovely old things go, but I knew I couldn't keep up that big house after my husband died. The people who bought the house weren't into antiques, so I just had those auction people sell everything. I have a lovely condo here in The Dalles now, with a lovely view of the river too. You bought the desk at the auction?"

Yes, definitely the chatty type. Abby had the feeling that if she wanted to know anything from the price of condos in The Dalles to what Liberty had for breakfast, the woman would be happy to tell her.

"No. A friend I work for at the local nature conservatory bought it for my office in the museum. He got it from the woman who bought it at the auction."

"He must think you're very special." Liberty sounded approving, maybe even a bit wistful. "As I recall, the desk brought quite a nice price."

"I'm wondering . . ." Abby wasn't sure how to handle this. Should she tell Liberty Washington everything? While she tried to decide, she realized one question might solve everything. "Do you have a daughter named Claudia?"

"No, there's just my son Matt. I've been staying with Matt and his wife Debbie over in Hood River ever since I broke my hip. Today is my first day home. It's so good to be here! Not that I didn't enjoy Matt and Debbie and the grandchildren," she added hastily. "But there's nothing like being in your own home."

"Do you have any other relatives or know anyone named Claudia?"

"No, I don't believe so." The woman sounded puzzled. "Does this have something to do with the desk?"

"I'm not sure. The thing is, I found something hidden in the desk. Something quite valuable. A necklace, actually. A card in the box suggests it was meant as a gift for someone named Claudia."

"Really? How exciting! Like finding buried treasure. I wonder how it got there?"

"I was hoping you could tell me. I thought perhaps you or your husband had hidden it there at some time."

"I certainly didn't." She laughed cheerfully. "I'm a bit forgetful these days. Would you believe I couldn't find one of my shoes this morning, and it turned up in Debbie's broom closet? But I'm fairly certain I wouldn't hide a valuable necklace and then forget it. What does it look like?"

Abby's quick impression was that the woman was curious, but not *greedy*-curious. Just to be safe, however, she said, "We're keeping that confidential until we locate the owner who can identify it."

"Of course. I understand."

"How long did you own the desk?"

"Oh, it had been in the family for a long, long time. An aunt had it before I got it years ago."

There was no chance that a former owner may have hidden the necklace there, given what Gordon Siebert had said about the blue diamond having surely been reset fairly recently. "What about your husband? Could he have bought the necklace and hidden it in the desk, perhaps intending it as an anniversary or birthday gift for you later?" Although that wouldn't explain the card to Claudia.

"Oh, I doubt that. I've never cared much for fancy jewelry, and if Norbert wanted to surprise me it would be with a cruise to the Caribbean or a week in London, something we could share." She laughed again. "Norbert was a very solid man, more inclined toward assets such as real estate and stocks and bonds than something frivolous such as jewelry. Which I can certainly appreciate, now that he's gone. But someone other than either of us must have hidden the necklace there after I sold it."

Such refreshing honesty! So many people were making up preposterous stories and trying to claim the necklace, and here was Liberty Washington, who was certainly in a position to make a credible claim to the necklace, denying all knowledge of it.

A second, rather disturbing thought suddenly surfaced in Abby's mind. Could husband Norbert have known a Claudia who *did* like expensive jewelry, someone Liberty had no idea existed? Could Norbert have hidden the necklace in the desk with the intention of giving it to that unknown Claudia, but suffered the heart attack before he could do so?

Abby didn't want to think anything so devious of Liberty's husband, and it was certainly not a possibility she intended to bring up.

"How about the people who owned the desk between the time of the auction and the time you got it?" Liberty asked, obviously wanting to be helpful. "Maybe one of them hid the necklace there."

"We've checked on that, and no one knows anything. But it's possible someone put the necklace in the desk after it was brought to my office." Abby could tell the woman would happily chat longer, but now she was rather anxious to end the conversation. Liberty Washington obviously knew nothing about a necklace or a Claudia, and Abby didn't want this conversation to raise unpleasant suspicions in Liberty's mind about the possibility of Norbert's past relationship with some unknown Claudia. "Thank you for taking the time to talk with me."

"Oh, that's fine. I've enjoyed it. A mysterious necklace. So exciting! I'm sorry I can't be more help. Perhaps you could tell me when you find out who owns it? I'd love to know."

"I can do that."

"I miss the island, you know. We had such good times there, fishing and walking on the beach and hiking the trails. And the people were so wonderful, so friendly. I had a flat tire once, and it wasn't two minutes before someone came along and fixed it for me. But it wouldn't have been the same without Norbert."

"I'm sure it wouldn't have," Abby agreed. "Thanks again for talking with me. And I hope your hip doesn't give you any problems."

"Do call me again if I can be of any help."

IN THE NEXT COUPLE OF DAYS, several more claimants for the necklace contacted Abby, a couple of whom she gave four stars for creativity but none higher than a single star for believability. A young man and a middle-aged couple actually went on to talk to Henry, but no one made a formal claim, all apparently turned off by the need to provide actual proof of ownership. Then something peculiar happened to Abby.

It was Friday afternoon and she had left the museum a few minutes early so she could stop by the bank before it closed. She was just crossing the bank's parking lot to return to her car when she had the strangest feeling that someone was watching her. It was an uncomfortable feeling and she turned uneasily.

She scanned both the parking lot and cars passing on the street. For a moment she thought a tall, lean man in denim jacket and pants across the street was looking at her, but a moment later she told herself she must have imagined the odd feeling. An expensive sports car had pulled in next to her in the parking lot and she gave the little car an appreciative glance. When she looked up, the man was headed next door to the post office.

Mary had dinner started by the time she got home. Abby added the broccoli she'd bought at The Green Grocer's.

Afterward, Mary took off for a meeting of her reading group, which had shifted to Friday for this month, and Abby relaxed with a copy of a Seattle newspaper she'd picked up at the grocery store. When Mary got home, they shared companionable cups of tea, and Mary laughingly told her about the rather heated discussion about which book the group would read next.

The phone rang just as Abby started upstairs for bed. Mary was headed for her bedroom, and Abby picked up the phone, surprised that anyone would call this late.

"Yes?"

"Stanton?" a male voice said.

No *Ms.* or *Dr.*, not even a misplaced *Mrs.* An odd way to start a conversation. Could it be Jules Gamino? Abby hadn't talked to him enough to be certain whether or not she'd recognize his voice.

"This is Abigail Stanton," she said, her tone cautious.

"You found the necklace."

"I found *a* necklace."

"And you know about the curse."

*Doesn't everybody?* Abby thought wryly. But what she said was, "I don't believe in curses."

"That could be a mistake. There may be something to this one."

She still didn't know if the caller was Gamino. He wasn't wheezing or rasping, but that may have been some temporary condition that had passed. But if it were Gamino, why wasn't he identifying himself? He'd done so readily enough before, had, in fact, tried to act rather chummy. Or was he just chang-ing tactics?

"What do you want?" she asked. "Why are you calling me?"

"I'm calling because the necklace is mine."

"Then all you have to do is take your proof of ownership to the authorities, to Sergeant Cobb at the local sheriff's sub-station, to be specific." Abby had said those words so often that she was beginning to wish she could just press a REPEAT button to send them out.

"I'm dealing with *you*, lady, not the authorities. I've been hearing people want you to get the necklace off the island. This is your chance."

"I give it to you, and you considerately take it off the island, thereby saving me and all the other inhabitants from doom?"

Her sarcasm apparently escaped him. "You got it," he said. "And it does belong to me."

"Exactly what is your claim to the necklace, Mr. . . . ?"

He laughed. "Nice try, but I'm not falling for that sly little trick, lady. You don't need to know my name."

Apparently not Gamino, then, because she certainly already knew *his* name.

"I do need to know why you think the necklace may be yours."

Another silence, but no rasp or wheeze, until he apparently decided he had to tell her something.

"I helped Van Horn get it. I was supposed to get a commis-sion, because I helped him make a good deal, but I never got a dime. In fact, I'm out some cash myself on the running around I did for him. So with Van Horn gone, I figure the necklace is mine. I'm entitled to it."

Abby was surprised. This was a very different story, one without a grandma, and it had a new name attached. Van Horn.

"Who's Van Horn? And by 'gone,' do you mean that he's passed away?"

"Van Horn is the guy who found out the curse on the necklace is real, big-time real. I would have thought you'd have found out about his accident by now."

Abby didn't see any point in trying to bluff. "I don't know anything about anyone named Van Horn or an accident. Perhaps you could tell me."

"All I'm telling you is that I want what's coming to me. The necklace. And you're the person who can get it for me."

"No, I can't," Abby said firmly, not adding that she wouldn't even if she could, with no more proof than this. "There are proper legal channels you'll have to go through with the authorities."

Abby didn't understand why so many people thought if they could just convince *her* that they were entitled to the necklace, she could blithely hand it over.

"Van Horn wasn't all that concerned about legal channels," the man growled. "Although he didn't come out too well, of course, in the end."

"Aren't *you* afraid of the curse?" Abby asked, stalling for time while she tried to figure out what was going on here.

Another silence, as if the man indeed had some qualms about the curse, then a rough laugh. "For what the Blue Moon is worth, I'm willing to risk it."

He'd called the diamond the Blue Moon. Was he just parroting the rumors going around or did he really know something?

"I'm sorry, but this conversation is really rather pointless," Abby finally said firmly. "The necklace is not in my possession now and I don't have the authority—"

"But you know where it is. I'm guessing the bank, tucked away in a safe deposit box."

Abby's breath caught. She suspected he really was just guessing, but it was a guess that was too accurate for comfort. She reverted to the bottom line that people never wanted to hear.

"You really will have to discuss all this with Sergeant Cobb at the sheriff's substation. I can't do anything for you."

"We'll see about that, Dr. Stanton." His tone was oddly confident, as if he knew something she didn't. Then he hung up.

He'd made no threats, but she now suspected that his calling her simply *Stanton* at the start of their conversation had been a deliberate rudeness, no doubt intended to intimidate her.

At some point Mary had come out of the bedroom, apparently realizing this wasn't some pleasant social call. Finnegan stood beside her. "Someone else calling about the necklace?"

Abby nodded. "At first I thought it was that Jules Gamino who called before, but now I think it may have been someone new." She repeated to Mary what the man had said. "I'll be so glad when the real owner turns up. I think I've had more phone calls in the last couple of weeks than in all the time since I returned to Sparrow Island."

"You're a popular lady, Abby Stanton."

Abby smiled ruefully. "All it takes is a three-million-dollar necklace, and then you're Miss Popularity."

"Are you going up to bed now?"

"No, I seem to be wide awake. I think I'll get on the Internet and surf for a while."

Mary yawned. "Okay. See you in the morning then. How does French toast sound?"

"Great!"

# Chapter Sixteen

ABBY SURFED THROUGH several Web sites on blue diamonds that she'd visited before, along with some new ones. One site she hadn't seen before was a "Where are they now?" site devoted to various high-profile gems with locations presently unknown. The Blue Moon was mentioned along with a comment she hadn't seen elsewhere, that this gem was supposed to have two small but distinctive flaws that could be used to identify it.

Gordon Siebert had mentioned a couple of small flaws. A tingle of excitement skittered up Abby's spine. Could this definitively determine whether the stone was the Blue Moon? The site invited anyone with information on any of the gems to contact the Web site. Abby clicked on the e-mail address and was about to write a message when wariness kicked in.

There were so many scams on the Internet. Was this Dr. Emmett Kingston legitimate? Or was he some kind of con man trying to get information about valuable gems for ulterior and not necessarily ethical purposes? He listed a professorship and two books he'd written. She looked on a book-buying

Web site and found the books did exist. She might also be able to check Kingston's credentials with the university he claimed to work for. But she was still hesitant about e-mailing a stranger with information about a blue diamond that, whether or not it was the Blue Moon, was extremely valuable and already had various imposters trying to claim it.

Another thought jumped in on the heels of Abby's concerns about Dr. Emmett Kingston, and with it a tide of dismay. Yes, she'd encountered some unscrupulous claimants for the necklace, but she didn't want to become a person who suspected everyone she encountered of dishonesty and underhanded schemes. This case was making her lose her faith in her fellow humans and she couldn't allow that to happen.

Reluctantly she decided she'd have to think about this. She printed out the additional information from the Web site and turned off her laptop without writing the e-mail. Maybe she'd try to contact the university later.

By morning she had come up with a different approach.

It was Saturday and she didn't have to go in to the museum, but after breakfast she drove into Green Harbor. She parked a couple of doors down from Siebert's Jewelry. A heavy fog had settled over the island, but Abby found it invigorating rather than depressing.

Gordon Siebert was alone when she went inside, looking as suave as ever in a dark suit and burgundy tie. A discreet sign posted near the register said "Experienced sales help wanted."

Abby came directly to the point. "I know our last meeting

was rather awkward, and perhaps you'd rather not have any further involvement with me or the necklace, but—"

Gordon made the little movement of his upper body that wasn't quite a bow, but almost. "On the contrary, if I can do anything to help stop all the wild rumors going around, I'd be delighted to do so. To hear some people tell it, the diamond's very presence means Sparrow Island is in danger of anything from sinking like Atlantis to suffering a biblical plague." He rolled his eyes.

"I'm sure no such calamities are going to happen, but we do seem to be getting an invasion of people making wild claims to ownership of the necklace," Abby said ruefully. "The reason I'm here today is because of something else I found on the Internet."

She spread the new computer printout on the counter. Gordon picked up the pages and studied them with interest.

"I'd like to contact this man, this Dr. Emmett Kingston, and see what he could tell us about identifying the Blue Moon, but I'm reluctant to do so without knowing if he's legitimate. I thought you might know or could find out. He's located in Chicago."

"I can't vouch for the absolute integrity of anyone but myself," Gordon Siebert said with a touch of pomposity, "but I can certainly find out if he's considered reputable. Kingston . . . Dr. Emmett Kingston," Gordon repeated. "*Hmmm*. Actually, the name sounds vaguely familiar, but I can't think in what context."

"Hopefully not as some famous jewel thief."

Gordon smiled. "I don't think so, but I have contacts in Chicago. I'll check him out."

"I'd appreciate that."


ABBY DIDN'T EXPECT TO HEAR from Gordon Siebert for several days, but he wasn't a man to waste time. He called her at home that very afternoon. She was outside raking leaves when Mary came to the sliding glass doors and held the phone out to her.

Abby leaned her rake against the deck and went up the sloping ramp to take the phone.

Gordon Siebert identified himself and then said, "I thought the Kingston name sounded vaguely familiar and I'm embarrassed that I didn't fully recognize it immediately. Dr. Kingston is with the University of Chicago, a professor of geology with a side interest in gems. He's very well known and considered quite an authority. I talked with a couple of people who vouched for him. He's now in the process of gathering material for a new book on the mysteries surrounding various lost gems."

"I'm glad to hear he's reputable. I'll e-mail him tonight at the address on the Web site."

"If it would be of any help to you, I can contact him. I'd really like to do something to help make up for that unfortunate breach of confidentiality." The hint of pomposity had now turned into what sounded like honest regret. "He also sounds like a most interesting man to get to know. But if you'd rather contact him yourself—"

"Actually, I'd appreciate it very much if you would contact

him. You can certainly talk more knowledgeably with him about gems and flaws than I can."

"I'll do it, then."

THAT EVENING there was another phone call. Henry had come for dinner. They'd had salmon stored in the freezer, a product of one of Henry's successful fishing trips, and Mary had baked it with butter and garlic. He'd brought along a DVD to watch afterward. It was an unexpectedly charming comedy, and afterward they were eating Mary's delicious cherry cobbler in the kitchen and discussing how Hollywood really could make something clean and fun if they wanted to. Abby answered the phone and carried it across the room so as not to interrupt Henry and Mary's conversation.

"Hello?"

"Is this Abby Stanton?"

Abby braced herself for another necklace story, but then she realized that she recognized the woman's soft voice. "Liberty?"

"Yes!" The woman sounded pleased. "You didn't leave your number, but I got it from Information. I hope you don't mind?"

"No, of course not. I'm happy to hear from you."

"And I hope I'm not calling too late?"

"Oh no. My sister and a friend and I were just enjoying a snack."

"Well, the thing is, I remembered something."

"Oh?"

"Yes. You remember I told you we had that desk in the guest room? Well, we had lots of guests, of course. When you have an island place, suddenly you seem to have all sorts of friends you never had before."

"I've heard that." She'd had some hints herself from friends and acquaintances at Cornell about how they might like to visit the islands, although those were all welcome hints from people she'd love to see again.

"Anyway, I don't know why I didn't think of it right off, but we had a guest who stayed in that room only a month or so before Norbert died. The very last guest we ever had, in fact. Not one of our usual friends. A most unusual guest, actually."

"Unusual in what way?"

"I never met him personally. I was down visiting Matt and Debbie when he was at the house. We had a boat for sale, you see, a very nice thirty-seven-foot cabin cruiser. Norbert had been having heart problems for some time and we weren't using the boat anymore, so we decided to sell it. We hadn't actually gotten around to advertising it yet, but we'd told a few people, and this acquaintance of a friend of Norbert's heard about it and came over to see the boat."

Abby made a small murmur of encouragement.

"He planned to stay at The Dorset, but when he tried to make a reservation, they were full that weekend. A wedding party or something. So Norbert told him to come anyway and stay at our house."

"And you think he may have hidden the necklace in the

desk in your guest room?" Abby asked doubtfully. Even more doubtfully adding to herself, *A three-million-dollar necklace? And then just walked off and left it?*

"I wouldn't think so except for a couple of things. The man's daughter was supposed to come over and meet him there on the island, and they were going to celebrate her birthday together."

Abby's interest suddenly sparked. She paced along the end of the room. "And the daughter's name was Claudia?"

"I don't know what the daughter's name was, unfortunately," Liberty admitted. "Actually, at the time, from the way the man talked, Norbert thought the man was thinking of buying the boat as a birthday present for her. Norbert and I talked on the phone every evening, of course, and he said the man wouldn't actually commit to buying until she came over and saw the boat. But maybe the real birthday present was a valuable necklace. Or maybe he intended to give her both a boat and a necklace. Norbert said he was a rather flamboyant type of person and apparently quite wealthy. He drove one of those enormous pickups, the kind with enough chrome on it to blind you, Norbert said. And he talked about traveling to all kinds of exotic places. Nairobi and the Seychelles and Corfu. I also remember Norbert saying that he wore an enormous emerald ring. Very flashy."

A flamboyant person, with a flashy emerald ring. That fit. The blue diamond necklace was definitely the kind of thing a flamboyant person would choose. But a sticking point intruded just as the pieces of the puzzle seemed to fall into place.

"But surely he wouldn't hide the valuable necklace in the desk for his daughter and then never come back for it or never even contact you about it again."

"He couldn't," Liberty said. "He was dead."

"*Dead?*" Abby repeated. Liberty, she realized, was not only chatty; she also had a flair for the dramatic.

"Dead," Liberty repeated.

"You mean he died soon afterward? Or right there in your house?"

"Well, neither, exactly. He didn't die in the house, but he died while he was staying there at the house. He was interested in hang gliding, you see, and he'd brought his equipment along intending to use it on some other island after he left. There's some place on one of the islands where they do a lot of hang gliding, I guess. But then one day he and Norbert were driving around in his pickup, because he wanted to see the island. They drove up that mountain. I forget the name—"

"Mount Ortiz?"

"Yes, that's right. Ortiz. And he decided to go hang gliding from up there."

"Right then, on the spur of the moment?"

"Yes! Right then. Norbert said he tried to talk the man out of it, saying he should talk to someone who'd done it from up there, someone who knew the wind currents. But he wouldn't listen."

With a rush of recognition, Abby suddenly knew where this was going. She remembered Henry talking about the rash of unpleasant incidents that happened about the same time as the man dying of a heart attack. She didn't interrupt Liberty's telling of her story, however.

"So he did it. Norbert said the man got his equipment out of his pickup right then and rigged it up right there. You can see Wayfarer Point Road from up there."

"Yes, I remember." When she was a girl it had been a strenuous climb up Mount Ortiz, but now there was a good road almost to the top of the mountain. From the parking area a trail went on up to the very peak, where a scenic-view platform had also been built.

"He intended to land on the road. Norbert was supposed to drive the pickup around and meet him there. He climbed over the guard rail and then he just started running! That's how they take off, you know. Norbert said he ran right off the edge of the mountain. He said he couldn't believe it, that his own stomach did a big flip-flop when the man did it."

"Was this man an experienced hang glider?"

"I have no idea. But he did have all the equipment. Norbert said the hang glider was gorgeous, with brilliant red and yellow stripes."

Flashy, Abby thought. The way this man liked things.

"I don't know what they're made of," Liberty went on. "Nylon or something like that, I guess, with a metal framework for the pilot or whatever he's called. Norbert said he looked fantastic floating out there for a few minutes, like a big butterfly. He said he was even thinking maybe he ought to learn to do it himself. And then the man seemed to be having some kind of problem, and the front part of the hang glider tipped way up."

Abby knew that the way a hang glider landed was to stall it slightly by tipping the nose of the glider upward. But if the pilot did it at the wrong time, or a wind draft caught and raised the nose too much, the craft could be in trouble.

"And then it just plummeted, Norbert said, like a big fist had grabbed it and dragged it down. It hit the tops of some trees first, but then a gust of wind jerked it away and it crashed in an open space, right on some rocks. Norbert called on his cell phone for help, but there was no road where the hang glider crashed and it took the deputies and medical people quite a while to get to him. I got home that evening, so I heard all this secondhand, but Norbert was really shaken up."

"Yes, it must have been a terrible shock for him. Do you remember the man's name?"

"Oh yes. Van Horn. Nelson Van Horn. I remember thinking it a rather elegant sounding name."

Van Horn! The same name mentioned by the man on the phone!

"Do you know anything more about him? Where he was from? What he did for a living? What he looked like? How we might locate his daughter?"

"Nothing at all, I'm afraid. As I said, I never met him personally. I have no idea what he looked like. But, as I said, I think he must have been quite wealthy. He was going to pay cash for the boat."

Quite wealthy indeed, if he was going to give his daughter an expensive boat and/or a three-million-dollar necklace for her birthday.

"Except there was one other thing. I hate to mention it, because the man is dead and all . . ."

Abby remained silent. It sounded as if Liberty had something negative to say about the man. She didn't want to encourage the woman to make a derogatory comment, but neither did she want to stop her from offering information that might be helpful.

"Norbert thought there might be something kind of shady about Van Horn. You asked what he did for a living and I recall Norbert wondering too. Van Horn just seemed to be *rich*, you know, without any specific source of income. And when I say he was going to pay cash for the boat, that's what I mean, actual cash dollars. Norbert was rather taken aback by that. Banks tend to ask questions if you come in with a lot of cash, he said. But I guess he intended to do it. We really needed to get rid of the boat because Norbert tended to work too hard trying to keep it clean and polished up, which he shouldn't have been doing, with his heart trouble and all."

People inherit money, Abby thought. Or they make good investments and become wealthy. A source of income didn't have to be obvious to be legitimate. Although cash dollars tended to suggest Van Horn had some less upstanding source of income. "What became of the boat?"

"I sold it after Norbert died. For a lot less money than Van Horn would have paid," she added wryly. "Anyway, I hope this may be of some help to you in locating the owner of the necklace."

"Oh, one more thing. When I remembered Van Horn, I got to thinking that, after the accident, I'd boxed up his things that were still in the guest room. We thought perhaps the daughter would want them, but she never showed up. We didn't know how to contact her or even what her name was. Perhaps we should have tried harder, but none of it looked particularly important anyway. There were just some clothes and shaving gear, plus pamphlets about boats and the islands that he'd left scattered on the desk. Although I see now that there are a few old receipts here too. They're all crumpled, as if he'd just emptied them out of his pockets. And here's a catalog of hang gliding equipment. After Norbert had his heart attack, none of this seemed important."

She sounded suddenly pensive, and Abby said sympathetically, "I can understand that."

"I hadn't thought of it again until you called and started me thinking."

Then Abby realized an important fact tucked into Liberty's chatter. Her pulse quickened. "You still have these items, the pamphlets and receipts?"

"I'm as surprised as you are but, yes, I do. I don't know where the clothes and shaving gear went. I probably donated them along with Norbert's clothes when I moved. But

Norbert was very conscientious and efficient, and he'd put the pamphlets and things in a manila folder in our filing cabinet, so they got moved with me. And there they were when I looked this afternoon, in a file actually labeled 'Van Horn.' I can't think that anything here would be of any help, but I'll be happy to mail it all up to you if you'd like."

"I'd be most happy if you would." Abby gave her a mailing address. She could hardly hope there was a receipt for a blue diamond necklace among the items, but who knew? There might be *something*.

"I'll get it in the mail to you on Monday, then."

"Thank you very much, Mrs. Washington."

This made a viable scenario, Abby reflected as she hung up. This man named Van Horn bought a fabulously expensive necklace for his daughter's birthday, possibly making the purchase under shady circumstances or with money that didn't go through regular channels. Possibly making the deal with the help of the man who'd called Abby and claimed the necklace was his because he'd never received his commission.

Van Horn then brought the necklace to the island, intending to surprise his daughter with it when she arrived to celebrate her birthday. He taped it in that hidden part of the desk for safekeeping until he could give it to her. But he was killed in the hang gliding accident and no one else knew anything about the necklace.

A viable scenario indeed.

# Chapter Seventeen

"THAT WAS QUITE A CONVERSATION," Mary observed when Abby rejoined Mary and Henry at the table where they were still drinking coffee.

"A most interesting and informative one." Abby refilled her own cup and relayed what Liberty Washington had told her.

"And so the necklace stayed right there, hidden in your desk all this time. Just think, if your drawer hadn't got stuck that day, the necklace might still be there," Mary mused.

"And apparently no record of the purchase turned up after Van Horn's death, so no one ever came looking for the necklace," Henry added.

"And even if he'd insured it, no one would ever have reported it missing and made a claim because no one even knew it existed!" Mary said.

"Perhaps we're making some assumptions here that may not prove true," Abby warned.

Henry tapped a finger against the handle of his coffee mug. "Interesting, very interesting, that the name Van Horn has now turned up twice. Too bad Claudia didn't turn up too."

"Would what the man on the phone said, the one who mentioned Van Horn, entitle him to claim the necklace?" Abby asked.

Henry considered the question thoughtfully. The overhead light gleamed on the balding area that he'd long ago given up trying to conceal and did nothing to detract from his handsome face. "He'd have to have something to document it, of course. But I think that situation would go beyond the jurisdiction of the sheriff's department to decide. In fact, it sounds to me like something a judge might have to decide. The heirs, especially Claudia, would surely have a valid claim."

Mary smiled wryly. "Nothing is ever simple, is it?"

"When you first said that caller mentioned the name Van Horn, I ran it through the system," Henry said. "Nothing turned up. So if he was involved in something shady, it apparently wasn't serious enough to attract the attention of the law."

"Or else he was very clever and simply never got caught," Abby suggested.

"Possibly. In any case, I didn't until now connect the Van Horn name with the hang gliding accident."

"Was there an investigation into the accident?" Abby asked.

"Very minimal. There was a witness, who must have been the husband of this woman you've been talking to. I can look up details in our files on Monday, but as I recall it was quite clearly a tragic accident."

"Caused by overconfidence on Van Horn's part?" Mary asked.

"Overconfidence, misjudgment, maybe pure foolishness."

"Did you notify next of kin?" Abby asked.

Henry tilted his head and looked off into space as he searched his own mental files. "No, I'm sure we didn't. The witness identified the man as Nelson Van Horn but, as I recall, that was about all he knew about him. I certainly don't remember anything about a Claudia. Van Horn probably had a wallet and identification on him at the time of the crash, but I never saw it. He was in very bad shape and the medics immediately airlifted him to Seattle. He died either on the way to the hospital or shortly after arrival, and the hospital must have taken care of the next-of-kin notification."

"What became of the pickup?"

"You know, I just don't remember. Although the information may be in our files."

"Would it be possible to get the name and address of next of kin from the hospital?" Abby asked.

"Possibly. I'll check it out. But there are so many privacy regulations these days that it could take time. Or maybe even a court order. But I may be able to find out something through the Department of Motor Vehicles. Van Horn must have had a driver's license."

"What about a hang glider's license?" Mary asked.

Abby could answer that question. She'd run across the information when she looked into hang gliding for the new exhibit. "No license is needed to hang glide."

"Maybe there should be," Henry suggested dryly.

ON MONDAY AFTERNOON, Abby had an unexpected visitor. Ida led him into her office. As usual, Gordon Siebert looked debonair and suave in a well-cut dark suit, today with a blue and silver striped tie. In his hand was an attractive leather briefcase, his initials GDS in gold on it.

Abby was surprised to see him. "Mr. Siebert! What brings you here?"

"I guess I haven't said it before, but do call me Gordon."

"And almost everyone calls me Abby."

He looked around her office with interest, apparently having been too disturbed the other time he was in it to notice details. "This really is a beautiful old desk. My wife is quite fond of antiques." He turned briskly, as if that was enough chitchat. "I've been in contact with Dr. Kingston. He's quite excited about the possibility that the Blue Moon is right here on Sparrow Island."

"Does he know anything that can be used specifically to identify the stone?"

"No interior photo. The gem dropped out of sight before that technology came into use. But he does have a hand-drawn diagram of what are supposed to be the two small flaws in the Blue Moon. He faxed me a copy of it." With a dramatic flourish Gordon opened the briefcase and drew out a sheet of paper. He handed it to Abby. "This is why I came out rather than calling. I wanted to show you this."

She studied the diagrams, considerably larger than life-size, showing a complicated web of fine lines, rather feathery in appearance. "I surely wouldn't be able to identify anything from this."

"I think I can," Gordon said with modest confidence. "At least, if the flaws in our stone are much different than these diagrams, I can fairly easily determine that the gem *isn't* the Blue Moon."

Abby smiled to herself at his reference to "our stone." Gordon was apparently taking a rather proprietary attitude toward the gem since it was here on the island.

"This will be big news in the gem world if this really is the Blue Moon," he added.

And a bit of prestige for the suave jeweler's connection with the find, Abby knew. Which was fine; he deserved recognition if he could bring off an actual identification.

"Of course, this does create a problem," he went on. "I'll have to see the necklace again to compare the stone with the diagram, and I need to do it in my store, where I can have all my equipment available. Do you think Sergeant Cobb will allow that?"

"Why don't we find out right now?" Abby suggested. She reached for the phone on her desk. "I'll call and ask him."

She dialed the substation and repeated to Henry what Gordon had said about needing to do the comparison at the store. "Could that be arranged?"

"It sounds like a workable idea to me, but I'll have to get

authorization from Sheriff Dutton. He's taking a very protective attitude toward something worth three million dollars. Is there any particular day or time Gordon Siebert wants to do it?"

"Here, I'll let you talk to him."

Abby handed the phone to Gordon. He gave it back a few moments later.

"We've tentatively set it for Wednesday morning, if the sheriff approves. Sergeant Cobb will let me know as soon as he hears from the sheriff. Will you be there?"

Abby hadn't thought about that until this moment, but the prospect came with a surge of anticipation. "I will be if Henry says I can." She had to admit it; she wanted to be among the first to know if the gem really was the Blue Moon.

"Good. I'll ask Dr. Kingston to overnight me a better copy of the drawing for exact comparison." Gordon slid the sheet back into his briefcase. Sounding a little embarrassed he added, "I'm really quite excited about this."

Gordon Siebert, Abby was almost certain, didn't get excited easily. But a bit of excitement definitely showed now in the animated sparkle of his eyes. It was rather nice to see a break in his usual suave reserve. "I am too," she said.

Gordon closed the briefcase and fastened it securely. "I think I'll just look around a bit while I'm here. There's more to the place than I realized."

"Stay as long as you like."

WORD CAME FROM HENRY the next morning when he called

to say that Sheriff Dutton had okayed taking the necklace to Siebert's Jewelry for identification.

"With qualifications, of course. It isn't to be left there overnight. I'm not even to let it out of my sight, in fact. Have to babysit it every minute."

"And you're going to do this tomorrow morning?"

"Right. I've already talked to Gordon Siebert again. As soon as the bank opens, I'll go in and pick up the necklace. Gordon's going to close the store temporarily while he compares the blue diamond with the drawing this expert in Chicago sent in the overnight mail."

"Do you think there's any danger? Is that why the store will be closed?"

"No, it's just so Gordon can devote his full attention to this without having curious customers crowding around watching. Although Sheriff Dutton wants a second deputy around, just to be on the safe side, so Deputy Niven will be along."

"I'd really like to be there too." Abby searched her mind for some way she could be helpful in this plan. "Perhaps I could identify the necklace as definitely the one I found in my desk?"

Henry chuckled as if he recognized that as a rather flimsy argument, but he said, "*Hmmm.* You found the necklace, you did your good-citizen duty in turning it over to the authorities rather than keeping it for yourself, as some people might have done, and you located the expert whose information may make identification of the stone possible. I'd say you've earned the right to be there at the official identification. Meet us there at the bank right after it opens at nine o'clock. We'll all go over to the jewelry store together in the cruiser, where we'll then wait breathlessly for Gordon Siebert to make the great announcement."

Henry's teasing tone suggested he was being a bit facetious about the breathlessness, but all Abby said was, "Thank you, Henry."

"Oh, one more thing. I checked back through the records of Van Horn's accident. We don't have any record of next of kin. There is a note that the pickup was claimed by his daughter, but a name isn't specified. There doesn't seem to be anything on ownership of the pickup or a driver's license, which may mean Van Horn lived out of state, or at least maintained a legal residence elsewhere."

"A rather mysterious man," Abby murmured.

"Yes," Henry agreed. "Mysterious indeed."

WEDNESDAY MORNING, Abby was at the bank almost on the dot of nine o'clock, the third customer of the day through the doors. She didn't want to be late for this. She went immediately to the counter in front of the safe deposit vault. A clerk came over, but Abby waved her off. "Thanks, but I have to wait for someone."

The flowers in the brass vase that always stood on the counter looked fresh. Elegant irises and glads, tall enough to balance the size of the heavy vase. Abby moved down the counter to admire the bouquet, reminding herself to be sure to tell Mary how nice the flowers looked. Mary had taught her manager Candace almost everything she knew about flower arranging, and she took pride in Candace's accomplishments. Interesting vase, Abby also thought as she touched the elaborate engraving lightly. A wide base for stability, then a narrow section that swelled into a graceful sphere.

Her hand was still on the counter when something touched her back. She started to step aside, thinking it was another customer who wanted to get by her. Muttered words in her ear stopped her short.

"Don't move, don't say a word. Act natural. I have a gun."

He moved in closer and a hard object pressed deeper into her side. Abby had never felt a gun in her ribs before, but she had no doubt he was telling the truth.

"Wh—what do you want?"

"Don't ask questions. Just do what I tell you. We're going into the vault together. We'll get the safe deposit box and take it to one of those little rooms where you can look at your box in private."

"But—"

"Be quiet. In the room, you hand over the necklace. Then we walk out of the room and out of the bank together. Very calm and nice. Just two old friends handling a little business deal. You don't give me any trouble and no one gets hurt."

Was this Gamino? She tried to inch her head around to look at his face, but all she could see was a cap with a visor pulled low on the man's forehead. A jab in the ribs stopped further inspection.

"Smile," he said. "Pretend you know me. Here comes the shaved-head guy."

Now Abby had to wonder how he knew she'd be at the bank this morning. This surely couldn't be some impulsive action, thought up on the spur of the moment. Was it possible she hadn't been imagining things that time she'd felt as if someone was watching her?

Whoever he was, he seemed to have his plan carefully choreographed. Except for one crucial fact he apparently didn't know.

"I can't get in the safe deposit box." Abby kept her voice to a whisper. "Sergeant Cobb rented it. It's in the name of the sheriff's department, not mine."

She felt his body tense. "You're lying."

"Wait and see. They won't let me in it."

Steven Jarvis was almost to the counter now, smile as broad as if he were greeting a million-dollar customer. Abby felt panic rising in the man holding the gun on her. This wasn't going as he'd planned. But if she thought this new information was going to make him back down, she was mistaken.

"Ms. Stanton and I need to get something out of a safe deposit box," he said to Steven, his voice sounding surprisingly calm and normal. "You're going to open it for us."

Steven Jarvis looked more puzzled than alarmed. "The box you and your sister have?" he asked Abby. "Did you bring your key? We'll need it to open—"

"The box with the necklace in it," the man growled.

"Forget about keys. Just open it. *Now*. I have a gun."

Comprehension dawned in Steve's saddle-brown eyes. His jaw dropped open.

Abby swallowed and confirmed the man's statement. "He has a gun."

"But I can't—"

"You *can* or something very bad will happen. We all go into the vault together. You open the safe deposit box."

He was improvising now, Abby knew, grabbing at straws to rescue his scheme. Her mind raced frantically and a fight-or-flight surge of adrenalin slammed through her body.

Steven lifted his hands, palms outward, as if trying to soothe the man. "Okay, okay, don't get nervous. We can do that. No problem."

Steven reached for the buzzer that released the small gate in the counter. Out of the corner of her eye, Abby saw the man turn his head slightly to watch the gate. Her hand was still on the counter.

It was now or never.

She didn't inch her hand toward the vase. She simply reached and grabbed and swung with all her strength.

# Chapter Eighteen

Flowers flew. water splashed. Someone screamed. The vase collided with something solid, hard enough to send a lightning bolt of pain up Abby's arm. The vase shot out of her hand. Then there was a *crack* of noise as it hit the floor and spun across the polished tile like a maniacal top.

Abby spun, too, her body following through on her swing at her assailant. Spinning. Tipping. Falling. The floor rushed up to meet her. She put out an arm to break her fall. It crumpled beneath her.

The crash sent a universe of stars careening and colliding in her head.

She stared upward trying to get some perspective on a world that seemed to have spun off its axis, not quite certain how she'd gotten into this strange position with her back against a hard floor. Odd, too, how she'd never noticed the interesting pattern of recessed lights in the bank's ceiling before . . .

A man with a gun stood over her. She pressed her body back against the floor, momentarily fearful.

But then she realized that this was not a strange, threatening man with a gun.

She blinked. "Henry?" She peered at the star on his uniform. "When did you get here? What happened?"

"I was just going to ask you that. We were supposed to meet here, but not like *this*."

Abby raised herself to a sitting position, pausing along the way as her head momentarily whirled dizzily and a faint nausea churned in her stomach. She looked around uncertainly. An unfamiliar man lay sprawled on the floor a few feet away, eyes closed. Jeans covered his long legs. A bulky jacket wrapped his torso. With his toes turned toward the ceiling, she had an interesting view of the complicated pattern on the soles of his beat-up sneakers.

The vase had landed against a potted rubber plant. Incongruously, the straps of her purse were still neatly draped over her shoulder, just as if she were all ready for a shopping excursion. Everyone, from customers to clerks to bank manager Steven Jarvis, Henry and Deputy Niven was staring down at her as if they were all part of some frozen display.

The display broke into action.

Henry knelt beside Abby. Steven roared through the gate. Deputy Niven grabbed the gun off the floor. Excited chatter sounded like surf in the background.

"Abby, are you all right? What happened?" Henry asked.

Abby eyed the prone man again. He still hadn't moved. "Did you shoot him?"

Henry looked at the gun in his hand. "No. Deputy Niven and I were just outside the door and I heard a sharp noise. I thought it was a shot . . ." He looked around and spotted the vase. "Maybe it was the vase hitting the floor."

"You should have seen her!" Steven said. "He had that gun on her and he demanded I take them into the vault to get the necklace, and she just grabbed that vase and clobbered him with it!"

"And down he went!" a woman clerk behind him echoed.

"I didn't do it to keep him from taking the necklace," Abby protested, remembering those moments just before she'd swung. A necklace wasn't worth that kind of action. She'd done it only to keep him from hurting anyone.

Steven planted his hands on his hips. "Who is he?"

Abby squirmed around on the floor so she could get a better look at the unconscious man. Gamino? He didn't match Bobby's description of the bicyclist at the door. That man was dark-haired, unshaven or bearded, Bobby had said. This man had a narrow, clean-shaven face, short brown hair and a ragged scar near his ear.

Henry knelt beside the unconscious man and checked his pulse and respiration. Abby wanted to go to him too. After all, she was the one who'd put him in this unconscious condition, and she'd never done that to anyone before. She started to get up, but Henry came over and gently put a hand on her shoulder to restrain her.

"You just take it easy for a few minutes," he said. He stood up again. "Anyone know him?" he asked.

There were shakes of heads and negative murmurs. Abby watched Steven pick up pieces of the vase and set them on the counter. The clerk started gathering up spilled flowers, and a man came with a mop and started sloshing up the spilled water. One vaseful of water, Abby realized, turned into an impressive lake when spread across a floor.

Deputy Niven stepped forward. He put the man's hands together and snapped handcuffs around his wrists. Only after that precaution did he start patting pockets looking for identification.

He pulled keys and some change from a pants pocket, a wrinkled handkerchief from another. "That's it," he said. "No wallet, no ID."

"We'd better get him over to the clinic," Henry said. "We'll have to figure out who he is later. You did quite a job on him, Abby."

Abby wasn't proud of resorting to violent physical action, but she was glad the Lord had given her the strength to prevent worse violence to others from this man.

She started to stand up, then realized her knees were showing an alarming tendency toward behaving like seaweed. Henry started to offer her a helping hand, then stopped.

"Abby, your arm!"

Abby looked at her left arm. An ache was starting deep inside, but at the moment the feeling was more numbness than pain. But should an arm look like that, off-kilter just above the wrist? Her mind still felt a little fuzzy, but she didn't think so.

"You're going to Dr. Randolph too," Henry said. "That arm's broken."

"My car's out in the parking lot. But I'm not sure I can drive . . ."

"Of course you can't drive. Deputy Niven will take this guy in the cruiser. I'll drive you in your—"

"What's going on here?" a big voice boomed.

Hugo! Abby had never been more glad to see anyone. "What are you doing here?" she asked. Even as she spoke the words she realized what an absurdly mundane question it was for an extraordinary situation.

"I stopped in to deposit a check on my way to the post office—" The answer was also mundane until Hugo broke off sharply. "What am *I* doing here? What are *you* doing here? *On the floor?*"

Hugo turned to look at the man now making some twitchy movements that suggested he might be regaining consciousness. "Who is this guy?" Hugo looked bewildered, but then his tone turned ominous when he peered at Abby again. "Did he hurt you?"

"Other way around," Henry said. "Our slugger took a bad fall, but she pulled a first-round knockout punch on him. Though I don't think he's badly hurt, more like a boxer knocked out briefly."

"What about the necklace?" Abby asked, remembering how this had all started. "We were going to take it to the jewelry store."

"The necklace," Henry said firmly, "will have to wait. I'll let Gordon Siebert know we won't be bringing it over today. Right now we need to get both of you over to the clinic."

"I'll take Abby," Hugo said instantly. "Unless she needs an ambulance?"

"No ambulance," Abby said. She was still a little shaky, but she was upright now, her mind and vision clear.

But before she could say anything else, Hugo had scooped her up in his arms and was carrying her toward the door.

"Hugo, put me down right this minute!" Abby said, aghast. "I don't need to be carried around like—"

A flashbulb popped in her face stopping the rest of her words. And there was William Jansen, ace editor/reporter for *The Birdcall*, snapping photos in all directions. How did he find out about this? Abby knew it was all too likely this ridiculous photo of her and Hugo was going to show up on the front page of *The Birdcall*.

Hugo paid the editor no attention as he shoved past the man. He didn't put Abby down until she was installed in the front seat of his car and safely buckled in.

Abby spent the next two hours at the clinic, Hugo at her side whenever possible. Dr. Randolph examined the bump on her head, where she'd collided with the floor, and found it tender but not a serious injury. No concussion, no treatment necessary.

The arm was a different story. Definitely broken. After X-rays, Dr. Randolph gently straightened the arm and gave her a pain pill when the pain began overriding the numbness. The arm had started to swell, but Dr. Randolph assured her it was a simple break and should heal nicely. She did, however, say she'd have to wait a couple of days until the swelling went down before putting on a cast. Abby left the clinic with her arm immobilized with a brace and protected with a sling, plus a stern warning that she must be as careful with it as if it were made of porcelain.

She could be thankful for one thing, she realized as they walked out to Hugo's car, his hand gently supporting her. It was her left arm that was broken, not her right. Her activities might be limited, but she could certainly do more than if it were the other way around.

Abby thought she could drive now, but Hugo wouldn't hear of that. He was driving her home, he said in a no-arguments-allowed tone as they walked out to his car. He'd arrange to bring her car out to the house later. He wanted to take her straight home, but Abby had done some thinking in the past two hours.

"Let's go down to the marina," she said.

"The marina?" Hugo sounded astonished. "This is no time for a boat ride."

Abby managed a chuckle in spite of the events of the past few hours. "I'm thinking that this guy with the gun must have had a plan of some kind. He couldn't have thought, with or without me as a hostage, that he could just saunter down to the ferry for a getaway. So he must have come by boat, with a plan to leave the same way."

"Good thinking," Hugo admitted.

Abby knew the manager at the marina slightly because her

father kept his fishing boat in a slip there. They stopped at the office to talk to him. He said there had been no new slip rentals recently, and, at this time of year, there weren't even many boats docking at the temporary sites reserved for visitors.

"One came in last night, though," he said. He motioned toward the visiting-boat area, and through the big window Abby could see a nice-looking cabin cruiser tied up at the dock. "Actually, it's been here a couple of times in the last few days."

"You don't know the owner?"

"No. He's never come in to ask about renting a regular boat slip, so I suppose he's just passing through. I don't think I've seen him today."

"It's just one person, not a couple or family?"

"That's all I've ever seen. Tall guy, kind of lanky, not very friendly."

A description that fit exactly, Abby thought.

"Let's go take a look," Hugo said.

Abby thanked the manager, then walked down on the dock. The cabin cruiser was larger than her father's boat, probably twenty-eight or thirty feet.

"Nice looking boat," Hugo commented. "Probably not more than a couple of years old. And not a cheap one."

Very nice indeed, Abby agreed. Spotless white paint and polished brass. Jaunty red curtains at the cabin windows, crisp flag flying, deck scrubbed and clean, ropes neatly coiled. The thought struck Abby that she wouldn't have expected the man at the bank to have such a clean, well-kept, even luxurious looking boat. Or perhaps, she had to admit, she had a certain prejudice toward the sort of person who'd hold a gun to her ribs.

"Looks as if it's registered in Washington," Hugo said.

He pointed to the number beginning with a WA on the side of the boat. All boats had to carry an easily readable registration number for identification purposes. The name on the boat read *Island Toy*.

"So, I wonder where the owner is?" Hugo asked.

"I suppose he could be asleep inside the cabin." The curtains were closed. "Or running errands in Green Harbor."

"Or," Hugo suggested wryly, "he could be at the clinic recovering from a blow from our local ornithologist. Or on his way to a holding cell at the substation."

HUGO DROPPED ABBY AT THE HOUSE, but he drove back out in Abby's car that afternoon. He arrived right behind Henry, apparently having arranged to ride back to town with Henry in the cruiser.

Abby was lying on the sofa in the living room when the two men came inside. Another pill was keeping the pain at bay, so she wasn't uncomfortable, but neither did she feel up to anything more strenuous than lying there. Blossom was snuggled up beside her and Mary was fussing over her. Was she warm enough? Did she need another blanket? Another pillow? How about some juice? A magazine?

"So, how's the slugger?" Henry asked as he looked down at her. He was still in uniform, still wearing his gun.

Abby had enough energy to retort, "About to slug *you*, Sergeant Cobb, if you try to pin that nickname on me."

She deliberately used his formal name and title to make her displeasure with the nickname stronger, but she doubted it worked.

He was smiling when he said, "Everyone is very proud of you, you know."

Abby groaned. What would her friends at Cornell think if this got back to them? *Slugger*. Maybe if she just didn't respond to the new nickname, it would go away.

Hugo pulled up a chair and sat close beside her as the conversation continued.

"Is the man in custody saying anything yet about who he is?" Mary asked.

"Silent as a clam. But I took his fingerprints, so if he has a record, we'll know who he is before long."

"I don't see his point in trying to conceal his identity," Abby said. "It doesn't seem very smart. He must know you'll find out sooner or later."

"Anyone who tries to pull what he did has to be long on greed but short on *smart*," Hugo observed.

Henry nodded. "Right. I suspect his refusal to give his name is because there's some outstanding charge against him, and he's hoping we won't run across it. But we will, of course, and, whoever he is, he's in one big mess of trouble."

"What happens to him now?" Abby asked.

"We'll hold him overnight here. Deputy Niven will stay

on guard. Then we'll transfer him to Friday Harbor where they have the facilities for holding prisoners for a longer period of time."

"I told Henry about the cabin cruiser down at the marina," Hugo said. "We drove over there, but the owner still wasn't around."

"Do you think there's a connection between the boat and the man in custody?" Abby asked Henry.

"It's certainly a possibility. A boat seems like the only way he could have planned to get himself and the necklace off the island after he'd been seen in the bank. It's a fair distance from the bank to the marina, but he probably figured with you as hostage, he could do it." As Abby had thought earlier, he added, "He couldn't plan on using the ferry. In any case, I'll run the boat registration numbers through the Washington State Marine Board and see what turns up. It's too late to do it today."

"And you don't worry about coming in to work," Hugo added sternly to Abby. "You take off all the time you need."

"It's just a broken arm, and a left one at that," Abby protested. She waved her good right arm vigorously. "And there's work I need to do on the new exhibit."

"Don't worry about that. You just take care of that arm. Orders from the boss."

JUST BEFORE BEDTIME, Mary brought a cup of hot chocolate to Abby on the sofa.

Abby smiled. "You're spoiling me. With special treatment

like this, I may decide to become a lady of leisure and just lie here," she teased.

"I'm sorry you got hurt. But it feels good to do something for you, after all you've done for me." Mary reached over and gave the blanket over Abby's legs a fractional tug to smooth a nonexistent wrinkle. "Have I ever told you how much I appreciate everything you've done for me? And that I love you very much? When I think of that terrible man, holding a *gun* on you, and what might have happened . . ."

Mary shook her head, and Abby saw a glint of tears in her sister's eyes. Abby felt a fullness in her own. They'd never been the kind of sisters who talked much about loving each other, but shortly after Abby returned to the island, they'd settled the differences that had caused tensions between them for many years. Right now her heart overflowed with sisterly love for Mary.

Mary blinked, as if she were a little embarrassed at letting her flood of feelings show so openly. With a deliberate attempt at tartness, she added, "So you'd better enjoy it while you can, you know. Because I'm sure I have a limited capacity for this maid stuff."

"I intend to take advantage of it every minute I can as long as it lasts," Abby assured her. "So, with that in mind, how about a few marshmallows to add to this hot chocolate?"

Mary made a little face at her, then smiled. "Whatever you wish, ma'am."

Then, as Mary headed her wheelchair for the kitchen, Abby called after her, "And you know what? I love you too."

# Chapter Nineteen

ABBY WENT BACK TO Dr. Randolph two days later. She had protested to Mary that she could certainly drive her own car now, but Mary had insisted on taking her in the van. The swelling in her arm had gone down, and the doctor took more X-rays and put on a cast. She recommended Abby also keep on using the sling because of the weight of the cast.

Mary took her home and made Abby lie down on the couch and rest for a while. "Trust me. It takes time for bones to recuperate. I know."

"I'm fine," Abby argued. To prove it, she sat up on the sofa rather than lying down. Her injury was so minimal compared to what Mary had gone through with her accident and the loss of the use of her legs. Abby felt fairly normal now, but she had to admit that she did tire much more easily than usual. Healing a bone fracture, even a simple one, apparently took more bodily energy than she would have guessed.

Mary dropped the mail they'd collected from their mailbox onto the coffee table in front of the couch. "If you feel you have to be doing something useful, you can go through the mail while I'm fixing lunch."

"Nothing more energetic than opening envelopes is allowed?"

"Exactly."

There wasn't much of interest in the mail. A couple of bills, magazines and catalogs. Then Abby spotted a large envelope with her name written in a rounded, feminine handwriting. She ripped it open eagerly.

"Something interesting?" Mary called as she was setting the kitchen table with place mats and cloth napkins. Mary always took time for those little niceties.

"It's the pamphlets and things Liberty Washington said were in the guest room where Nelson Van Horn had been staying when he visited them."

She quickly scanned through the items. The receipts were inconsequential, just printed store receipts without Van Horn's name on them. Two pamphlets about expensive brands of boats, two more about the San Juan Islands, and a hang gliding magazine. Nothing about expensive necklaces.

"Okay, lunch is on the table," Mary called. "Anything helpful in what the woman sent you?" she asked when Abby sat down at the table.

"Not that I can see. I knew it was probably too much to hope that there would be, but I'd hoped anyway."

Just then the phone rang and it was Henry with news regarding the registration of the boat moored in the marina.

"Turns out it's registered to a man named Gregory Wakefield, with an address in Anacortes. Not surprisingly, the fingerprint report on our man in custody also matches to Gregory Wakefield. He has some fairly serious traffic violations, but I think the reason he wouldn't give us his name is because there was a warrant out for his arrest on a burglary charge."

Abby was happy to have some information on her assailant, at last.

"Thanks, Henry. I appreciate all the work you're doing," Abby said.

After Abby and Mary digested this new development, as well as their lunch, Mary decided to drive back into town for some bookkeeping work at Island Blooms.

"You'll be okay?" she asked anxiously before she left.

"I'll be fine," Abby assured her. "I'll probably nap."

Abby did nap and woke feeling considerably refreshed. She went through the items that Liberty had sent again, carefully shaking out the pages of the pamphlets in case anything had been tucked inside. One of the boat pamphlets had the word *Washington* scribbled on it. Her first thought was that the notation simply had something to do with the state of Washington, but then she realized it might be connected with Norbert and Liberty Washington's last name. Could Van Horn have been comparing the boat the Washingtons had for sale with new models of the same brand? It was a long shot, but Abby dialed the phone number of the dealer stamped on the back.

To her disappointment, the call went nowhere. The man she talked to asked several others, but no one knew anything about someone named Van Horn.

What now? Keep trying, she told herself determinedly. Sooner or later, something helpful had to turn up.

In the meantime, Henry and Gordon Siebert had rescheduled the inspection of the diamond to verify whether or not it was the Blue Moon and discovered that indeed, it was.

Now all Abby had to figure out was who the rightful owner was and how to get the necklace back to them.

# *Chapter Twenty*

$A$BBY HAD SPENT THE first two days of the week at home. She hadn't really wanted to stay away from work this long, but Hugo had joined Mary in insisting on it. She slept late, read, strolled down to the beach and surfed the Internet. Mary, making them both feel like kids again, experimented with a new hairdo for Abby that had them both laughing.

But by Wednesday morning, Abby had had enough of recuperating. Her arm still ached occasionally, but she wanted to get back to work. A life of leisure was not for her! Mary wanted to drive her to the museum, but Abby was determined to start doing her own driving again. "My fingers work fine." She illustrated, wiggling them at Mary.

"Okay," Mary agreed reluctantly, "but you call me if you need me. I may lie down for a nap after a while. I didn't sleep very well last night. But I'll keep the phone right beside me so I'll hear it in case you call."

As Abby drove through Green Harbor, she made a quick detour at *The Birdcall*.

At the front desk, she asked if she could look at old issues from a year or so back. *The Birdcall* was cutting-edge modern in some ways. They were hooked into the LexisNexis system, and their computers had sleek flat screens, rather than the bulky kind. But they had never updated to a modern computerized archives system, and if you wanted to see something in a back issue you had to plow through old copies of the newspaper. The woman led her to a back room. She'd rather hoped to avoid editor William Jansen, but less than ten minutes later his inquisitive brown eyes peered into the room.

"Della said you were back here. Looking for something?"

Abby's tart thought was, *No, I just like to wallow in dusty old newspapers.* But what she said was more congenial, but uninformative. "Lots of interesting things here."

William was not to be put off that easily. "Maybe I can help you find what you're looking for."

Abby sighed inwardly. It was all going to get out sooner or later. What she didn't like were the connections that would inevitably follow. The Washingtons had had the necklace in their home; Norbert Washington had soon died of a heart attack. Van Horn probably owned the necklace; he died in a hang gliding accident. *The curse at work again*, the nervous Nellie types would think. Along with the thought, *The island is doomed.*

But William was probably going to hang around until she found what she wanted, so she may as well tell him.

"I'm interested in a hang gliding accident on Mount Ortiz, but I haven't found anything yet. I'm not sure of the date."

"I remember that." As William spoke, he was shuffling through earlier editions. "I think it may have been farther back than you're looking . . . Yes, here it is. Information on what happened was sketchy, too, though I did interview a man who witnessed the crash."

"Norbert Washington?"

William ran his finger down through the article until he came to the name. "Right. How did you know?"

"I've been checking into some things."

William smiled, as if that didn't surprise him. "The victim, let's see, what was his name?"

"Nelson Van Horn."

"Right again. He was a guest of the Washingtons, but apparently they didn't know him very well."

The article had a large headline. "Man Dies in Hang Gliding Crash," with a relatively short article below. It said no more than what Abby already knew.

"You didn't come up with more information about Van Horn for a follow-up article?"

"He seemed to be something of a mystery man. I was curious, of course, but since he wasn't a Sparrow Islander, I didn't go into any deep investigation."

"I'm also interested in Norbert Washington's death. He had a heart attack a month or so after the hang gliding accident."

William looked alert. "There's some connection?"

"Just checking."

That article, when they found it, also didn't tell Abby anything more than she already knew. William put the papers back on the shelf for her.

"I take it all this has something to do with the necklace you found?" William asked.

When in doubt, Abby's theory was, answer a question with another question. "What makes you think that?"

William laughed. "Newspaperman's nose for news and a certain knowledge of you, Abby Stanton, and your sleuthing ways. By the way, I'm working now on the article about the necklace and your adventure at the bank. I hear your new name is Slugger."

Abby glowered at him.

"But I won't put that in the article of course," he added hastily.

"What about that photo you took at the bank?"

"Oh, I took several photos," William said blandly. "They'll all be in there."

Abby sighed inwardly. "Would you like to interview me for the article?"

"Oh yes, indeed. I thought about asking, but I've heard you're a little touchy about all the rumors going around." He smiled. "As well as the nickname."

"Then this is an opportunity for both of us to set the record straight."

"Let me get my tape recorder."

LATER THAT DAY, Abby knew she wasn't at her most efficient at the museum, with the use of only one arm, but she got caught up on various things. Ida fussed over her solicitously, insisting on opening the mail for her and bringing her coffee—although Ida didn't hesitate to tease Abby a little bit too.

"Anything more I can do for you, Slugger?" she inquired.

Abby just sighed to herself. Slugger. How long would it take to live *that* down?

Even Hugo stopped into her office twice to check up on her, although, thankfully, he bypassed the Slugger moniker. She used one of his visits to check up on him as well.

"I'm wondering if you've heard any more from the specialists over in Seattle?"

"I have. They've decided the medication isn't doing as much as they'd hoped. There are various other treatments these days, as you probably know. Radiation, implantation of radioactive seeds, even gene therapy. But for me they've decided on the good, old-fashioned knife."

"Oh, Hugo, I'm sorry to hear that."

"I understand it's a different type of surgery than what used to be done. Not quite as drastic, though I'm not exactly looking forward to it."

"When?"

"Next week. I'll probably be in the hospital for several days." He hesitated, then, sounding apologetic, added, "I know it probably sounds, oh, antisocial, but I'd just as soon not have visitors." He lifted his eyebrows questioningly.

"I understand. But if there's anything I can do to help, anything at all . . ."

"I'll let you know."

"What about follow-up treatments?"

"First, we see how the surgery goes."

"I'll be praying."

"That's what I need most."

MARY HAD SAID ABBY SHOULD CALL if she needed anything, but it was not, however, Abby who called Mary that day. It was Mary who called Abby about 4:30, her voice frantic.

"He's missing, Abby, Finnegan's missing! I let him outside to play for a while, and I fell asleep and now he's missing!" Mary's hoarse words tumbled over each other like rocks rolling down a hillside.

"Mary, slow down—"

"I know he wouldn't run away. I'm *positive* of it. But I've called till I can hardly talk. Abby, I'm so worried!"

Abby was as positive as Mary was that Finnegan wouldn't run away. The backyard wasn't fenced, but a board fence ran along the property line with the McDonalds. There was nothing to keep Finnegan from going down to the shore and possibly circling around the end of the fence, but Abby had never known him to leave the area right around the house by himself. He was too well trained.

"Have you talked to Henry?"

"I called and he's coming over, but he's over on Lopez so it will take him a while."

"I'll be home as soon as I can get there."

Abby grabbed her coat and ran out the front door, calling, "Finnegan's missing!" as she flew by Ida at the front desk. She had to dodge the black cat, Eclipse, on the front steps. What she didn't need was another fall! At 4:30, darkness was already approaching. Not a good time to be searching for a lost dog.

At the house, Abby was out of her car and running into the house through the laundry room even before the garage door was fully shut behind her.

The sliding glass doors to the deck stood open, the yard lights on. Even though it was difficult for Mary to get around in the heavy grass with her wheelchair, she was still out searching for her beloved dog.

Abby ran to her sister and hugged her. "We'll find him," she promised. She realized Mary was shivering, her face lined with exhaustion and worry. "You go inside and warm up now, okay? I'll do the looking."

"Abby, what if he's gone for good?" Mary's voice cracked with worry. "What if he got out on the road and a car hit him?"

This was the biggest danger, Abby knew. Even if Finnegan had uncharacteristically wandered to the rocky shore behind their property, he wouldn't be in any particular danger there. But the road was a different matter. She hadn't spotted him as she was coming home, but he could have gone in the other direction.

"I'll go drive along the road. You call the neighbors, okay?"

To her relief, Abby found no sign of Finnegan anywhere along the road. So where *was* he?

"No one's home at the McDonalds'," Mary reported when Abby returned. "The Wetherbees have been gone all afternoon and haven't seen him, but Lars said he'd go out and take a look around their place. But I think if Finnegan was just over there, he'd have heard me calling and would've come to me."

"You stay by the phone, okay? If he did somehow wander off, surely someone will spot him and try to call. Almost everyone knows Finnegan. I'll go out and search down to the shore."

Darkness had fallen by now. Abby took a flashlight and searched the property as best she could with the handicap of darkness and her cast, afraid she might find Finnegan injured or ill. She pushed shrubs aside so she could peer underneath and walked purposely through the tall grass they left unmowed to protect the habitat for the birds, flashlight swinging from side to side. No sign of him anywhere.

She had just returned to the ramp going up to the back deck when the doors slid open. "Abby, are you out there?" Mary called. "I've found something."

From both words and tone, Abby knew it wasn't a good something. She ran up the ramp. Wordlessly, Mary handed her a scrap of paper. The edges were ragged and the paper stained, as if it had been torn from a notebook that had been wet at some time.

I HAVE THE DOG. YOU GET THE NECKLACE. YOU'LL RECEIVE INSTRUCTIONS ABOUT WHERE TO MAKE THE EXCHANGE. I GET

THE NECKLACE OR YOU NEVER SEE THE
DOG AGAIN.

"Somebody *kidnapped* Finnegan?" Abby said, aghast.
"Where did you get this?"

"I opened the front door to call for Finnegan again. I
hadn't been out that way before. Somebody had stuck the
note there."

This had to be Gamino, Abby thought. When he came to
the house on the bicycle he'd been checking them out. And
he'd learned enough to hit them where they were most vulner-
able, through Finnegan.

They were still in the living room, looking at the note they
had placed on the coffee table in an effort to preserve any fingerprints on it, when Henry arrived with his cruiser lights
blazing. Abby ran to the front door to let him in.

Henry stopped short when he stepped inside and saw
Mary's distraught face. "What's the matter?"

"Someone left this on the front door." Abby gestured to
the note on the coffee table. "I guess you'd call it a ransom
note. Fortunately, Mary only touched the note briefly so there
may still be fingerprints on it belonging to the kidnapper."

Henry took another quick look at Mary as if to make certain she really was okay. Henry then touched the note by a
corner only, careful not to add his own fingerprints.

"If the guy's smart, he probably wore gloves. But we'll dust
it to be sure. Might get lucky." After he'd read the note, he

asked Mary, "No car in the driveway or commotion behind the house?"

"Not a thing," she said, her voice barely holding back her tears. "I should have brought Finnegan in before I fell asleep, but I didn't. And now he's *gone*!"

Abby squeezed her sister's shoulder reassuringly. "We'll get him back."

"Yes," Henry said, a note of grim determination in his voice. "We will."

He got an evidence bag from the car and carefully sealed the note inside. Abby knew he doubted it would provide any useful prints, but it was evidence. Abby told him her suspicion that the kidnapper was Gamino.

"He must have had a car this time," Mary said, her mind still functioning in spite of this shock. "He couldn't have carried Finnegan off on a bicycle."

"I suppose he could have led Finnegan alongside the bicycle," Henry said, frowning. "Although that seems unlikely. Finnegan would surely have put up some resistance."

"But even if he somehow managed to lead Finnegan off, where would he go with him?" Abby asked. "He must realize someone would surely spot him."

Mary lifted a finger. "A boat," she said suddenly. "You've already figured out that the man in the bank arrived by boat so why not this guy too?"

"A boat?" Abby repeated, thinking the house was a long hike or bicycle ride from the marina. Then a sudden excitement hit her. "Yes, a boat! He came to shore right down there on the Wetherbees' little dock. He knew about it from having been here on his bicycle before. Then he just walked up to the house . . ."

". . . grabbed Finnegan, left the note and walked back to his boat again," Henry said grimly.

Abby could only wonder why she hadn't already thought of this. Getting permission to put in a dock was extremely difficult these days, but the Wetherbees' dock had been built years ago, and old Lars generously allowed anyone in the neighborhood to use it. The dock wasn't visible from other nearby houses, and Mary had already said the Wetherbees had been gone all afternoon.

"A boat would explain a lot of things," Abby said thoughtfully. "Why Gamino didn't contact me again as soon as he said he would. Because of the storm and the small-craft warnings, he and his boat were stuck over at Friday Harbor. Then when he did come, he brought the bicycle on his boat."

Henry nodded. "And I couldn't find where he was staying here on the island because he *wasn't* staying on the island. He was sleeping on the boat." Henry expanded on the idea. "He probably docked at the marina to begin with, then he rode out here on the bicycle. But I doubt he stayed there overnight. I'd guess he took the boat offshore, tossed out an anchor and spent the night out there somewhere."

Abby knew that the seats on many boats opened out to make a kind of bed. Not necessarily the most comfortable way to spend the night, but an effective way for Gamino to keep out of sight.

"So how will we ever find him?" Mary asked. "We don't have a boat name or description, and his boat probably looks like hundreds of others."

"The water's shallow here, not like at the marina. Which means it can't be a very large boat, or he couldn't have gotten it into the Wetherbees' dock," Abby pointed out.

But they all knew this deduction didn't narrow the possibilities much. There were how many hundreds of small boats in the San Juan Islands, even at this time of year?

Now Abby also realized something else, what that odd noise she'd heard on the cell phone was. Gamino had called her from the boat, and that was the sound of the engine in the background. Movement of the boat out of an area of good cell phone transmission was what had caused his voice on the phone to break up.

"I'll put the information out all over the islands. Every deputy will be on the lookout for a small boat with a golden retriever mix on board," Henry said.

"Oh, I almost forgot," Abby said, "has Greg Wakefield said anything more about Van Horn?"

"We brought that up, but now he's claiming he never called you and has no idea who Van Horn is. But we know the kidnapper is going to call again to make the arrangements about exchanging Finnegan for the necklace. I'm going to arrange for a tap on your phone."

But before the tap could be installed, Gamino called again.

# Chapter Twenty-One

THE CALL WAS SHORT, so short Abby doubted it could have been traced even if the tap had been in place. It came right after Abby got home from work the following day.

"Abby?"

Abby tensed. She recognized the voice now. "Yes."

"Sunday night. Seven o'clock. You have the necklace. I'll have the dog. No cops. You don't even *talk* to the cops about this or the deal is off."

"Where do I meet you?"

"Oh no. I tell you that now and you'll have a trap all set up. This is just to let you know *when*, so you can be ready on short notice. You'll receive instructions just beforehand about *where*. Good-bye, Abby," he ended abruptly.

"Wait! We're worried about Finnegan. Is he okay?"

"He's fine. Not too happy being away from his people, of course, but I'm taking good care of him. Oh, and another reminder. This is your only chance. If you don't show up, you never see the dog again."

Abby swallowed hard, but all she said was, "You'll be coming by boat?"

He hesitated, as if deciding whether or not he wanted to give even that small bit of information. Finally he said, "Yes, by boat." Unexpectedly, she heard him laugh. "But that's not a big help, is it? The sheriff's office can't have every landing spot on the island covered. Talk to you later, Abby."

Abby repeated the contents of the call to Mary, including that Gamino had said Finnegan was in good shape.

"Can we believe him?" Mary asked.

In spite of her worries about Finnegan, Mary hadn't fallen into a depression, as Abby had briefly feared she might. This was a harsh blow, but Mary was a fighter. Plus, they'd spent much time in prayer for the precious service dog's safe return, as had other members of Little Flock, and Mary's faith that he'd be back with her soon was sustaining her.

Abby considered Mary's question about trusting Gamino. "In this case, I think so. He isn't going to let any harm come to Finnegan. He figures Finnegan is his ticket to getting the necklace."

"But he isn't, is he?" Mary said, and Abby could hear fear creeping into her voice. "We don't have the necklace to give him. And he warned us not to tell the 'cops' anything."

"But we have to tell Henry," Abby said gently.

Mary hesitated only momentarily. "You're right, of course. We have to tell Henry." She glanced at her watch. "I'll call his cell phone right now."

Blossom twined around Abby's legs as Mary made the call. Abby scooped up the cat and sat on the sofa with her. With her playmate Finnegan gone, the lonely cat wanted more attention than ever.

"He was already on the ferry on his way home," Mary reported when she hung up. "He wants to know the minute you hear a location where Gamino wants to meet you. He says they'll be ready and even on short notice they can move in and nail the man and rescue Finnegan. The way it sounds, once Gamino calls, you won't actually be involved."

"I'm not sure it's going to work if I'm not involved," Abby said slowly. "Gamino was quite specific that I had to show up to make the trade."

"Henry pointed out, and it's true, of course, that the situation could turn dangerous if you actually meet Gamino and don't have the necklace to make the trade. And Henry can't authorize such a trade, of course." Mary swallowed uneasily.

"I've been thinking about that," Abby said. Actually, she'd been thinking about it ever since Gamino first called about making the trade. "Maybe there's a way. Remember that brooch Mom had when we were kids? It had a kind of blue-green stone? Well, glass, I suppose it was, not really a stone."

Unexpectedly, in spite of the tension built into the situation, Mary laughed. "Oh, I remember. It was a huge thing, with big, heavy, gold-colored curlicues around the center-piece. And a pin on back big enough to poke holes in shoe leather. I always thought that blue-green glass looked like some fossilized bird dropping that had washed up on the beach."

"A bird dropping!" Abby repeated indignantly. "I gave that brooch to Mom for Mother's Day one year!"

Mary put her fingertips to her mouth. "Oh. I'd forgotten."

"But you're right. It was big and ugly. As I recall, I thought it would show up nice on a white dress Mom had. But I guess taste in accessories has never been one of my strong points, has it?"

"You were probably only seven or eight years old. And your taste is fine now."

"Thanks. I wonder if Mom still has it."

"Oh, I'm sure she does. She seldom gets rid of anything."

"So what are you thinking?" Mary asked.

"Didn't you once have a rhinestone necklace?"

"Rhinestones pretty much went out of style years ago, but yes, I'm sure I still have it tucked away somewhere." She lifted her eyebrows as if puzzled by this odd train of thought.

"Okay, what I'm thinking is this: we could remove that piece of blue-green glass or whatever it is from Mom's brooch. You could take some stones out of that old rhinestone necklace. I'm not much good with crafts, but you are, and you could fasten the rhinestones around the center piece some way, add a chain and make it all look pretty good."

"And try to fool Gamino with it, so he'd make a trade for Finnegan?" Mary asked doubtfully.

"Yes. That way Finnegan would be safe with us before Henry went after him. Gamino doesn't know what the necklace actually looks like now. Apparently that information has never leaked out."

"He knows the stone is blue. A blue *diamond*. This one would be that peculiar blue-greenish color. And no way is it going to look like three million dollars worth of necklace."

"He'll be in a hurry and, hopefully, won't stop to examine it closely. It'll be dark, which will also help."

Mary stroked Blossom, who had jumped into her lap now. She was frowning but also nodding slowly. "It might work." The nod became more emphatic. "It's crazy, but it just might work! But I still don't think Henry is going to want you there."

"Then we'll just have to persuade him. And afterward, of course, we'll put the brooch back together and return it to Mom."

MARY CALLED THEIR MOTHER immediately and asked if they could borrow the brooch for a project. Ellen was going to a meeting, but she said she'd set the brooch out so they could pick it up. Abby made a quick trip over to the farm, just as glad Ellen wasn't there so she didn't have to give details about their project.

Mary was in her craft room when Abby returned. Mary had located the old rhinestone necklace while Abby was gone and was now in the process of removing the square-shaped rhinestones from it. Abby set the brooch on the table.

Abby set about trying to take the brooch apart while Mary worked on the rhinestone necklace. Using the small, sharp-nosed pliers Mary used in her crafts work, Abby pried at the prongs holding the center stone in place. When they were loose, she tapped the brooch against the table, gently, then harder. "Whatever the brooch lacks in beauty, it apparently makes up in sturdiness."

"That was my thought too," Mary said with a sideways glance at the piece of jewelry. "The thing looks as if it could survive being run over by an eighteen-wheeler."

"Which would probably have been an appropriate fate for it."

Abby couldn't help it. In general, she wasn't much of a giggler, but now, thinking of the brooch popping up unscathed after an encounter with an eighteen-wheeler, she started laughing. A moment later Mary joined in.

"A mother really has to love her child to actually wear something like this," Abby said.

When Abby finally got the stone out of its setting she put the blue-green oval on the table, and Mary arranged the rhinestones around it in rough imitation of the real necklace.

"With bad eyesight, a dark night and no idea what good jewelry looks like, it may work," Mary said. She sounded skeptical but hopeful.

"How can we make the rhinestones stay in place? Glue?"

"I think what we need is something to hold the center piece so I can fasten the rhinestones to that rather than gluing them right onto the stone. And then we need an eyelet at the top to run a chain through."

Abby thought a moment, then dashed to the kitchen,

rummaged in a drawer and came back with a small metal object with a handle.

Mary looked at it. "A *tea infuser*?"

The tea infuser was designed in the shape of a hinged spoon, punctured with tiny holes to let the water flow through tea leaves inside.

"Well, why not?" Mary added philosophically. She picked up the stone from the brooch and slipped it into one side of the spoon. It fit neatly, with just enough room for the rhinestones to encircle it.

"Looks pretty good!" Abby said.

They took a break for dinner, a ham casserole that Mary had cooking in the oven. Afterwards, Mary went to work dismantling the tea infuser. Struggling to get a good grip, she dropped the tiny pliers. When they clattered on the floor, both sisters stopped short. Abby knew they were thinking the same thing. In the past, Finnegan would have quickly retrieved the tool for Mary.

Mary swallowed hard but said nothing. Abby silently leaned over and picked up the pliers for her.

Abby went upstairs and removed an inexpensive, gold-colored chain from an old necklace. Working together, they first cemented the large stone into the spoon-shaped tea infuser, then glued the rhinestones around it. The two sisters also talked, talked more than they had in a long time. Talked about past, present and future, laughed some more and drank numerous cups of tea.

As a finishing touch, Mary gave the blue-green centerpiece a thin gloss of blue fingernail polish. The result was unexpectedly good.

Abby contributed a fancy purple and silver striped box that had held the parting gift from her associates at Cornell, a silver medal honoring her work there. With sudden inspiration Mary used glass cutters to cut a section out of a piece of mirror from her supply of crafts materials and lined the box with it.

"It's what interior designers do sometimes, use a mirror to give a room the illusion of more space. Now if Gamino shines a flashlight in there to look at the necklace, he'll get enough dazzle to blind him."

They finished the presentation with a silver ribbon that would slip off easily. They didn't want Gamino frustrated with complicated knots.

Finally Mary held up the completed project, necklace nestled in mirror-lined box with a border of blue velvet to hold it in place. "Voilà!" she cried.

"Eureka!" Abby agreed.

They grinned at each other, one of the closest moments Abby had ever felt with her sister.

Sobering, Mary added the most important point. "Now if Gamino just falls for it."

HENRY SHOWED UP AT THE HOUSE right after breakfast on Saturday morning. He said he'd already eaten, but when Mary offered coffee and a slice of toasted, home-baked cinnamon raisin bread, he readily accepted.

As they all sat drinking coffee, Henry reported that through state records he'd located a registration number for a boat belonging to Gamino. Deputies all over the San Juans, as well as the marinas, had been notified to watch for the boat and Finnegan.

"But I don't have high hopes that's going to work," he added somberly. "The guy seems pretty crafty about keeping out of sight. So the basic plan is this. The sheriff's department boat will be ready to go Sunday afternoon. Deputy Niven and I will be on it. As soon as you hear from Gamino with a location, you call me by cell phone. Then we'll close in on him." He gave Abby a sharp look. "And if you're having any thoughts about actually meeting this guy yourself, forget it."

"There's a possibility Gamino could get away when he realizes you're trying to capture him. He'll surely make a run for it, in which case we won't get Finnegan back. And Gamino made it plain that this would be our only chance. But if I could get Finnegan *before* you go after Gamino . . ."

Abby let her voice trail off and Henry hesitated, as if reluctantly seeing the value in her argument. But that didn't keep him from saying, "No. Too dangerous. When he realizes you don't have the necklace, you and Finnegan could both be in danger."

Mary and Abby exchanged glances. "Not necessarily," Abby said.

Mary wheeled toward the craft room. A moment later she returned with the necklace dangling from her fingers.

It didn't look like the real necklace, Abby had to admit. Far from it. But the rhinestone-ringed piece of stone hanging from the imitation gold chain did, if you didn't look too closely, look glittery and lovely and even valuable.

Henry's jaw dropped open. "Where did you get that?"

"We made it," Mary said. "And Abby's trading this to Gamino for Finnegan is the only way we can be sure we'll get him back."

Henry rocked back in his chair. "I don't like it," he muttered.

"None of us likes it," Abby agreed. "But it's the only way. Unless I actually have Finnegan in my possession before you move in, too many things can go wrong."

"Things can go wrong anyway. What if this creep takes a look at your necklace and immediately realizes it's a phony? You don't know what he might do."

A possibility, Abby had to admit. But for Finnegan she was willing to risk it. She managed to say calmly, "I have full confidence in your and Deputy Niven's abilities to handle the situation after the trade is made."

Henry didn't suddenly embrace the idea of Abby's meeting Gamino, but he did say with grudging reluctance, "I suppose we could discuss some ideas on how we can make this work. A lot depends on where Gamino wants you to meet him."

And then they settled down with more coffee to work out a plan.

# Chapter Twenty-Two

AFTER HENRY LEFT, Abby felt restless. She asked her sister if she'd like to take a drive up Mount Ortiz, but Mary said she wanted to work a bit at Island Blooms. Abby started to make the drive alone but on impulse stopped by the McDonalds' house and asked Bobby if he'd like to come along. He jumped at the chance, of course. He looked at his mother, who had come to the door with him. Sandy tilted her head, smiled and nodded.

"Should I bring the ornithopter?" he asked Abby. "It's all put together. I could show you how it works."

"It works?"

"Oh yeah. Dad and I tried it on the beach. It's kind of weird, flopping its wings like a big bug. It's a good thing people figured out a better way to fly than that!"

"Then I think you should keep it in good shape for the exhibit. As I recall, the wind can be quite strong on the mountain and something might happen to it up there."

Something had happened to Nelson Van Horn's hang glider up there, which was what today's trip was really all about.

"How about bringing your camera?" she suggested. "Maybe we'll see some birds."

"Yeah!"

Bobby dashed off to his bedroom to get the camera and Abby chatted for a few moments with Sandy. Her father seemed to be adjusting to the new room at the nursing home, she said, and there had been no more emergency calls.

The road wound up the side of Mount Ortiz, widening to accommodate spectacular viewing spots in several places. It wasn't a high mountain, only 1,155 feet—nothing like snow-clad Mount Rainier and Mount Baker over on the mainland, but the views of islands and water were magnificent.

When they reached the parking area and Abby turned the engine off, Bobby jumped out of the car, camera in hand. Abby moved more slowly, having to reach her right arm across her body to open the door. Dr. Randolph had said the cast had to remain on for six weeks.

She walked to the guardrail on the edge of the parking area. From there the island lay below them like a green jewel surrounded by water that was incredibly blue today. Like a blue diamond turned to liquid, with the green of other islands like emeralds floating on its shimmering surface. The graceful shape of Cedar Grove Lake lay to the south and Oyster Inlet, like the blade of a knife, slashed deep into the northern end of the island. Wayfarer Point Lighthouse stood as a lonely sentinel off to the northwest. And somewhere out there, Nelson Van Horn's hang glider had crashed.

What location had he used as a jumping-off point for his hang glider? This wasn't the actual peak of the mountain; you had to climb higher on a trail to reach that. Abby didn't know how bulky or heavy hang gliding equipment was, but she suspected it was too much for Van Horn to carry up there. So he must have taken off right here. But he had to have space to run to get started.

There was some space between the guardrail and the steep drop-off, but a sign on the guard rail read DANGER DO NOT VENTURE BEYOND THIS POINT. A sign that Van Horn probably ignored, Abby realized. He must have climbed outside the rail and run alongside it to make his takeoff with the hang glider.

After becoming airborne Van Horn would have had to do some maneuvering to reach a suitable spot on Wayfarer Point Road, but Abby knew from her research that a hang glider pilot could change course to some degree by shifting his weight on the control bar.

But it all seemed such foolish recklessness, just running and jumping off into space.

Yet at the same time, Abby could almost see why Van Horn had done it, why he was so eager to take off from here. At this moment, everything was so quiet and serene and peaceful, almost as if you wouldn't even need a hang glider to float off into the sky.

Even as she thought about the appealing serenity, a sudden gust of wind whipped Bobby's Seattle Mariners baseball cap from his head. He raced after it, laughing as it bounced along the paved parking area as if deliberately teasing him.

"Hey, look, there's an eagle!" Bobby yelled when he captured his cap. He stopped short. "No, it isn't. It's a vulture! Two vultures!"

He lifted his camera and got off three quick shots. Vultures, of course, were scorned by many people as ugly creatures with a disgusting appetite for dead and rotting flesh, but Abby saw them differently, beautiful in their own way. They were the designated cleanup crew, diligently performing a vital duty. And, just now, they were floating on an updraft and circling lazily, incredibly majestic and graceful. One didn't need to be an eagle to soar with regal grace, she thought with fresh appreciation for the wonderful demonstration of the Lord's creativity.

Yet even as she watched, something happened. A cloud appeared, seemingly from nowhere, and drifted across the sun. So swift the change! The blue waters changed to steely gray, and a raw wind suddenly whipped the tops of trees below and made Abby pull her jacket tighter around her.

The invisible updraft on which the vultures floated changed too, seeming to spill one of the graceful birds on its side, like some great carnival ride carelessly tossing off a rider. The bird tumbled only a short distance before those powerful wings took hold and righted it.

*But*, Abby thought, *if that had happened to a hang glider, without flapping wings to come to the rescue, the results would be disastrous.*

"Did you get that?" Abby asked.

"I think so. But I'm not sure. It happened so fast! I'm going to save up my money and buy a video camera."

The vultures were gone now, the sky empty, clouds thickening like murky gray gravy congealing in the sky. A few drops of windblown rain spattered Abby's face.

"I guess it's a good thing I didn't bring the ornithopter," Bobby said. "I would've crashed it for sure."

Much like the hang glider of Nelson Van Horn.

ABBY'S NERVES WERE TIGHT when she and Mary went to church the next morning. Today was the day. When would Gamino call? Would the weather turn bad and prevent him from coming? Could she pull off a successful exchange? But by the time they emerged from the church she'd relaxed.

The earlier blustery wind had calmed, but Abby knew it wasn't just the better weather that had calmed her nerves. Many people had inquired about Finnegan, offering sympathy and hope. Rev. Hale had even included Finnegan in his prayers for the day.

But mostly, Abby knew, her calm came from knowing they could trust in the Lord with this as in everything. As Hebrews 13:5 promised, "Never will I leave you; never will I forsake you."

Mary, too, seemed serene after the service. "I think I'll have Finnegan back by tonight," she whispered confidently on the way down the ramp at the church.

Abby briefly wondered what would happen if things went

wrong and somehow they *didn't* get Finnegan back, but she didn't dwell on it.

George and Ellen invited them over for dinner, but Abby and Mary exchanged quick glances and Mary declined for both of them. They needed to be home whenever Gamino decided to make that all-important call.

Their father looked curious, but he trusted them and asked no questions.

They were home by 12:30. Much too early for a call, Abby was fairly certain. But she didn't want to get far from a phone anyway.

The clock showed 2:30, 3:30, 4:30. At 5:03, the phone rang. But it was Henry, tersely wanting to know if they'd tried to call him and hadn't been able to reach him.

"No, we're still waiting to hear from him."

"Okay."

Henry closed the connection abruptly. He knew the line had to be kept open. Gamino was definitely going to cut it close, Abby realized, as the minutes inched by. At 5:58, the phone rang again.

"Abby Stanton speaking," she said curtly.

He didn't bother to identify himself. "Okay, you know where Paradise Cove is?"

"Yes."

"You've got the necklace?"

Abby took a deep breath. "Yes."

"Okay. Seven o'clock. The dock at Paradise Cove."

Gamino had chosen well, Abby knew. Paradise Cove had only tent camping, no recreational vehicles, so at this time of year it was undoubtedly empty. The road ended a few hundred feet from the dock, so he knew she'd have to be on foot. He figured he could make a quick getaway and be miles from the island in minutes. He had it all planned.

"That doesn't give me much time—"

"You'd better hurry, then. Blink your flashlight on and off three times when you reach the dock so I'll know it's you."

"Three times," Abby echoed.

"And no cops. You got that? No cops. I see a cop and everything's off."

No good-bye, but the conversation was over. Time for action. Abby punched in Henry's cell phone number.

"Paradise Cove," she said crisply. "Seven o'clock. I'm supposed to signal him with three off-and-on blinks of the flashlight when I arrive."

"Okay. We'll get over there right now and hide behind the rocks on the north side of the Cove. You make your trade. As soon as you have Finnegan in your possession, you wave the flashlight and we'll come in like gangbusters."

Abby felt a tap on her arm. She glanced at her sister, who'd wheeled up close beside her.

"One more thing," Mary said. "I'm coming along."

"No, you can't do that!" Abby gasped. "No way!"

"What's that?" Henry asked, and Abby realized she'd spoken into the phone.

"Hold on a minute," she said to Henry. She put her hand over the phone. "Mary, you can't come with me. The whole idea is . . . preposterous. It's out of the question. Impossible."

"Yes, I *can* come. The guy said 'no cops,' not 'no sister.'"

"Maybe he didn't say it, but I'm sure he meant it. No *anybody*. He wants me to come alone. I don't think this is a time to argue semantics."

"Is that the only reason you don't want me along?" Mary challenged. "Or is it because I'm in a wheelchair and you think I'd be more liability than help?"

Abby uneasily examined her objections to her sister's presence. "The road doesn't go quite all the way. There's only a trail for the last couple hundred feet or so to the dock."

"But it's an easy trail." Mary argued. "The church had a picnic out there a couple of years ago, and I remember women there with baby strollers. And aren't you the one who tells me I shouldn't let a wheelchair limit my activities? That I can do whatever I make up my mind to do?"

Abby groaned inwardly. What a time to have her words tossed back to her.

"Abby, what's going on?" Henry asked in her ear. "Is something wrong?"

"Something else," Mary said. "Your arm. It's in a cast, in case you've forgotten. And that does put certain limitations on what you can do. But both my arms work fine." Mary waved her arms—strong from using the wheelchair—over her head. "And your legs work fine."

Abby couldn't help smiling. "So you're saying that we both have our limitations, but between us we have two good legs and two good arms?"

"Three, actually. Two good legs and three good arms." Mary took her sister's free hand. "Please, Abby? I want to be there to do whatever I can. For you. For Finnegan."

Abby looked at her sister for a long moment, then took her hand off the phone. "Henry, Mary wants to come along."

The noises coming across the line sounded like ricocheting popcorn. Finally they turned into comprehensible words. "No. Absolutely not."

Abby took another look at her sister. She'd much rather Mary stayed safely at home. She'd a thousand times rather Mary stayed at home. But she also knew Mary needed to do this for her own sense of worth and her love for Finnegan.

"I think she should come along, Henry," Abby said quietly into the phone. "It's important."

There was a moment of hesitation until Henry finally said gruffly. "We haven't time to argue about it. Just be careful. Both of you. And call me again when you reach the parking lot."

# Chapter Twenty-Three

MARY PARKED THE VAN in the empty parking area at the end of the road. The dense forest swallowed the headlight beams like some black hole in space.

"Well, here we are," Mary said. She sounded a little uncertain.

"I have to call Henry."

Mary dug the cell phone out of the embroidered denim bag hanging on her wheelchair and handed it to Abby. Abby punched in the numbers. Henry answered with a terse, "Yes?"

"We're here. You're all set?" Abby asked.

"All in place and ready to go. You okay?"

"We're fine." Except for the fact that her heart felt as if it might pound right through her chest, like some pendulum gone berserk. In the bank, she hadn't had time to panic. She'd just acted on reflex to clobber her assailant. But she had plenty of time to panic now. *Lord, keep me calm. Be with us. Watch over us. Keep Mary safe! Guide us in what to do. Amen.*

"Okay. Be careful."

Abby handed the phone back to Mary. Making one last effort she said, "There's no need for you to go any farther. I appreciate your coming, but I think it would be safer if—"

"If I let you go off and leave me behind just when the excitement's about to start? No way!" Mary expertly moved the wheelchair from its position behind the steering wheel to the exit lift.

Abby glanced at the red numbers of the digital clock on the dashboard. Plenty of time to get to the dock. But no time to waste. She pulled the blue stocking cap she'd brought down over her ears.

Five minutes later, they were on the trail. Abby carried the heavy-duty, square flashlight. Mary had another smaller flashlight in the denim bag. Extra batteries for both flashlights were also stashed in the bag. They moved along the trail without speaking, the only sound the whisper of the wheels. The forest seemed eerily silent.

Out in the parking area, shifting clouds had flirted with the half-moon and stars, but here on the short trail, under a heavy canopy of branches, only the beam of the flashlight kept the darkness at bay.

Old fir and pine needles padded the trail, but the going was apparently harder than Mary had expected. Exposed roots crossed the trail in places, and she grunted with the effort of getting over them, her sister unable to push her because of the cast.

Abby didn't look at her watch while they were on the trail. It seemed as if the trip was taking much too long. But when they broke into the narrow, grassy clearing around the end of the cove and she did peer at her watch, she was surprised to find they had several minutes to spare. A cloud slid away from the moon and its silvery light revealed a white boat bobbing gently in the calm waters of the Cove.

"That must be him," Mary breathed. "Do you think he really has Finnegan with him?"

"We'll know in a few minutes."

Abby peered toward the picnic and camping area back in the trees. The tables and fireplaces were hidden in the shadows, not visible now. She hadn't expected anyone would be camped there now and she was relieved to find this was true. They didn't need an audience.

When they reached the dock, Abby carefully lifted the flashlight and made three slow and distinct off-and-on clicks with the switch.

By now the moon had disappeared behind another cloud, and the indistinct shape of the boat looked ghostly as it slowly moved toward the dock in response to the signal. The engine sounded unnaturally loud in the silence of the cove.

Abby picked a cautious path along the dock. Mary wheeled alongside her, the wheelchair making scraping noises on the wood. The tide was out, the water lapping gently at the pilings supporting the dock.

The dock shuddered lightly when the boat crunched into it. Either Gamino wasn't the most expert of boat operators or he was as nervous as they were. Abby wanted to shine her flashlight directly on the boat and see if she could spot

Finnegan, but she didn't know how Gamino might react, so she aimed the beam near her feet and kept going.

"I'm going to get my flashlight out too, just in case," Mary whispered.

"Don't turn it on yet," Abby whispered back. "I want to tell him who you are, so he won't do something drastic when he sees there's someone other than just me."

A verse popped into her head from Psalms. She whispered it for Mary's benefit too. "He is my refuge and my fortress, my God, in whom I trust."

And Mary instantly came back with another verse from Psalms. "The Lord is my strength and my shield; my heart trusts in him."

"We're in good hands," Abby whispered.

The boat, Abby could see as they moved farther out on the dock, was perhaps eighteen or twenty feet long. A canvas top covered the front section, shadowing everything within, but the back end was open. A rope had been tossed loosely around a metal cleat on the dock, but the engine was still idling, apparently poised for a fast getaway. Water bubbled up from the engine at the stern.

"We . . . we're here." Abby heard her voice come out in a hoarse croak as she called to Gamino. Hastily, before he could jump to some dangerous conclusion, she added, "My sister came along. She's very anxious to get her dog back."

"I . . . I've missed him very much," Mary added.

A commotion unexpectedly erupted from within the boat.

Something was flailing around in there. Then a bark sounded, sharp and clear. Finnegan! Finnegan reacting frantically to the sound of familiar voices.

"Get down!" a voice commanded.

Abby knew Finnegan must be tied inside the boat or he'd have jumped out to get to Mary.

"Let's get this over with," the man growled. He stepped into the open section of the boat. A shifting flicker of moonlight exposed his muscular figure in dark clothes. He matched the description Bobby had given of the man at the door. Moonlight glinted on something in his hands. A gun.

"Gimme the necklace," he commanded.

Abby had the box in her hands. The silver stripes on the box in which they'd packed it also glinted in the moonlight. The barrel of the gun targeted on her midsection made her knees go jellyfish weak, but she held firm. "No. We want the dog first."

"You're not getting the dog till I get the necklace. Take it or leave it." In a halfway conciliatory tone he added, "I've got no reason to keep the dog once I get the necklace. You'll get him."

Abby didn't trust him, but she had no choice. She stepped closer to the boat and reached across the narrow expanse of water between dock and boat to hand the box to him.

He reached for it, gun still in his other hand and still pointed at her. Finnegan went into a frenzy, jumping and barking. Abby stretched her good arm as far as she could to get the box to Gamino. His hand touched it, but a jiggle of the boat turned the touch into a bump instead of a grab.

They both looked down as the box splashed into the water.

"You dropped it!"

Abby thought she could argue the point with him. *You* dropped it. But at the moment the distinction didn't matter, because the box and necklace were gone, down there in the water somewhere. She and Gamino both stood there peering into the dark water, as if neither of them could quite believe what had just happened.

Behind her she heard Mary whisper frantically, "What's going on? What happened?"

Abby didn't take time to explain. "Look, just give us the dog," she said to Gamino. She tried desperately to think of some persuasive reason he should do that, but all she could come up with was, "You can find the necklace later, in the daylight. No point in your keeping the dog until then."

"No. You're gonna find the necklace. *Now*."

Abby stared at him, as much bewildered as frightened. She glanced down at the dark water, then back up at him. "There's no way I can find—"

"If you want the dog, you're gonna find it."

Abby couldn't believe what she was hearing. "This is preposterous. I won't be able to see down there in the water! I can't possibly find the necklace."

"I've got a waterproof flashlight here somewhere." He turned back into the boat and rummaged around. A moment later a light flicked on as he tested whether the flashlight was working. In the brief flash Abby saw Finnegan. He'd managed to jump into the operator's seat behind the steering wheel, not barking now but still frantically pulling and twisting on the rope that tied him.

The light went out and Gamino stepped out of the boat and onto the dock. Abby handed her flashlight to Mary and accepted the other flashlight Gamino held out to her. She wondered if Henry and Deputy Niven were puzzled by this strange movement of lights. *Don't come roaring in now*, she begged silently. With the gun in his hand, no telling how Gamino would react if they did.

Gamino motioned with the gun. "Get going."

Abby looked down at the dark water. She saw no way this could work, but she hadn't much choice. She momentarily thought about taking off her shoes so they wouldn't weigh her down, but then decided she'd need them to walk around in the water. The bottom of the cove was rough and rocky.

She headed along the dock back toward shore. The water would be shallower there, and she could work her way out to where the box had plunged into the water, though it was surely over her head there. Maybe she would have to take off her shoes.

At the end of the dock she waded in. At the halfway point she expected the water to swallow her up, but it was only waist deep. She should be glad the tide was out, she realized. If it weren't, she'd be in over her head right here. But it was cold, so cold. She'd be numb within minutes.

"Quit wasting time," Gamino muttered.

As if this were some refreshing seaside dip and she was taking time to enjoy it!

She pushed the waterproof flashlight underwater and turned it on. Yes, she could see the rocks around her feet on the bottom here. Maybe, just *maybe*, if the water wasn't too deep out where the box had fallen in . . .

She edged forward, holding the flashlight in her one good hand. She tried to hold her cast above the water, but it was useless. The waves were mild here compared to the open coastline, but still they sloshed over her chest and almost threatened to knock her off her feet.

Mary, apparently unable to be quiet any longer, cried out. "Abby, be careful!"

The anguish in Mary's voice sent Finnegan into a fresh storm of leaping and barking.

And then, the engine changed pitch and the boat started moving. Abby looked up in astonishment to see the rope spin around the metal cleat and then fly into the air. How could that be? Gamino was still on the dock. What was happening? Who was operating the boat?

"Hey!" Gamino yelped. He stood frozen for a moment, as if he couldn't believe what he was seeing, then thundered toward the boat. "Stop—"

The boat was sliding away from the dock now. Gamino lunged for it and skidded on the boards. He threw out his hands as he hit the end of the dock, but it was too late to stop his momentum.

Abby heard the heavy splash even over the sound of the boat engine. It sounded like a cannonball hitting the water.

Mary's wheelchair suddenly shot forward. Abby thought it was going over the edge of the dock too, but Mary somehow braked it. She leaned over and grabbed something off the dock.

Abby floundered back to shallower water and managed to scramble out and onto the dock. She stared in astonishment at the boat now making a lazy circle out in the center of the cove. Splashes and yells rose from the water beyond the end of the dock. Abby looked at Mary and gasped when she saw what was now in Mary's hand. The gun!

"I'm drowning!" Gamino yelled, splashing furiously. "The water's over my head here! Help!"

"You're not drowning," Mary said calmly. "Grab hold of the piling under the dock. But you can't come up here. I have the gun."

Abby wasn't certain Mary knew how to use the gun, but it was also obvious that Gamino wasn't certain she *didn't* know how to use it. She looked over the end of the dock and saw him glowering up at them, one arm wrapped around a piling.

And still the boat circled lazily as yelps and barks echoed from it. Abby vaguely realized she was dripping wet and shivering, but she was too flabbergasted by the moving boat to pay attention to the chill.

"You have an accomplice in the boat?" she asked Gamino, bewildered. Waves from the boat's wake were hitting both him and the dock now.

"All that's in the boat is your dog, Finnegan or whatever his name is. He must have hit the control lever when he was jumping around and knocked it out of neutral." A wave washed over Gamino's head and he came up sputtering.

"Finnegan is guiding the boat?" Mary asked doubtfully.

"No, of course not," sputtered Gamino below her. It's going in circles because that's the way the wheel was turned."

"Now isn't that something?" Abby asked no one in particular as they all watched the boat idly circling.

"Wave the flashlight, Abby," Mary said suddenly. "Wave it!"

And Abby realized that in the wonder of watching Finnegan making a solo boat ride, that was exactly what she had forgotten to do.

She raised the flashlight and waved as wildly as if she were signaling to the Lord Himself.

# Chapter Twenty-Four

LIGHTS FLASHED WITHIN the cluster of big rocks at the north side of the wide entrance to the cove. Seconds later, a boat with official lights blazing roared out of its hiding place. It zoomed toward the circling boat but had to pull up short to keep from hitting it.

"This is the sheriff's department," Henry's voice boomed over the loudspeaker. "Stop the boat immediately."

The boat continued its leisurely pace. The spotlight on the official boat flared on and targeted Gamino's boat.

"Stop!" Henry yelled over the loudspeaker again. "You must stop now! Come to the back of the boat with your hands up!"

The boat moved past them unheedingly. The spotlight, apparently guided by Deputy Niven, followed it. Suddenly his voice in the background also blared over the loudspeaker.

"Hey, there's nobody in there. We're talking to a *dog*!"

"What do you mean there's nobody in the boat?" Henry asked. The loudspeaker magnified his tone of indignation. "Somebody has to be—"

"I mean, I can see from where I am that there's no one in the boat. Just the dog standing on the seat. Wheel must be stuck. What do you think we should do?"

Abby, in spite of her wet, disheveled condition, couldn't help smiling. The two men were obviously unaware the loudspeaker was transmitting their conversation all across the cove.

"I wonder what happened to—" The loudspeaker cut off abruptly and a few moments later the spotlight suddenly moved again, this time targeting the dock. Abby waved frantically.

The loudspeaker boomed again. "You okay?"

"We're fine!"

"Where's Gamino?" Henry said shining his light over the water.

The official boat cautiously edged forward, coordinating its speed with that of the circling boat. With the big lights from the sheriff's boat lighting the way, Deputy Niven jumped between the two boats. A moment later the noisy engine in Gamino's boat quieted to a rumbling idle. And a moment after that a freed Finnegan appeared at the back of the boat, tail waving victoriously.

*Thank You, Lord*, Abby breathed, and she knew Mary was offering the same thanks. She flicked the flashlight beam over the edge of the dock to check on Gamino again. He'd moved over to where a ladder led up to the end of the dock and was holding onto it.

"You okay?" Abby asked Gamino cautiously.

Gamino had only one sour comment to make. "I wish I'd

never even seen that dog. I'm getting out of here," he added suddenly. He pulled himself up one rung on the wooden ladder.

"No, you're not going anywhere until the officers get here. In case you've forgotten, *we* have the gun."

"You're not gonna shoot me," he said with unexpected confidence. "People like you don't shoot people." He moved up another step.

"That's true," Abby conceded. "We'd aim over your head and try to scare you. But I'm sure neither of us is a very accurate shot, which means there's a good chance we might accidentally hit you even if we didn't mean to."

For a moment Gamino's upturned face looked as if he might try to escape anyway. But then he apparently decided the wild aim of two inexperienced women was too great a risk and settled down to wait for the officers.

Gamino's boat, with Deputy Niven now at the helm, headed for the dock. Finnegan went into a frenzy of excitement as they approached and he spotted Mary. As soon as the boat was within jumping distance of the dock, the dog leaped.

Finnegan raced to Mary for an ecstatic reunion. He was usually a rather reserved dog, except when playing in the backyard at the house, but now he jumped and danced and wiggled and licked like a puppy, so glad was he to see his family again. Mary embraced him like the old friend he was. Abby went over to join in the reunion and got a happy slurp on the ear.

Henry maneuvered the sheriff's boat so he could tie up at the dock. Lights from the boat lit up the whole dock.

"The necklace fell in the water, but we're fine," Abby assured Henry before he could even ask when he jumped to the dock and tied the boat to one of the metal cleats.

He went over to check on Gamino. "You okay?"

"I cut my hand on the piling," Gamino grumbled. "I'm getting hypothermia. And I've swallowed enough water to float a yacht."

"Considering what you tried to pull here, those may be the least of your problems," Henry said. He turned back to Mary and Abby. "That wasn't exactly fair. Telling me about Mary at the very last minute," he added reproachfully.

"We didn't think of it until the very last minute," Abby said honestly.

He muttered something that sounded like *humph*.

Mary simply held out the gun to him. "It's Gamino's gun. I've probably ruined the fingerprints on it, but he dropped it and I had to grab it when I could."

Henry accepted the gun, inspected it briefly and passed it along to Deputy Niven for safe storage in the boat.

"Let's see. Finnegan is safe and sound. You two had the gun. The perpetrator is all ready for us to take into custody." Abby expected this to turn into a stern lecture, but Henry just stood there shaking his head. Finally, sounding somewhere between resigned and admiring, he said, "I'd say the Stanton sisters have struck again."

Giving the sisters no time to comment, he ordered Gamino to come up onto the dock with his hands up.

Gamino complied. Deputy Niven snapped handcuffs on him, then draped the shivering man in a blanket from the boat. The deputy tossed a second blanket for Abby, and she accepted it gratefully as Henry pulled it over her shoulders and waterlogged cast. In the excitement, she'd almost forgotten how cold she was, but now she was beginning to feel as if she'd stepped from an ice bath into a refrigerator.

Deputy Niven was taking Gamino to the sheriff's boat when the would-be extortionist yanked to a stop in front of Abby.

"You're a fool, you know that?" he sneered. He was definitely in need of a shave tonight. "If you had any brains you'd never of told these jerks anything about the necklace, just kept it for yourself. You could have been rich!"

"I'm already rich."

He eyed her blanket-clad figure and squishy old shoes, which she now realized were draped with bits of kelp. "You don't look rich to me."

"Being rich isn't about what you have here on earth," Abby said gently.

In the glare of lights from the boat Gamino momentarily looked puzzled, but he just shrugged. "And now the necklace is down there in the water somewhere. It'll probably wash out to sea and no one will have it. Good joke on ol' Van Horn." He laughed humorlessly.

Abby and Mary, Henry and Deputy Niven all stared at Gamino.

"You knew Van Horn?" Henry asked finally, and Abby knew he was as surprised as she was.

"I had some dealings with him. He's the one who cut me out of the deal on the necklace. Me 'n' Wakefield both, actually. Though Wakefield was trying to cheat Van Horn too. As well as me and his wife."

Another shock wave. "You and Wakefield were working together with Van Horn?" Henry asked.

"Work with Wakefield? No way. I wouldn't trust Wakefield any farther than I could throw my boat," Gamino said scornfully. "I'm just glad he didn't get the necklace either."

"Actually, the real necklace isn't down there in the water," Henry said. "That was an imitation."

"An imitation?" Gamino sounded indignant, as if they hadn't played fair with him. Then, turning resigned, he added, "Just as well I didn't try to go down after it, then. I'd probably have drowned for nothing."

Deputy Niven prodded Gamino on toward the boat, but another question jumped into Abby's mind. She called it after him.

"What's Gregory Wakefield's wife's name?"

"Ex-wife, actually. Claudia. Van Horn's daughter. Lives over on Orcas Island."

No one said a word, and Gamino apparently didn't realize what a bombshell he'd just dropped on them. He was more concerned with getting into the boat with his wrists handcuffed.

"We'll talk about this later," Henry said in a low voice to Abby and Mary. "Right now, you two better get on home before Abby catches pneumonia."

"Are you angry with us?" Mary asked.

Henry frowned. "I'm thinking about it. I certainly have a right to be, don't you think?" But Abby could see a smile tugging at the corners of his mouth. "Maybe we should post warning notices for all the local criminal types. Tell them the Stanton sisters are on the loose and they'd better watch out."

"We're harmless," Mary protested.

Henry jerked a thumb toward the prisoner. "Tell that to our friend here. He didn't come out too well in this caper. Neither did the guy with big ideas about a heist at the bank."

"These things happen," Abby said in a philosophical tone, and Henry just shook his head and smiled.

Finnegan was still wearing his collar. Mary snapped a leash on it, and together she, Abby and Finnegan started back to the van. Abby's shoes and socks squished with each step. Her wet slacks clung like just-pasted wallpaper.

At the edge of the clearing, she paused to look back. The sheriff's boat was headed for the mouth of the cove now, Gamino's boat dragging behind at the end of a cable.

Abby looked at her sister and smiled. "I'm glad you came along."

"Not a bad night's work for all of us," Mary suggested with satisfaction.

"With the Lord's help. I think we owe Him a big thank you."

In spite of the blanket, Abby was shivering, but they stopped right there and each offered prayerful words of thanks—thanks for keeping them safe, thanks for bringing Finnegan back safely.

Back at the house, the night held one more success. Abby looked in the San Juans' phone book and there it was. When Henry called a little later to check on them, Abby gave it to him: Claudia Wakefield's phone number.

# Chapter Twenty-Five

THE NEXT MORNING ABBY was up early. When Mary came in the kitchen, still sleepy-eyed, she looked at Abby's old jeans and sneakers. "You're going to the office in those?" She blinked at the clock. "And what are you doing up so early?"

Abby slipped the oatmeal into the microwave and punched buttons. "I'm going out to Paradise Cove."

"To Paradise Cove? What for?"

"To look for the necklace."

"You can't go out there and plow around in ten or fifteen feet of water! And there's no telling where the necklace is by now. It could be halfway to China!"

"Sometimes things wash into shore, not out. Anyway I have to try. Mom is going to be really upset if she doesn't get the brooch back." She eyed her sister as she got bowls out of the cupboard. "Do you want to be the one to tell her we lost it and it's now at the bottom of Paradise Cove?"

"Well, no," Mary said.

"I shouldn't be gone more than a couple hours. I'm taking along some extra clothes in case I get wet."

Mary sighed. "Okay, I'm coming along. Can't have just one Stanton sister running off on a wild goose chase."

The tide was out when they reached the Cove. A breeze riffled the water, but the sun felt unseasonably warm on their backs. Not exactly warm enough for a dip, however, Abby thought, not looking forward to what she had to do. Mary immediately spotted something sloshing in the water just a few feet from the dock. She released Finnegan and pointed to it. A moment later he returned with the stocking cap Abby had completely forgotten about and hadn't even missed until now.

"Good dog!" Mary held up the dripping stocking cap and wrinkled her nose. "Why don't I just knit you another one?"

"I always really liked this one."

"I'll knit you a better one." Mary rolled over to a trash can near the dock and dropped the stocking cap inside.

Abby walked out to the end of the dock and looked down. The bottom was indistinct but she caught a flash of something down there. The necklace? No. But the glitter might be from a shard of the mirror that had lined the bottom of the box!

Mary joined her and together they strained to see the rocky bottom on both sides of the dock from one end to the other. Nothing. Abby then carefully walked the high tide line on the beach. She wasn't hopeful. The necklace wouldn't have washed "halfway to China" by now, but it could have washed into deeper water in the cove and maybe even have been carried off by some curious crow or other bird. Which meant that sooner or later she was going to have to make that plunge into the cold water.

And then she spotted it, trapped in a clump of debris at the high tide line! She knelt to disentangle the chain from bits of driftwood and kelp, then stood up to wave it at her sister.

"It's missing some rhinestones, but the center part is here!" she called. "I told you that stuff was indestructible!"

Back at the house, they tried to reassemble the brooch, but without success. Finally they decided there was no getting around it. The brooch was not repairable. They'd have to confess to their mother what they'd done.

"No point in putting it off," Abby said.

"None at all," Mary agreed dolefully.

They drove over to the farm, feeling much like they had as girls when they'd had to confess something.

Abby presented her mother with the dissembled brooch and Mary handed her the necklace they'd created, which now looked rather worse for wear, the lost rhinestones having created gaps, like teeth missing in a grin. Abby explained what they'd done and why.

"We're very sorry," she added. "When we borrowed the brooch we thought we could put it back together. But it just won't work."

Ellen studied the old brooch and the new necklace as she listened to their tale.

"Well, no disaster," she said briskly. She disappeared and came back with a small box and a card. She dropped the gap-toothed necklace into the box, then bent to write on the card. Abby and Mary looked at each other, puzzled. They watched their mother set the box on a shelf in the living room and propped up the card. Together they read, "Tribute to my daughters' resourcefulness and courage. The Blue Moon II."

TWO DAYS LATER Abby and Henry were standing by the rail watching the whitewater wake roll away from the big ferry headed toward Orcas Island. The sheriff's department cruiser was down below.

Abby reported to Henry that after their successful retrieval expedition to Paradise Cove, Mary had taken Finnegan to the vet for a checkup and he was fine. He'd slipped easily back into his usual routine of helping Mary.

Now she added, "I'm a little surprised that you asked me to come along today. I appreciate it."

Henry looked a little guilty. He'd taken off the hat he usually wore with his uniform, to keep it from blowing away in the wind, and the stiff breeze ruffled his fringe of white hair. "I appreciate all you've done. You asked the right question of Gamino or we wouldn't be doing this. But I asked you to come along to see Claudia Wakefield mostly for another reason."

"Oh?"

"She sounded nervous about my coming. I think having you along and telling her how you found the necklace will set her at ease."

"You told her about the necklace?"

"No. Only that we want to talk to her about an item we think belonged to her father. All the circumstantial evidence points to him as the owner, but Sheriff Dutton says we're going to have to have something more concrete before we can release it to her. And there's still the possibility it was acquired under shady circumstances or with illegal money, which would complicate things. I'm hoping she'll have a receipt or something to prove ownership."

"I wonder why she'd be nervous?"

"A visit from a law officer makes a lot of people nervous. She asked if she should have her lawyer present."

"Seems like an odd question."

"I'd say it suggests she may not be totally unaware of her father's shady dealings. "

Henry was familiar with Orcas Island and had no diffi- culty locating Claudia Wakefield's home. It sat on a forested hillside with a spectacular view overlooking East Sound, the deep bay that cut the island almost in half.

The house was large and elegant, but not ostentatious, a blazing white against the green woods around it, with a wall of windows and a huge brick patio. The large yard had a well- cared-for, but not manicured, look, as if it were meant to be used. A sign at the end of the driveway said Hillside Manor Bed & Breakfast.

The woman who came to the door was in her late thirties, Abby guessed. She was an attractive woman, with short brown hair, a slender figure in brown slacks and sunny yellow blouse, discreet makeup and a wary but not unfriendly expression on her face. In his uniform, Henry probably didn't need identification, but he provided it anyway and introduced Abby. The woman gave Abby and her cast a quick, curious glance, then motioned them inside.

"Come into the living room. I had several guests over the weekend, but no one's here at the moment. This is a slow time of year." She led them to the big room with the wall of windows overlooking the sound.

"Would you like coffee and croissants?" Claudia smiled. "If you don't mind leftovers. I made more than enough for the weekend guests."

Henry declined the refreshments, so Abby did, too, although she rather regretted turning down homemade croissants.

"The reason we're here, as I told you on the phone," Henry began, "is because the sheriff's department is in custody of an item we believe belonged to your father and was intended as a gift for you. I'll let Abby explain what it is and how she found it."

Abby did that, and also brought out the computer printouts she'd downloaded from the Internet. "We've recently established that the diamond is in fact the Blue Moon."

Claudia studied the printouts carefully. Abby saw her eyebrows lift when she reached the section about the curse.

"This appears to be a very valuable necklace," she finally commented. She did not sound overjoyed about it nor did she jump in with eager questions.

"The photo doesn't show the necklace as it is now. The blue diamond has been put into a more modern setting. A rough estimate of its current value is at least three million dollars," Henry said.

"It's also an incredibly beautiful necklace now," Abby said. "Quite breathtaking, actually."

Claudia looked more troubled than excited. "And you think this has something to do with me?"

"A number of people have tried to claim the necklace, but our investigation has led us to believe it was intended as a gift for you from your father," Henry said.

Abby explained about the roundabout trail that they'd traced from the desk in her office to the Washingtons and then to Nelson Van Horn.

"Although this isn't definitive proof that the necklace was his and that he actually hid it in the desk," Henry warned. "Some definite proof will be required before we can turn the necklace over to you. We're hoping there may have been a receipt or something among your father's things."

"No. Nothing. I have no proof," Claudia said flatly. "After his death, I received the emerald ring my father always wore, but I don't know anything about a necklace. And I'm sure if the lawyer handling the estate had seen anything concerning it in my father's papers, he'd have said something."

"Your father never mentioned the necklace to you?" Abby asked.

Claudia shook her head. "I know he had something special

in mind for my birthday. We were planning to get together on Sparrow Island to celebrate it." Claudia's expression went mistily reminiscent. "It was my thirty-ninth birthday, and Dad said it was time for something big before I turned forty. My marriage had ended a few months before. Greg was an . . . unfortunate choice in husbands, but I was pretty broken up over the divorce anyway. After Dad's death, I assumed the gift was supposed to have been that cabin cruiser he was looking at on Sparrow Island. We'd done a lot of boating together when I was a young girl."

After giving Claudia time to lose herself in memories for a few moments, Abby ventured to say, "You don't seem eager to claim the necklace."

Claudia's smile was quick, but she nervously fingered the plain gold chain at her neck. "I'm not sure how much to tell you."

"About your father?" Abby asked.

Claudia didn't answer the question. Instead she asked, "How did you connect me with my father since my name isn't Van Horn?"

"Two men who are in custody for trying to obtain the necklace illegally have both mentioned your father," Henry explained. "They seemed to think they had some claim on the necklace because of a connection with him. One of the men is Gregory Wakefield, although it was the other man, Jules Gamino, who actually mentioned you as being Van Horn's daughter. Wakefield himself declined to furnish even his own name, and we had to trace it through fingerprints."

Claudia's smile was wan. "Which I'm sure were on file, given some of Greg's past activities."

"He's in bigger trouble now," Henry said.

"Did Greg do that to you?" Claudia asked in dismay as she looked at the cast on Abby's arm.

"Not directly. Actually, I hurt it in a fall."

"A fall she wouldn't have taken if it weren't for Wakefield," Henry put in.

Claudia reached over and squeezed Abby's hand. "I'm so sorry." Then she nodded as if the pieces of a puzzle had just fallen into place. "So this is what Greg was yelling about."

"Yelling about?" Abby repeated.

"Greg came here not long after the hang gliding accident, ranting that my father had cheated him and he wanted what was rightfully his. It was something about a necklace, but I had no idea what that meant at the time. I just asked him to leave."

"Did you tell him you didn't know anything about a necklace?" Henry asked.

"Oh yes. About ten times. But he seemed convinced that I was lying. I don't know why he'd think that, except that Greg's a liar, so he assumes everyone else is too. And he has a terrible temper. Plus an attitude that he's entitled, that whatever he wants, he's entitled to have. When he left I decided if he ever came back I was going to get a restraining order against him. But I haven't seen him again, thankfully. I guess he decided I really didn't know anything about a necklace."

"Wakefield claimed to Abby that he helped your father acquire the necklace," Henry said. "Do you think that's true?"

"It could be." Claudia looked down at her hands, and Abby saw that the nails were clipped short, no polish. She guessed Claudia did much of the work on the beautiful yard herself, not because she couldn't afford to hire help but because she liked working with the soil and growing things.

"Did he work for your father?"

"Off and on. They didn't like each other, but sometimes they had business dealings together—although I don't know what those dealings were."

Abby and Henry exchanged a glance. Claudia wasn't being secretive by any means, but it was obvious she'd rather not discuss her father. Abby wasn't certain knowing more about Nelson Van Horn was important, except for one point. Quietly she asked, "Do you think your father obtained the necklace by legitimate means?"

"I loved my father," Claudia said almost fiercely. "He raised me alone after my mother died when I was twelve. He was always so good to me. He always went to parent/teacher conferences and came to my school functions and took me to buy clothes."

"He sounds like a very caring father."

"He was." She smiled ruefully. "He also knew more about people than I did. I should have listened to him when he told me Greg would cause me heartache. But when I insisted I would marry Greg, even if we had to run off to Reno, he threw a huge, fantastic wedding for us. We lifted off in a helicopter at the end of the reception. And had a honeymoon in Rio de Janeiro."

*Exactly the kind of man who'd give his daughter a three-million-dollar necklace for her thirty-ninth birthday*, Abby thought.

"When we got back, he'd bought this place for us." Her gesture took in the house and grounds. "Greg tried to grab it when we divorced, but my father had a lawyer who wasn't about to let that happen."

"But?" Abby asked, because there was obviously a *but* attached to all these good things Claudia had to say about her father.

"But there were many things I didn't know about my father. There were things I *did* know, of course. About his various successful businesses, and how he often bought and sold real estate, usually very profitably. But there were other things I . . . I wondered about."

"Things not quite on the up-and-up?"

"I was afraid that was the case, yes," Claudia said. "And to get back to your earlier question, no, I don't know whether he acquired the necklace through legitimate channels. And if Greg was involved . . ." She shook her head.

Abby jumped to a different subject. "Your father enjoyed hang gliding?"

"My father enjoyed anything that was exciting and dangerous and death-defying. He'd only recently taken up hang gliding, but he'd done everything else, from sky-diving and bungee jumping to rock climbing and scuba diving. Once he hired a helicopter to take him and a friend way back in some Canadian mountains so they could ski out. When he heard about some huge storm surf in Hawaii, he rushed over there to surf it. He just loved taking chances." She spoke with affection, but also a kind of bewilderment, as if this attraction for the dangerous was beyond her understanding.

"I begged him not to do some of the things he did, but he'd just laugh and tell me I worried too much. He was such a stubborn man. You might even say bullheaded." She sighed, as if this had long been a trial to her. Then she smiled ruefully again. "Like father, like daughter, I suppose, considering my stubbornness about marrying Greg when Dad advised me not to."

"Your father never got hurt doing any of this?"

"Never. Which I suppose made him believe he was invincible." She swallowed. "And he wasn't."

"None of us is," Abby said softly.

They sat there in silence for a minute until Henry asked gently, "Do you want to make a claim for the necklace?"

"I'll have to think about it. If it wasn't acquired legitimately . . ."

"If it wasn't acquired legitimately, then we can't release it to you."

"Then perhaps we should just wait and see."

"Very well, then," Henry said. "If you come across anything, you let us know. And we'll do the same."

Just as they were going out the door, Abby thought of one more thing.

"I have a few things your father had left in the guest room when he was staying with the Washingtons. I didn't see anything important, but I'll be glad to send them over, if you'd like."

"I'd appreciate that. Thank you."

"WHAT DO YOU THINK NOW?" Henry asked reflectively as they waited in the short line at the ferry slip.

"I think Claudia Van Horn Wakefield is a woman with a great deal of class." Abby realized now that Claudia had never asked about the curse. Apparently she had no belief in such matters. Abby approved of that too. "I wish she'd had something to prove she was entitled to the necklace. I'd like to see her have it."

"So would I," Henry said.

EVEN THOUGH ABBY hadn't been present when Gordon Siebert examined the blue diamond, she made a point of stopping by his store to hear how he had made the verification.

Gordon welcomed her inside. "So I guess you heard that it is the Blue Moon." He motioned her toward his office, where he showed her the diagrams he'd made of the interior of the gem in the necklace. He placed them side by side with the drawings he'd received from the expert in Chicago.

"Of course these show the flaws much enlarged," he pointed out. "The actual flaws can't be seen without a microscope, and they detract nothing from the gem's beauty or value."

Abby knew she was no expert, but the enlarged diagrams indeed looked identical to her. The feathery designs even had a beauty of their own. She smiled to herself at the thought: *Even in flaws, the Lord created beauty.*

"I've been waiting to call Dr. Kingston and tell him," Gordon said.

"Yes, do that."

"Have you made any progress locating the owner?"

"We're reasonably certain we know who's entitled to the necklace, but coming up with enough proof of ownership to allow the sheriff's department to release it to her is something else."

"Personally, I'd like to see it in a museum somewhere." Gordon smiled ruefully. "But I imagine anyone who can prove ownership is going to want it for herself. I'm sure it's worth even more than my earlier estimate now that it's been positively identified as the Blue Moon."

"I'm glad we had your expertise available on this."

"I just wish some expert could convince some of the people around here that there's nothing to that ridiculous curse."

"You've been hearing more rumors?"

"I had to go into the drugstore a couple of days ago, and Ed Willoughby commented how he'd been hearing people say that it couldn't be coincidence that so many bad things had happened to people who'd been connected with the necklace.

Donna Morgan from Bayside Souvenirs happened to be there, too, and she was wondering if Van Horn had acquired the necklace because some tragedy had happened to the previous owner."

"That's troubling," Abby agreed.

"Oh, I haven't seen it yet, but I also heard the new issue of *The Birdcall* has an article about you and the necklace and the incident at the bank in it."

Abby could only hope that would quiet the islanders' concerns, not alarm them further.

LATE THAT SAME AFTERNOON, Hugo took the ferry to Seattle. His surgery was scheduled for the following morning. Again he said, "No visitors." But when Abby asked before he left if that also meant no phone calls, he relented. "Well, okay. But not before the day after the surgery. I don't want my head gummed up with pain pills."

Abby stopped at The Green Grocer to pick up a copy of *The Birdcall* on her way home. She eyed the headline on the front page when she paid for the newspaper at the checkout stand: "Famous Diamond Discovered on Sparrow Island."

The clerk looked at the headline too. "I don't think there's any point taking chances having that thing around. I mean if it could give a guy a heart attack and bring a hang glider down right out of the sky, no telling what it could do if it really went on a rampage."

"Is *that* what the article says?" Abby asked, startled,

because she hadn't thought William Jansen would write anything so inflammatory.

"Oh no. It doesn't say that. That's just what people are saying."

Abby was relieved to hear that William Jansen had lived up to her confidence in him. "The necklace didn't do any of those things," she said firmly. "It isn't a live, thinking thing. It can't go on a 'rampage.'"

"Well, strange things happen," the clerk said, obviously unconvinced.

ABBY READ THE ARTICLE in the car, under the parking lot lights. It was well done and quite comprehensive, covering everything from Abby's finding of the necklace to the efforts of people who had tried to claim it, the dognapping, the attack in the bank and the connection with Nelson Van Horn and his hang gliding disaster.

Abby had to groan when she saw the photo of herself and Hugo, however. It looked way too much like a man carrying a bride across the threshold. But the photo was, thankfully, buried among a half dozen others, including one of banker Steven Jarvis, which she doubted pleased him any more than hers pleased her. The light had hit his shaved head in just such a way that it had the pale gleam of an under-ripe melon.

Mary's only comment when she saw the photo was, "At least he didn't call you Slugger."

*Be grateful for small favors*, Abby reminded herself.

Even though the article made no mention of the curse in any way, the rumors continued to circulate.

Ida mentioned the very next day that she was hearing conversations at the Springhouse about how so many people connected with the diamond had suffered calamities. Later in the day, when Abby went in for a checkup on her arm at the clinic, she heard people in the waiting room discussing the same subject. Several comments were prefaced with some version of, "I don't really believe that stuff about a curse, *but*—"

Something needed to be done to get people out of this superstitious sinkhole, Abby thought in exasperation. But what? She could hardly stand on a street corner and shout that believing any of this nonsense was totally ridiculous.

That evening she called the hospital and talked with Hugo. The conversation was brief because he was still on pain pills that were making him a little groggy. "But not groggy enough to know I'd rather be home than here," he added with his usual good humor. His further statement that the surgery had gone fine sounded optimistic, but guardedly so, as if he didn't want to claim success prematurely.

Afterward, Abby remembered that she wanted to send the pamphlets and miscellaneous receipts Liberty Washington had sent her on to Claudia Wakefield. She glanced through them once more as she was putting them into a fresh envelope to mail.

She stopped short, receipt in hand, when she spotted something she hadn't seen before.

# Chapter Twenty-Six

Probably nothing, she decided, and stuck the receipt in the envelope. But the following morning she hesitated before adding the envelope to the museum's stack of outgoing mail.

It was just a name, Pragmire, and a phone number scribbled on the back of one of the receipts. Calling it would probably be as useless as calling the boat dealer named on one of the pamphlets had been. Surely Van Horn wouldn't have scribbled anything important on the back of a receipt from Wal-Mart, would he? And yet Van Horn was a strange and mysterious man . . .

And what did she have to lose by calling? Other than having someone think she was a little weird, of course! She was surprised when a brisk feminine voice answered with the name of an insurance company.

"Is there a Mr. Pragmire in this office?"

"Actually it's Ms. Pragmire. I'll connect you."

A moment later a friendly, slightly older sounding voice came on the line. "Genevieve Pragmire speaking. May I help you?"

Feeling more than a little awkward, Abby identified herself and then said she was trying to locate information about a man named Nelson Van Horn who may have been a client of the agency. A thought occurred to her. "Do you handle boat insurance?" Perhaps Van Horn had been investigating the boat he was about to buy.

The voice cooled. "We're a specialized company often dealing with Lloyd's of London. The only boat insurance we'd handle would be something covering a high-value yacht. But we don't give out confidential information about our clients."

"I realize that. But it's a peculiar situation." Trying to simplify it as much as possible, Abby explained about finding the necklace, Van Horn's death, and finding Ms. Pragmire's name and phone number among some things left behind by Van Horn.

"You think he may have insured a valuable boat with us?"

"Actually, I'm not sure what he was doing," Abby admitted. "But we think he owned a very valuable necklace. He may have been insuring that. The gem in it has been identified as the one known as the Blue Moon."

"This is very odd." The woman still sounded cool, but, reluctantly interested. "Who did you say you were again?"

Abby repeated her name and went on to explain her connection with the Nature Museum.

"I know the museum!" the woman exclaimed. "My husband and I were there last summer. It's a marvelous place. We were so impressed. I especially loved that Mount Saint Helen's exhibit. We wanted to go on one of the bird walks, but we ran out of time."

"If you'd come, we'd have met. I'm an ornithologist and lead the bird walks."

"Really?" The woman paused, as if taking a moment to digest that and perhaps realign Abby on her mental radar. "And you say you found this necklace in the museum?"

"That's right. Hidden in my desk. I've traced the possible ownership of the necklace to this man named Van Horn and his daughter Claudia. We'd like to release it to her, but we haven't been able to establish enough proof to make that possible."

Another hesitation. "There may have been something. Let me check our files. Hold on."

Abby scrunched the phone between jaw and shoulder, and with her one good hand she used the waiting time to clean out one of the pigeonholes in her desk. She could never understand how *stuff* accumulated with such speed. It was a good five minutes before Genevieve Pragmire returned.

"I'm sorry. It took me a while. Mr. Van Horn wasn't actually a client, so the file wasn't in with our regular files, but . . . Are the authorities involved in this, Dr. Stanton?"

"Oh yes. An officer named Sergeant Henry Cobb with the local county sheriff's department has been working on it. But a couple of incidents have happened that make me especially eager to see the necklace returned to its rightful owner as soon as possible." Briefly Abby explained about both the dognapping and the encounter at the bank.

"And you call these *incidents*?" the woman exclaimed. "I call them disasters! I'm sure I'd have fainted. But you're okay?"

"I'm fine. But I'd like to avoid anything similar happening in the future."

"I can understand that." On a friendlier note than before she added, "Well, I can tell you a little of what we have here. Mr. Van Horn did contact us, and it was a necklace he wanted to insure, a quite valuable necklace. As I said, we specialize in this type of high-value policy for individual items not covered by regular policies, which is why he came to us, of course. But we never actually handled the insurance on the necklace."

"Can you tell me why?"

"Basically, it was because, although he provided figures and documents showing a rough value of the necklace based on the value of property he traded for it, we needed a certified appraisal of the necklace itself. Mr. Van Horn was supposed to do that and get back to us, but we never heard from him again. I'm not sure why the folder's never been discarded rather than being in our pending file all this time. Just an oversight probably."

"Is the daughter named Claudia mentioned?"

"Yes. This indicates her name was supposed to be on the insurance policy too. Except that it was never issued, apparently, from what you say, because he died before he could get back to us."

"But you do have proof there that Mr. Van Horn obtained the necklace legitimately?"

"Oh yes, a documented trade, but—" The woman broke off. "Look, I know you're totally trustworthy and reliable, and I wish I could tell you more, but I just don't think I can give you any further information. But if you'd have the authorities, this Sergeant Cobb you mentioned, or perhaps Claudia Wakefield herself contact us—"

Abby hid her disappointment, because, actually, she was as exhilarated as disappointed. "I'll do that. And thank you! If you get over to the museum again, look me up."

"I'm looking forward to it."

Abby immediately relayed the information to Henry. He said he would contact the insurance company right away.

"Good work, Abby," he added appreciatively.

She decided to hold off on sending the envelope over to Claudia Wakefield just yet.

HUGO CAME IN TO HIS OFFICE briefly on Monday afternoon. He said he wasn't feeling up to anything as vigorous as mountain climbing or scuba diving just yet, and he'd have to continue to have PSA blood tests regularly, but the doctor had assured him the surgery had accomplished exactly what it was supposed to. He was cancer free, no follow-up radiation needed. Abby was so glad to hear this that she came out from behind her desk to give him a warm hug of congratulations, which he returned with equal warmth. Then they sat in her office drinking tea while she gave him a full rundown on the events that had taken place while he was away.

"So Finnegan is home safe and sound, Van Horn's daughter is located, the Blue Moon is positively identified, and both the extortionist and the robber in the bank are safely in custody." Hugo nodded with satisfaction. "Sounds as if, with your usual efficiency, you have the situation all wrapped up."

"Not quite. Sheriff Dutton and the county's legal counsel are still considering the evidence provided by the insurance company about Claudia's right to the necklace."

"I'm sure they have to cover all the legalities."

"And I'm still hearing rumbles about the dangers of the Blue Moon's curse. I can't believe people are still concerned about it, but apparently they are."

Hugo nodded. "I stopped in the drugstore to pick up a prescription and heard three people in there talking about it."

"I suppose we could ask Henry to move the necklace off the island, to a safe deposit box somewhere else, until everything is settled," Abby said. "But that doesn't address the real problem."

"Which is that people are believing superstitious nonsense."

"Exactly. As if the Blue Moon had yanked Nelson Van Horn's hang glider right out of the sky!"

Hugo leaned back in his chair, his thoughtful gaze looking off into space through Abby's office window. "I have an idea . . ."

Abby listened and agreed.

BECAUSE OF THE LIMITATIONS of having only one working arm, Abby enlisted Ida Tolliver's help to hurry the project along. Hugo brought several items from home to add. Abby hired handyman Rick DeBow to help too. She spent considerable time on the Internet and also conferred with Bobby McDonald. The two of them returned to Mount Ortiz where he took more photos, and she studied the wind drafts and bird movements more thoroughly.

She placed a display ad in *The Birdcall* and made some special invitations by phone to a few people who seemed most vocal about the dangers of the Blue Moon. She arranged with the Springhouse Café for catered hors d'oeuvres, plus sparkling apple and berry juice beverages. Ida made a huge banner to drape above the outside doors of the museum.

But before the big night on Friday arrived, another short project intervened. Henry contacted Abby to say Sheriff Dutton and the legal counsel were finally satisfied and arrangements were all made.

"We're keeping it all very low-key," he added. "Steven Jarvis is going to let me into the bank before regular opening time. Then an ordinary ferry ride over to Orcas."

Abby laughed. "Although carrying a three-million-dollar cargo takes it rather out of the ordinary. Does Claudia know?"

"I told her we were bringing something, but I think she thinks it's just those things you had of her father's. As I said, this is going to be very low-key. Sheriff Dutton didn't want to take any chances on word getting out, not even through Claudia."

"That's good. But you be careful anyway, Henry, okay?" Then she hesitated, a certain word Henry had just said jumped out at her. "You told her we were bringing her something? We as in . . . ?"

"As in you and me. You were in on finding this treasure. I think it's only fair that you're in on seeing it go to its rightful owner. Sheriff Dutton agrees."

They arranged to meet at the ferry the following morning.

# Chapter Twenty-Seven

CLAUDIA WAKEFIELD STOOD up from where she'd been working in a flower bed when the cruiser pulled into the driveway. She pushed back the sleeve of her blue chambray shirt with the back of her other hand. Abby and Henry got out of the cruiser and walked toward her.

"Oh my. It's ten o'clock already isn't it? I didn't realize that." She smiled as she looked down at the grass stains on the knees of her old jeans. "Well, this is the real me. I guess you'll have to take me as I am. All smudged and dirty. And maybe smelling of compost too."

This time she took them in through the kitchen, dropping off her dirt-stained sneakers at the door and going into a bathroom near the back door to wash her hands.

"Coffee?" she asked when she rejoined them in the kitchen.

This time Henry accepted and so did Abby. Claudia motioned them to chairs around a round maple table with pale cream placemats. A plate of oatmeal-raisin cookies accompanied the mugs of coffee when she brought them. She sat at the table with them, her mug in her hands.

"So you've brought those items my father left in the Washingtons' guest room?"

"Yes, we did. Liberty apologized for no longer having the clothes. So this is what there was." Abby handed over the envelope she had never mailed. "I don't think there's anything of importance, but I thought you might want to look through them."

"Thank you. I appreciate your thoughtfulness. I've been wondering about Greg and that other man—what was his name? Gamino? Whom you said were in custody." Claudia skimmed through the items in the envelope as she spoke.

"Neither has been able to post bail and they're still in custody. They've been arraigned on various charges. It will probably take a while, but eventually they'll go to trial." Henry reached for briefcase at his side. "We have something else for you."

He opened the briefcase at his side and set a plain-colored, oblong box on the table. "Open it."

Abby hadn't seen the necklace for a while and she felt awed all over. The vivid color of the blue diamond, its incredible depth and sparkle. The elegance of the glittering diamonds surrounding it and the sheer opulence of the entwined strands of tiny diamonds. She glanced up and saw Claudia staring at the necklace with equal awe.

"My father planned to give me *this* for my birthday?"

"That was his plan, yes," Abby said. "The blue diamond was identified just a couple of days ago as the famous gem known as the Blue Moon. It's almost perfect, only two tiny flaws, which were what made identification possible, actually. It has quite a history, from first being found in India to belonging to a French king, various noblemen and even a famous wine-making family."

"May I take it out of the box?"

Henry laughed. "It's yours. You can do whatever you want with it."

Claudia reached for the dazzling chain, then stopped. "But I thought I had to have proof of ownership before I could have it. And I don't have any proof."

"We do," Henry said. He reached into the briefcase again and spread various documents across the table. "What we have here are copies of an agreement trading property that your father had owned in Italy for a number of years, with a value that translates to approximately 2.7 million U.S. dollars, for a necklace containing a twenty-one carat blue diamond."

It was the first time Abby had seen the documents. If Van Horn was into anything shady, this gift meant for his daughter was not involved. Had Wakefield and/or Gamino been involved in the transaction? Or had they somehow known about it and tried to cut themselves in when the necklace surfaced after Van Horn's death? They were not mentioned in these documents.

"Where in the world did you get all this?" Claudia asked, obviously astonished.

"Your father was making arrangements with an insurance company to insure the necklace at the time of his death. Abby here—" Henry motioned to Abby sitting beside him. She still felt a little dazzled looking at the necklace again. "—located them and got the information for us to work with. Then I contacted them and the insurance company faxed everything over to us. The county legal counsel took it a step further and looked up your father's probated will to make certain you were the legal heir."

"I . . . I really don't know what to say," Claudia murmured, as if she was a little stunned. "Thank you, Abby. And you, too, Sergeant Cobb. And everybody else who had a part in this."

"I think the first thing you should say is that you're going to get the necklace insured immediately. And get it to some safe place as soon as possible. In fact, if you'd like, Abby and I can accompany you to a bank for safekeeping."

"Actually, I have a wall safe here at the house. Dad had it installed a few months before he died. It's hidden and quite secure, I'm sure. I wonder if he had this planned even then?" she mused.

Could be, Abby thought. A strange man, Van Horn. Cautious about some things. Reckless about others.

"Well, we'll be going then," Henry said. He stood up.

"Actually," Claudia said thoughtfully, the dazzling necklace dangling from her fingers now. "I won't be keeping it in the safe for long anyway." She smiled. "I can't quite see myself wearing this when I'm out there digging up the flower beds or in here making breakfast for my guests, can you?"

"It's worth a great deal if you plan to sell it," Abby said.

"I've been thinking since you were here the last time," Claudia said slowly. She let the necklace twist and turn in her fingers, letting the light catch it. "And now that I've seen the necklace and know its name and heard its history, I'm sure of it."

"Sure of . . . ?"

"I don't think it should be stuck away in a dark safe deposit box where no one can see it. I'm going to donate it to a museum, where everyone can see and enjoy it."

A woman with class indeed, Abby thought.

# Chapter Twenty-Eight

FRIDAY NIGHT. The time for the big event had arrived.

The weather was cooperating, stars sparkling overhead and the waning moon riding high in a clear sky. Inside and out, every light in the museum blazed. Ida's outdoor banner announcing *New Exhibit Opening Tonight!* developed a droop at one end but Rick DeBow brought out a ladder and quickly straightened it. The parking lot started to fill.

Inside, people milled around drinking sparkling juice and eating hors d'oeuvres, the cream cheese-and-salmon variety a strong favorite.

Promptly at seven o'clock Ida unveiled the new exhibit. A sign across the top identified it: Bird Flight and Early Human Flight. Inside, a carved model of an eagle in flight hung from the ceiling, beside it a tiny, colorful model of a hummingbird, showing two totally different styles of bird flight. Models depicting various forms of early human flight were hanging beyond them: Bobby's first model of an ornithopter, a model of the Wright Brothers' first plane from Hugo's personal collection, a miniature copy of a hang glider, and a hot-air balloon. A box kite in the shape of a castle, another contribution from Bobby, filled one corner.

The display below included individual feathers with diagrams of how they affected flight, enlarged sketches of various outrageous ornithopters people had tried to fly in the early years, plus enlarged photos of birds in flight, several of which Bobby had taken on Mount Ortiz.

Rick had built a small platform for Abby, and she stood on it to talk to the crowd about what was in the exhibit.

She talked first about bird flight and the early assumption that man could fly only by imitating the flapping of a bird's wings.

"One fable carried this idea of copying birds to the extreme, in that it actually used birds. A king named Kai Kawus wanted to fly, and, being a king, he wanted to do it while sitting on his throne. So the scheme was to put a tall pole on each corner of the throne, with large chunks of meat on top. Hungry eagles were chained at the bottom of the throne, and their attempts to fly up to get the meat were supposed to lift the throne." She looked over the group. "Does anyone think this worked?"

"About as well as the time I tried to fly using pillowcases and a bunch of balloons from my birthday party when I was a little kid," Aaron Holloway said. He patted a hip, which was apparently where his own early attempt at human flight had landed him. He'd shown up early this evening to help Ida with some last-minute details.

Abby went on with other details about how man had tried to make flapping-wing machines, usually powered by pedaling or kicking, and made of everything from actual feathers to taffeta. Other hopefuls had tried oversized kites and found that though a huge box kite might lift a man off the ground, where the kite and man went was no more controllable than the whim of the wind.

"Actual flight had to wait until the forces of lift, drag and gravity—and how each affects flight—were better understood," she explained.

Abby didn't want to get too technical in her talk about flight, but she thought she had to go into some detail in order to explain the tragic death here on Sparrow Island that had some of the more superstitious residents concerned.

"The hang glider came about when people began to understand more about the technical aspects of flight. You have only to look at an eagle or vulture floating effortlessly to realize that flapping wings aren't always necessary. With a hang glider the pilot runs down a slope to get air moving across the wing, which generates lift. Gravity and the pilot pull the hang glider down, of course, but also moves it forward, creating more air flow over the wing. The hang glider pilot can, as the eagle and vulture do, also take advantage of the thermal lift in rising hot air or air deflected upward by a cliff or ridge."

Abby pointed to Bobby's photographs showing the vultures they'd seen at Mount Ortiz, so graceful and elegant in the sky.

"But sometimes things go wrong. Updrafts are not necessarily consistent. Sometimes there are downdrafts or other irregularities, which can be disastrous. Bobby was fortunate enough to catch a photo when that happened to one of the vultures we were watching." Here she pointed to his photo of the tumbling vulture. "The bird, of course, simply flapped its wings and recovered quickly."

She paused a moment to be sure she had everyone's attention. "But when an updraft changes and a hang glider starts to plummet, it doesn't have wings to flap and save itself. The only control the pilot has in a hang glider is the bar he's holding onto. If the pilot pulls back on the bar, tipping the nose down, the glider speeds up and he may escape the downward pull. But, if the pilot is inexperienced or panics and pushes forward, which is rather an instinctive move to make, like putting on a brake, the nose of the glider tips upward. The glider then slows down and may even stall. In a stall, air stops flowing over the wing and the hang glider sinks. And crashes to the ground."

The audience was silent, as if they were indeed thinking of what had happened on Mount Ortiz. Al Minsky put it into words.

"That's what happened to that Nelson Van Horn when he crashed here on Sparrow Island, not some curse?"

"Yes, I think that's what happened. It would have happened whether or not he'd ever had any connection with the Blue Moon necklace because it was caused by the shifting updraft and possibly an error in judgment. It could have happened to anyone who made the mistake of trying to hang glide from the mountain that day. The necklace is beautiful and valuable, but it has no power to hurt or destroy lives. Or harm anyone here on our island."

There were small murmurings in the crowd, some of which sounded approving, some still questioning.

This time it was young Aaron who uneasily brought up the subject of other local people who had been affected by the curse. "But what about the man who had the necklace in his house and then had a heart attack? What about the two guys in jail now? Their luck was really bad. And even you, Abby, you got a broken arm! And Donna Morgan hurt her neck. That's a lot of coincidences."

It was quite a speech for rather shy, sometimes tongue-tied Aaron, and Abby actually admired him for having the courage to speak up about something that apparently bothered him.

"I don't believe I'd call them coincidences. All these happenings had specific causes. Norbert Washington certainly did die of a heart attack. But his wife told me he'd had heart trouble long before the necklace came to be hidden in the desk in their house. The diamond didn't cause his health problems. James Gamino and Gregory Wakefield never had any close connection with the necklace and have only their own greed to blame for their troubles."

"I can tell you what caused my injured neck and it wasn't that necklace's being in my store a good year ago," Donna broke in. "It's taken me a while to see it, but it was my own procrastination about getting that back room in my store cleaned up." She glanced around and added wryly, "As a couple of people have pointed out to me."

"And me?" Abby lifted her cast-covered arm and considered it. Not caused by any curse, but how to explain it?

Hugo moved up to her side and put his arm around her shoulders. "Abby's broken arm also had nothing to do with a superstitious curse. That cast is her badge of honor for courage and quick thinking, and doing what had to be done to prevent a bigger tragedy."

Aaron grinned. "I guess it's better to be a slugger than superstitious."

Abby decided it was a good time to ignore the slugger reference. "God is always in control, Aaron. Never forget that." Abby gave that a moment to sink in, then said briskly, "Now a young man from right here on the island has a special demonstration for us. If you'll all just follow me outside—?"

Abby led the way to where Bobby and his father were waiting outside on the steps. Bobby had the ornithopter in his hands, the one he'd sent for that was much larger than the one in the exhibit. When the crowd was assembled he gave it a toss that sent it skyward.

All eyes followed the machine as it sailed over the parking lot, wings flapping wildly. It rose, it swooped, it wobbled, it turned. Abby glanced at Bobby uncertainly. Was it supposed to do that?

Bobby stood there with open mouth watching his creation. And then suddenly it made a giant U-turn, rose, dipped, zoomed back toward the crowd and crashed. Crashed like a bug smashing into a windshield, right on the museum steps only a few feet from him.

Abby looked at Bobby again. He must be so disappointed, devastated in fact. And he did, in fact, for a moment look quite devastated. But she had underestimated Bobby.

"I guess maybe that's why ornithopters never became a real good way to fly," Bobby said as he eyed the broken pieces of the crashed machine. He didn't sound devastated, merely young-scientist thoughtful.

As laughter rippled through the crowd, Abby realized something else was happening. A commotion arose in the crowd. Then she saw what it was. Eclipse, the black cat that had been hanging around, had apparently been frightened by the crash. He zigzagged through the crowd, ducked under the ladder Rick had left nearby, streaked directly across Aaron's somewhat oversized feet and then disappeared around the corner of the museum.

Aaron just stood there looking down at his feet as if trying to assess what had happened here.

"Hey, Aaron, you're in trouble now!" someone yelled. "Not only did a black cat cross your path, it ran under a ladder first! Double bad luck."

Aaron wiggled his feet, then broke into a grin. "Nah, those are both just more dumb superstitions. I'll show you!"

He held out his arm to Ida. She looked puzzled for a moment, then smiled and joined him, and together they ducked under the ladder and marched through together.

Hugo looked at Abby questioningly. He crooked his arm. Abby hesitated. It was a bit undignified. But why not? She tucked her hand around his arm and together they, too, slipped under the ladder.

On the far side, she and Hugo stepped back to watch a laughing parade pass under the ladder. Hugo gave her hand a squeeze and they both laughed.

Yes indeed, Abby thought, God was in control here. Just as He always was.

# MATHEMATICAL
# JOURNEYS